# DEVIL
## IN THE DUNES

**WENDY BYARD**

*Wendy Byard*

Devil in the Dunes

Copyright @ 2025 by Wendy Byard

All rights reserved. No part of this book may be reproduced in any form without permission from the author or publisher, except as permitted by U.S. copyright law.

ISBN: 979-8-218-60551-3

wendybyardauthor.com

"We are each our own devil, and make this world our hell."

-Oscar Wilde

# **FRIDAY NIGHT**
## CHAPTER 1
### The Weirdo

*I see you.*

Hidden behind tall tufts of spiked dune grass, the shifting sands and impenetrable pitch-black waters of Lake Michigan mere feet away, I watch – crouched and ready. Past the golden grasses and below the sloping dune, Cadie McLeod is twirling girlishly in the cool sand. She acts as if no one is watching her because, of course, she doesn't know that I am. Would she keep swaying around the flickering fire if she knew I was here – observing her - hidden from view?

I'm quivering with anticipation. It's midnight in Harbor Cove. Up above, a red supermoon casts rays through incoming clouds to shine a hazy spotlight on the endless beach. It allows me to study her every movement. I am transfixed; in the soft light, the popular young woman is more captivating than ever. Her face is toasted warm and glowing. Dancing in her flowing yellow sundress beside the crackling bonfire and red sparks shooting high into the night sky, she smiles brightly at her good friends – and eager eighteen-year-olds in expensive swim trunks who hope they'll get lucky tonight.

*Like all men: fools.*

A sudden gust of wind catches the young woman's long crimson hair, and it lifts upward, causing her and a friend to laugh and stumble in the wind-blown sands. The breezes are cooling, picking up. The smells of sweet fire and earthy lake water fill my nostrils as strengthening waves claw at the nighttime beach. I observe Cadie touch the gold necklace around her slender neck, the neck my fingers soon will be choking.

She's blissfully unaware. Just a lovely girl on an idyllic beach enjoying her end-of-school celebration. Completely at ease – well, maybe not completely. Her parents *were* murdered (but that's another story).

*Oh, how I despise her and her happiness.*

While I bide my time, a thought suddenly springs to mind. The little girl (Emily was it?) who disappeared from these very dunes ten years ago. Her tender body was never found. Some of the locals say the Devil in the Dunes got her.

*Poor little girl.*

Now shifting from knee to aching knee, I try to calm my excitement, waiting for the final minutes to pass, and feeling the syringe in my coat pocket move slightly. I pat it reassuringly. It's almost time.

*Be patient.*

Too many times to count, I've approached girls like her – beautiful girls with fit bodies, tan faces, and straight, white teeth. They've got it good growing up in Harbor Cove. Just being women, honestly. They're sweet at first, happily chatting with you for a minute, eyes animated, providing you a moment of their precious time. Then, slowly, that look appears: the dark shadow of recognition.

*Oh, this guy's weird.*

They're not smiling anymore. Nervous and uncomfortable, they scan the room. They're looking to be rescued. From me. The Weirdo.

Who do they think they are? I'm worth a million of them.

So, I made a vow to live free of them.

I've never been happier.

As I have for quite some time, I study Cadie from afar – always learning her patterns and routines. Finalizing my plan and choosing the perfect day. I chuckle as she dances a bit unevenly from too much beer. Ironically, "Cruel Summer" by Taylor Swift is playing on someone's speaker. I see Cadie leave the drunken group of silly teens and slowly make her way to the dark lake – the high winds tossing her hair. The glowing moon continues to allow me to observe her, and the circling light from the nearby Point Betsie Lighthouse occasionally travels across the sand. I can see Harbor Cove Pier in the distance and fondly remember all the times I've stalked her, quietly walking the wooden planks behind her.

*Invisible.*

*But growing in strength and conviction.*

She noticed me - once. It was a cool Sunday evening, and Cadie and her friends were eating ice cream as they strolled the pier – a Sunday tradition in Harbor Cove. The colder temperature didn't stop the carefree girls from wearing jean cut-offs and short tops. They were in high spirits, laughing about something they found extremely funny. It was hard to hear. I couldn't get too close. I thought I heard Julie mention her puppy, Murphy, but I couldn't be sure. They were all smiling so damn much.

*Must be nice to be that happy.*

As the threesome made their way down Harbor Cove Pier as it jutted deeper into Lake Michigan, I kept a steady distance behind so as not to seem oddly close. Stratus clouds creeped overhead, dampening the mood and making the people seem like shadows – soulless. Cadie brushed long hair from her face and took a lick of ice cream. I was mesmerized by her fleeting flick of tongue. So pink and little. Was I aroused or disgusted? It's hard to tell anymore.

Then suddenly, she looked right at me. Straight into my eyes. She saw me watching her intently. Yet, she didn't look away or scowl in disgust. She just smiled warmly - like she was doing me a huge favor – and I felt deep anger slice through me like a switchblade.

*Sure, grace me with your smile. You don't know what's coming.*

I continue to observe her as the strengthening winds sweep over me.

Cadie suddenly lifts her sundress and kicks off her matching yellow flip flops. I marvel at her long, graceful legs moving in the cool water. Years of running high school track has sculpted enviable calves. She is a strong athlete.

*That might be a problem.*

Then I notice her perfectly formed face seems darkly pensive and lost in thought as she toys with her necklace. Half a heart on a gold chain.

*Where is the other half, Cadie?*

It pleases me to witness her pain. Alone with her surely sad thoughts. I, too, have unpleasant thoughts - not that anyone cares. Unspoken, hidden thoughts about the people who have wronged me. No wonder my mind is consumed with vengeance and death.

*How do you let go of a grudge that destroyed your life?*

One bright Saturday in late May, I was shocked to see her. She was jogging down Laurel Lane, coming right at me. Her green eyes glowed, and her luxurious hair blew free in the Lake Michigan breeze. She was enchantment. In that very moment, the curtains parted, and I saw it all. She was everything: smart, beautiful, sexual - liked and loved by all. An exceptional person with big plans for her life.

*I hated her so much.*

I stepped backward behind a towering oak tree as she ran by. All the feelings I'd shoved down deep in my barren soul began bubbling upward: unrelenting pain, anger, resentment, and bitterness. I slid down in the grass and leaned against the tree. I closed my eyes, trying to remember the last time I'd truly felt hope and happiness. It was when I believed my soulmate liked me – maybe even loved me. Yet, I overhead the whispers. People saying I didn't stand a chance. That I was delusional. That she was too good for me. That I was even ugly.

Unfortunately, I knew they were right.

I sat there in the grass for a long time, maybe hours, ruminating in pain and simmering in my anger until every cell of my body was saturated in hate. Finally, as the evening clouds rolled in, blotting out the sun and making me shiver, I stood up. I began walking down the dark, desolate street. And just as I passed underneath a streetlamp, its mercury vapor light twitched to life, and the blue-green glow immediately illuminated my path – and my mind. That's the moment I truly understood. It didn't matter that she was all of those things. I was still better than her. I was better than all of them.

Now, as I watch Cadie wave goodbye to friends and walk away from the fire's dying embers, I take position and ready myself; the time has come.

*For me to be set free - to win.*

Is this a tale of simple vengeance? If only.

## CHAPTER 2
## Cadie McLeod

When I was a little girl, just twelve years old, the people who loved me best died in a car crash. Except, to be completely accurate, they weren't in a car. A car crashed into them. Harbor Cove police said the car that hit my parents was traveling fifty miles per hour. Aileen, my joyful, free-spirited artist mom and Thomas, my loving, hardworking scientist dad, were plowed into by a drunk driver on a spring evening as they ran across M-22. Aileen and Thomas McLeod – my own Scottish saints - were killed instantly. Obliterated. That's the word the newspaper used. They were only thirty-five. At least they were together. Police theorize they were holding hands.

*Does that make it less painful?*

Reportedly, they were celebrating my dad's work promotion. That evening, instead of raising a champagne toast, they headed to Frosty Bar for their favorite Traverse City Cherry Ice Cream. Always two scoops in a waffle cone with sprinkles. Unfortunately, they never made it. A drunk driver ran them down in cold blood and drove away. Police never caught their killer.

I try not to think about the cause of their death because all sorts of horrifying images take hold of my mind. The police said there were no brake marks at the scene.

*How drunk would you have to be to run people down and simply drive off?*

Every year, on the anniversary of their deaths, I'm racked with the deepest sorrow, but I conceal it best I can. All evening, I've pretended I'm enjoying myself, pasting on a smile and trying to convince even myself. I've laughed – even giggled. I've danced on the beach. I've even talked with a few guys I never really got to know and a few who make me uneasy.

*Boys will be boys, right?*

I also worked up courage to talk to Nick. (We haven't spoken seriously since that dreadful morning on Mackinac Island when he pushed too far.) Tonight, he's getting drunk and acting off. He has a bit of a temper lately.

All night, I try to behave like a normal 18-year-old girl the best I can, but six years ago, my parents were ripped away, I was orphaned, and my life changed forever. For so long, I have dragged profound sadness behind me like a heavy chain. I can never be the happy-go-lucky girl I once was.

*I can never truly be normal. But I am trying. I know my parents would want me to be happy.*

Suddenly, I feel as if someone is watching me. I survey the dunes but see nothing but dark, endless shapes of shifting sand. Maybe it's the Devil in the Dunes, I laugh hollowly. Actually, it's the cryptic note that's got me worried and the truck that sometimes parks outside my house late at night. The other night its bright lights flashed into my bedroom window, waking me up. Then the lights went dark. I got out of bed, crept to the window, and looked out over the yard to the end of the driveway. I could see the black silhouette of someone inside the truck - just sitting there, watching the house. I nervously got back in bed and heard the truck slowly back out of the driveway.

*Maybe it was turning around? Should I say something to Aunt Marie? I really don't want to worry her.*

I stop walking the beach and look up. Overhead, the strawberry moon is enormous and deep red. When it's like this, I reminisce about the many times I trekked the beach with my parents and sometimes arm in arm with my mom. Whenever there was a supermoon shining bigger and brighter, my mom would get excited and burst out singing, "When the moon hits your eye, it's a big pizza pie. That's amore!" I would join in, singing badly, and mom would look down at me and laugh. She had a distinct laugh for a woman: loud and bold. Sometimes, other beachgoers would turn and look at my boisterous mother, but she didn't care. She was confident.

Occasionally, though, I could sense anxiety in my parents. It was subtle; I don't think anyone else would sense it. But sometimes, I could overhear them talking quietly about something - maybe the past? Their faces would cloud over and darken, and my dad would touch the scar around his eye. I usually walked away when they were like that. It made me uncomfortable.

Aileen had mysterious, light green emerald eyes that were almost translucent when she was happy, but they could suddenly darken when she became passionate or upset. Just as quickly, she could be laughing madly. I think that was the Scottish in her: a full spectrum of feelings she was never fearful to convey. My dad never joined in the craziness, though. He was more reserved – the conservative scientist - and would roll his eyes at us, but there was often a broad smile on his handsome, tanned face (years of playing outdoor Lacrosse). He was protective of my mother, and he loved her fiercely. I knew he enjoyed her silly, spontaneous humor (although she could certainly be serious and strong). She was the playful ying to his more serious yang. He looked at her like she was his bonnie lass – his good fortune. He also looked at me that way.

I can picture them: my father's square jaw, sandy brown hair, and ice-blue eyes and my mother's sometimes transparent green eyes and thick red hair cascading down her shoulders. No wonder they were voted Most Beautiful Couple their senior year. Not to brag, but I'm thankful I look just like her. Whenever I look in the mirror, I see my mom. However, when I do, I'm also reminded I'll never see her – never see them - again.

The tears begin to fall.

I hear someone yell my name from far away. Even my name reminds me of my mother. As a child and adult, my mom adored Nancy Drew books. She admired their clever and competent heroine who was never afraid to speak her mind. My mom once told me, "Nancy Drew shows us all the ways a woman can be. Women can be powerful and strong and live an independent life. You're the smartest person I know, Cadie. You could live a life like that. You can be free."

I often wondered what she meant by that.

*Free how?*

She said I reminded her of Nancy Drew, which, coming from her, was the supreme compliment. (Mom claimed to have read all 175 books; I've read 25, I think.) The books were written under the pseudonym Carolyn Keene, so my mother named me Carolyn. My little cousin Isla had a speech impediment and could never pronounce Carolyn. She began calling me Cadie, and the nickname stuck. Dad wanted to name me Elspeth after his Mhamo – so old fashioned! Can you imagine me being named Elspeth? Then I'd be called Ellie or Pethie or Peth.

*Groan.*

"So, your name is Beth?"

"No, Elspeth."

"Seth?"

*Ugh.*

I have a hard enough time getting people to pronounce my last name correctly.

"It's Mc Lee-od?

"No, McLeod."

"Mac Load?"

"No, McLeod as in, 'I wish I was floating away right now in a cloud.'"

Thankfully, my strong-willed mother won out, and Carolyn - Cadie - it is.

Instinctively, I touch my necklace. It provides comfort and sends me back to my twelfth birthday. (A few months later we laid my parents to rest in a small cemetery in Manistee). They gave me the necklace in a little pink box: half a gold heart on a small chain. The other half was my mother's. I smile remembering how she always wore the other half on her slender neck. Her necklace was never found at the accident scene. I went there once to look for it, but it was too painful. All I could think about is the horror they must have felt when the car hit them. I always prayed that their deaths were instant, so they never suffered. I'm heartbroken for dad: In the end, he couldn't protect his wife.

*My parents - my friends – oh, how I miss you.*

My mind travels back to the night before they were killed. We were in my cozy bedroom - mom tucking me in for the night. Dad peeked in to say goodnight, patted me on the head, and gently shut the door. With bright eyes, mom told me about a book she bought. She always loved to surprise me with a new book. That's how my love of reading – and learning - began.

"Can we read it now," I pleaded. "I would love to hear a new story!"

I knew she probably planned on reading it with daddy on the porch swing tomorrow or a in a few days, but I was hoping to stay up a bit later.

"Oh, okay," Aileen smiled. "How can I refuse my precious Carolyn?"

My mother was so good to me.

That night, we cuddled together under my fluffy pink comforter and read *The Legend of the Sleeping Bear Sand Dunes*. The book told the Ojibwa story of a mother and her two cubs. The three of them, to escape a raging Wisconsin fire, jumped into Lake Michigan and swam for their lives. The bears were strong swimmers, but it was dark, and they swam for hours. The poor cubs became separated from their momma. Exhausted, they drowned before they reached the shore.

I looked up and saw a hint of tears in my mother's eyes - the last time I would see my mother cry.

Momma Bear was heartbroken. She climbed the high bluff and called out to her babies over and over, but received no reply. There she waited, atop that bluff, scanning the horizon, looking for her children. So, the legend goes, the Great Spirit Manitou created two islands – North and South Manitou - to honor the bear cubs' bravery and a single sand dune to represent the resilient Momma Bear who spent the rest of her life in vigil, waiting for her babies to return.

Of course, I started sobbing. My mother didn't think I would take the story so much to heart, but I did. Aileen stroked my hair until I fell asleep, her warm body snuggling with mine. She finally fell asleep as well, and I remember waking up later and hearing her steady breathing. I snuggled in closer, and she placed her arm over me. It brought me contentment, and I remember thinking how lucky I was to have her as my mom. I felt nothing but peace and love and safety.

That's the final memory I have of my mom - and dad. The next day they were dead.

Now when I drive by Sleeping Bear, I recall that Indian legend, but my story is reversed. I'm the solitary sand dune eternally keeping vigil – staring into the deep Lake Michigan waters - waiting for my mother and father to return to me. Of course, like the legend, they never do. They are gone forever. Not drowned at sea, but murdered.

Even though I'm not a religious person, I sometimes pray there is a Great Spirit, so one day I can see Thomas and Aileen once more. Whenever I go to Sleeping Bear and walk to the edge of its massive dunes, I look out over the vast waters and am reminded of my parents. I feel a sense of hope that someday we will be reunited.

I'm crying again and suddenly conscious that my wet feet are freezing and becoming numb. I'm at the deserted end of the beach, far from the laughter and dying fire. I have a weird, disquieting feeling. I think about the truck parked outside my bedroom last night, its lights briefly shining in my window before the driver turned them off. Did they leave me that strange letter? If so, why?

I have an instinct I should leave the beach and head for the safety of home.

The westerly winds are now colder and picking up, creating sizeable waves and swirling my sundress. I'm shivering, and I wonder if it's from a gust front or something more sinister. The moon makes the approaching tall clouds appear whitish, and I notice their wispy tops. I also smell the earthiness of the Great Lake. A thunderstorm is on its way. I wipe away the cold tears from my cheeks and pat down my dress. It's time to head back. Back to the cozy cottage. Back to my Aunt Marie who will be waiting up for me.

Turning north toward the bonfire, I see the solitary sand dune – momma bear - off in the distance, and my mood lightens slightly.

I run down the beach, faster and faster – actually sprinting - and feel the cool sugar sand between my toes. My speed gives me strength, and running helps me forget. The cool, incoming storm winds toss my hair, and my mind is clear, at least for the moment, of the deep, piercing sadness that visits me every year on this day.

As I continue to sprint down the beach, my heart pounding, I also feel my spirit, my powerful desire to live and to make my parents proud. I remember my mother's favorite quote by Nancy Drew: "Nothing is impossible. The word itself says, I'm possible."

*Thank you, mother, for all you taught me. I will never forget.*

As I near the waning fire, all I can think about is the promise I made to my parents six years ago: that I would get justice for them. That I would find their killer.

I finally reach the bonfire and slow down, walking toward the smoldering embers, trying to catch my breath and quiet my mind. My remaining classmates look up at me as I pass by - a determined look etched across my face as a final thought dominates my thinking.

*Six years ago, you murdered my parents. You ran them down like dogs in the street and never looked back. And whoever you are, wherever you are,*

*I WILL FIND YOU.*

## CHAPTER 3
## The Weirdo

Strangling her was not that hard, surprisingly. In seconds, she was unconscious. That educational *YouTube* video was quite accurate. She gargled slightly and then slumped like a bag of rocks. I about fell over a tree branch trying to keep her from flopping into the sand. When her head slumped over, some of her hair shoved into my mouth. I'm still picking her long red hairs off my jacket.

She was heavier than I thought. A hundred and forty pounds? A hundred and fifty? I knew she was tall – she towers over her friends - but she's thin. No, not thin - athletic. I guess I just thought she'd be lighter. They say muscles are heavier. They're not kidding.

*Who am I kidding? I loved it.*

If I'm honest, I'd have to say the moment she was in my control was thrilling – electrifying! I had positioned myself in the woods, just off the trail. Hidden by trees, I watched and waited. I stayed utterly silent, knowing she would take this trail back to her bike. Finally, I saw her. Long, flowing red hair and bits of her pretty sundress peeking through the trees. The overhead moon provided just enough light. And I heard her. She seemed somewhat tipsy and playfully yelled goodbye to her friends, taking a final selfie over her shoulder.

"Love you guys!" she waved. "Stop by Scoops tomorrow. "I'll be there all afternoon. I'll give you free ice cream. Just don't tell anyone." She laughed and turned, walking into the dark trail. Those were the last words she uttered before she became mine.

As she plodded by in the sand, humming to herself, I calmly stepped out from behind a tree, quietly advanced, and quickly encircled my left arm around her neck. I grabbed my left lower bicep with my right hand, and pulled hard. (This put pressures on both carotid arteries, cutting off blood.) She was clearly shocked and began to struggle but went unconscious fairly quickly – in five or six seconds. Then lights out.

As she drooped on the ground in front of me, I carefully put my hand into my coat pocket and removed the syringe. Staying very still, I leaned over and lifted Cadie's lifeless arm. Then I forcefully plunged the Ketamine needle deep into her muscle.

*Enjoy your ride down the K-Hole, Cadie McLeod.*

After putting the syringe back into my pocket, I worked my forearms under her armpits, and locked them together just above her small breasts. I was excited to have her under my control until I felt her moist armpits.

I don't like it when women sweat. It's not ladylike. Not that I should know. I've never really touched a woman.

I dragged her in the sand – long legs sticking out - over the uneven, twisting trail through the small dunes, rocks, and occasional tree branch past the bike rack to my truck that was parked behind large grasses. I could hear happy, drunken laughter in the distance. I had to hurry.

It took only six minutes to reach my vehicle, open the tailgate, and heave her up into the truck bed (not the easiest moment) and roll her in. It did take a minute to hoist up both of her long legs. Earlier, I had placed a black bookbag in the back of my truck. From it, I grabbed zip ties and bound her wrists. Then I tied a bandana tight over her eyes and head, securing my guest for the ride to her new – albeit brief - home.

I hope I didn't give her too much Special K. I don't want to kill her – *not yet anyways.*

Before I closed the truck's tailgate, I remembered I had one last thing to do. I leaned in and put my hand down her dress. I felt for the necklace and then grabbed it. I ripped the half a heart necklace from her slim neck and shoved it in my jean's pocket. Then I slammed the tailgate and was off.

Exceeding my expectations, in a little over twelve minutes, Cadie and I were on the road. As I peered over my steering wheel into the darkness, grinning like a damn fool, my mood began to darken. My smiled faded, and my eyes narrowed into steely slits.

This was really happening. My fantasy was really coming true – and coming to an end.

As I drove down that lonely road, raindrops now falling softly on my window, my thoughts turned to what lie ahead: to the next several days and what I was surely owed.

## CHAPTER 4
## Thomas and Aileen McLeod

Right up until the night the couple was murdered, Cadie's parents lived a mostly charmed life. The high school sweethearts were blessed with love and a strong marriage, a sweet daughter, their homey cottage in Harbor Cove, and good friends and neighbors on Laurel Lane – a happy existence along Michigan's west coast. The singing sand beaches and freshwater breezes as well as the deeply forested state parks and the world's largest freshwater dunes added joy to their lives as they loved hiking and weekends boating on Lake Michigan. They had no reason to believe their seemingly blessed lives would ever be any different.

However, as the saying goes, "Into every life rain must fall."

Often called the Third Coast of the US, the west Michigan coastline – all 130 miles - stretches from Silver Lake in the north to St. Joseph in the south. All along I-96 and up to M-31, M-109, and M-22, from the Indiana border to the northern tip of Leelanau County and Grand Traverse Lighthouse, the shoreline is lined with lush, emerald-green forests and wilderness islands, towering dunes that rise several hundred feet above Lake Michigan, and picturesque beach towns. Inviting hamlets and colorful, scenic communities like South Haven, Saugatuck, Holland, Grand Haven, Pentwater, Empire, Glen Arbor, Leland, Charlevoix, and Petoskey dot the coastline. In 2011, *Good Morning America* even named the Sleeping Bear Dunes National Lakeshore, "the most beautiful place in America." The marketing geniuses call it "Pure Michigan," and it is a lovely place to live.

However, no place is perfect. Even the Garden of Eden had its slippery snake.

After graduating high school, the Most Beautiful Couple attended Alma College. Like any good Scotsman, Thomas loved Lacrosse; he was the Scots' midfielder and helped win the MIAA title his senior year. The young man was strong and agile - in the best shape of his life. His teammates often joked that Thomas, the team leader who played both offense and defense, grew eyes in the back of his head as he could see everything on the field. He was fortunate to have loyal teammates who were more like a band of brothers, and they added depth to Thomas's life.

After college, when Thomas, Sam, Al, and the rest would meet up for the annual Highland Festival, their fists full of Glenfiddich, the men might get a little crazy and loudly sing "Onward Scotsmen" until they fell about laughing. Regardless of the previous night's reverie, though, every year the 'brothers' managed to win tug-of-war. Sometimes, the guys made it to Detroit for St. Andrew's Society Highland Games. After, they would all head to The Scotsman to share a wee dram. In the decade before Thomas was murdered, he was living a good life surrounded by the best of men, and every single one of them thought Thomas was the best guy they knew.

He was the type of favored young man, however, who might inspire jealousy in lesser men.

Thomas and Aileen married, and Aileen, who had earned an Art and Design degree from Alma, became a watercolorist. Her west Michigan landscapes, noted for their intense blue pigments and bold strokes, sold well throughout the Midwest. Several years after college, she opened an art studio in an historic building in downtown Alma next to Old City Hall. Aileen loved the building's Italianate architecture with its low overhanging roof and tall, narrow windows that allowed sunlight to flood her studio and colorful canvases. She even spearheaded the Alma Heritage Foundation to preserve Alma's historic buildings. Thomas, who ultimately earned a PhD from MSU, became an environmental chemist for the State of Michigan and worked twenty minutes away in Mt. Pleasant.

It was most definitely a good life - so far.

For a long time, the couple was content in their agricultural college town - until they weren't. As the years went by, they grew restless for a change, and their westside roots beckoned them home. Thomas and Aileen also decided they wanted Cadie to have the childhood they had – a sunny lake life filled with boating, beaches, and nighttime bonfires. So, when Cadie was eleven, they made the difficult choice to leave Alma behind and begin anew. They headed for the west coast of Michigan, specifically Harbor Cove.

The small coastal town is situated in Benzie County along Lake Michigan just northwest of Crystal Lake and south of the entrance to the Sleeping Bear Sand Dunes. The nearby lakes are quiet, secluded, and surrounded by lush forests just outside the National Lakeshore. Harbor Cove is a quaint, picturesque town with charming shops, a winery, bustling farmer's market, a much-loved ice cream shop, and, of course, a crystal blue harbor.

To Thomas and Aileen, Harbor Cove was Shangri-La – the truly perfect place to raise their only child. Of course, Shangri-La is a myth, and most people don't realize the fabricated literary town was in fact not paradise; instead, it was preparing for catastrophe.

So, in the end, the metaphor *was* fitting.

Their Shangri-La did experience catastrophe, and, like the cold rain that falls from a Lake Michigan storm cloud, bad luck finally fell on the McLeods.

First, it fell on Thomas and Aileen. Then their daughter Cadie.

Six years after the death of Thomas and Aileen, on a warm Friday night in June, when the community of Harbor Cove was celebrating its seniors, their beautiful and talented daughter left an end-of-school bonfire on the edge of Lake Michigan. She had her whole life ahead of her that included a full ride scholarship to Michigan State University to study chemistry and run hurdles for the MSU track team. It was a stellar future.

At midnight, their daughter left her friends and the fire's glowing remnants and walked down an isolated trail into the windswept dunes. All she wanted to do was retrieve her bike and ride home to the safety of Aunt Marie's cottage. But that was not to be; someone in the universe had other plans. That night the young woman never made it to the cozy cottage only miles away. Instead, in the desolate dunes under a now cloudy sky, Cadie McLeod came face to face with a devil in the dunes: pure evil in human form.

Then, in an instant, the exceptional young woman was gone. Thomas and Aileen's much beloved daughter simply vanished like an evening breeze blowing across the shifting sands.

## SATURDAY
### CHAPTER 5
## Nick Brennan

I yank the deep blue quilt up over my head, trying to go back to sleep, but I can't. The heavy June rain is now pelting the window behind my head. It sounds like an army of acorns attacking a coffee can. The storm they talked about is here, and my Saturday is ruined.

Man, does my head hurt. It feels like a pumpkin that's been dropped on a sidewalk. I know that sounds strange, but for some reason the word pumpkin just popped into my mind. And sidewalk. That's just how my brain works.

My right ankle is also killing me.

*What the hell happened last night?*

I can't remember a thing.

I rub my left foot on my aching ankle, hoping to dull the pain, but it continues to throb. My head also continues to radiate in misery, and I curse the alcohol at last night's party – like it was the alcohol's fault.

"I curse you, Traverse City Whiskey. Why did you let me drink so much?"

That wasn't my plan: to overdrink. I blame Glen Boer.

I rub my eyes and think about Cadie. I immediately feel a bit better.

Dark clouds make shadows on my bedroom walls. When the sun is high over Lake Michigan, Harbor Cove is the best. The deep blue water shimmers and reflects the sky above. Except for nearby Torch Lake, which many people compare to the Caribbean, I think our little cove is the most beautiful place on earth. However, when storms hit, and our small corner of the world darkens, Harbor Cove takes on a darker, stranger vibe. There's something eerie about a deserted tourist town.

Thinking about the rain makes me thankful for last night. The party was great. Yeah, it was a long, tiring day with two AP exams, helping at the church rummage sale, track practice, and then the party. But now that graduation day is getting closer, I'm thankful to spend time with friends – and Cadie – even if we are off right now. It's hitting me hard that life will never be the same.

*Did I say something to her last night? I feel like I may have gotten a little mouthy.*

Mike is going to Michigan Tech to study wildlife management. Dirk is going to study exercise science at Central (Dude, how is exercise a degree?), and Layne is going to OU - not sure what he's studying, though. I thought Blake would stay put and help with his uncle's marina, but his uncle thinks Blake needs a business degree, so Blake's going to Western. I like Blake; I mean we're friends, but he's a little off. Just kind of insecure and intense sometimes. If I were his uncle, I'm not sure I would want him involved in the marina. Then there's Cadie and her ambitious plans to earn a PhD in forensic science at MSU. Did I say she earned a full ride to run track and study science? She's amazing - and beautiful – and sometimes mysterious. What can I say? I love her.

And me? I've been waitlisted. At least it's the University of Michigan. Still, it's kind of embarrassing not to have a college nailed down by now. I did earn top honors in the Midwest Young Writers Challenge sponsored by Penn State. And I'm not stupid. So, yeah, I'm hopeful I'll get in. UM has a prestigious creative writing and literature program. I know - kind of an unexpected major for the son of a cop.

My two favorite books are *To Kill a Mockingbird* and *The Catcher in the Rye*. When you grow up with a dad who is the local town hero, your personality forms into a strange mixture of social awareness and teen angst. It keeps me constantly second guessing myself. (Not necessarily a bad thing, though.) One day, I hope to write a novel. I just need a worthy topic. Hopefully, once I leave Harbor Cove, my world will open up like everyone says it will, and I'll have a million things to write about. So, my small world is changing and growing – for the best, I guess.

*Yet why do I suddenly feel something is not right?*

I bury my head in the oversized pillow. I don't want to think about everything right now. I just need more sleep. Unfortunately, sleep seems out of the question as I now hear my father's deep, rich voice. He is out in the living room. I can hear him speaking emphatically to someone on the phone. He sounds worried; his voice is loud. I rarely hear him worried, so I can tell something's wrong. It must be a bad case. I strain to hear what he's talking about.

As I mentioned, my father Jake Brennan is a cop, more specifically, a police detective in Harbor Cove. He has worked for the Harbor Cove Police Department since he graduated from Harbor Cove High School. Being a cop was his first and only job, and he loves it. He began as a patrol officer but also has worked as a resource officer at my high school and as a training and recruiting officer. My dad puts in long hours because he really does care. He's kind of a Boy Scout lol.

To be honest, Harbor Cove can be boring. Not much goes on. Speeding tickets, a tourist peeing in the bushes, some kids spray painting lopsided penises on the *Welcome to Harbor Cove* sign - that's about it. But that's not to say nothing happens. Two years ago, my dad was driving 131 in a snowstorm on his way to Big Rapids when he came across a serious crash. Jake was the first responder at a bus fire. There was also a five-car pileup. It was bad. The bus driver was killed instantly. My dad climbed into the bus several times and saved the children from dying. Unfortunately, he never saw the little girl unconscious under a seat. I know her death still haunts him.

For his bravery, he was awarded Michigan's Medal of Honor – going above and beyond. We all attended the ceremony in East Lansing. Without getting too sappy, I'd say my dad is pretty darn cool. He's the best guy I know. Does that sound sappy? I imagine it does.

Jake's off the phone now, and I can hear his new combat boots hitting the hallway's wood floor as he walks towards my room.

"Hey Nick, I'm glad you're up," he says, his voice thick. As he opens my door, his large 6'5" frame fills the small doorway. (Everything in our cottage house is little: little doors, little rooms, little windows. Clearly, my petite mom picked out our house. My dad did try to make her happy.) My friends even poke fun: "Dude, how can you and your giant dad live in that tiny dollhouse?"

Jake enters my room. I can sense something is really wrong. He's unusually quiet; I feel his anxiety.

"I just got a phone call from Marie McLeod. She said Cadie never came home last night."

"What?" I'm still sleepy and trying to process the words he just spoke.

"Wake up, Nick!" my dad says forcefully. "Cadie didn't come home last night.

Marie just called. She's worried. You were at the party, right?"

*I can barely remember last night.*

"Yeah, I was there," I respond to my dad's strong tone and sit up, still groggy, trying to fully wake up and understand what he's saying to me. My brain finally clicks on.

"She probably spent the night at Tori's house. Or Julie's house. Her aunt should just give them a call."

"Marie already called them," my dad says, now pacing the room. "Marie said she's called all of Cadie's friends and asked them to call other friends, but no one's heard from her."

In the shadows of my bedroom, his face looks tired and drawn. Not normal for him. Jake's big brown eyes are usually smiling and upbeat – happy and trying to see good in everything – unless the past creeps into his thoughts. Watching his grim face is now making me nervous.

"Marie has been texting Cadie since late last night when she didn't return home. She said it's not like Cadie to not answer her phone."

"Her phone probably died," I respond, feeling more uneasy. "Let me look at my phone."

Cadie has been my crush for years, ever since she was my neighbor. She lived right next door to us in a blue house with a large white porch. We would spread a blanket out on the porch and play *Clue* while her mom planted flowers. Cadie loved her mother so much. Sadly, her mom and dad were killed by a drunk driver. Dad loathes the fact that he never found the driver and brought them to justice. He thinks he failed the McLeods. First the McLeods and then the little dead girl. But he did everything he could – for all of them. Sometimes, you just don't catch the bad guy. Life isn't like the movies. There's not always a happy ending.

I look at my phone. No word from Cadie. But I do have a bunch of texts from other people. I set the phone down and begin rubbing my aching forehead.

Ever since Cadie's parents were killed, dad and I have been super protective of Cadie and Aunt Marie. After their deaths, Cadie went to live with Marie a few miles away in Waters Edge, a subdivision not too far from where the party took place last night. Their deaths crushed me. I loved her mom and dad. When

Thomas and Aileen were killed and Cadie moved away, my whole life changed. It was like a dark blanket got thrown over my world, and it remained altered for a long time. Sure, with time, we all healed somewhat, but whenever I see Cadie looking down, I know she's thinking about her mom and dad.

*Why can't I remember last night? Jesus, what happened at that party?*

My pumpkin head is hurting again.

"I don't have any messages from Cadie," I say out loud. "But I do have a lot of other texts I need to read."

Dad is still pacing and reading his own text messages. I quickly reach over and pick my phone back up from the blue nightstand beside my bed. (Before she moved to Florida, my mom redecorated my bedroom in everything nautical.) Now my phone is completely blown up. I have a ton of texts – and still none from Cadie.

*This is not good.*

Scrolling through them, I can see they're all about Cadie. People are wondering where she's at and getting worried. The word is out that she didn't come home last night, and no one can get a hold of her. This is so unlike her. I'm starting to panic. I notice my breathing quicken, and my heart is beating faster. I send Cadie a text.

"Hey, girl, it's me. Will you call me? No one can get a hold of you. We're starting to worry about you."

Then I call her. The phone rings and rings and goes to voicemail, which is full.

As I put the phone down, I fight to remember last night. Finally, a memory comes to me.

"You know, dad, I spoke to Cadie last night."

My dad looks up at me, his face tight. He nods.

"Yesterday was the anniversary of her parents' death. Cadie seemed mostly okay, but later on I could tell she wasn't right. She left the party for a while to walk down the beach. When she came back, she still seemed a bit off, and I asked her if she was okay and if she needed a ride. She said she rode Marie's bike over, so she would just ride it home. I also just remember her saying she had to open Scoops this morning. I'm sure that's where she's at. She probably spent the night at someone's house and didn't have her phone charger. Now she's at work. I'm sure she's fine."

Now I'm trying to calm my own nerves. The fact that no one can find her and she went missing on the day her parents died is honestly pretty concerning. I should have been there for her. I should have made sure she got home all right. I just can't remember. Then an unwelcome thought pops into my mind: Emily Hadly – the little girl who went missing from the dunes years ago. I was only seven, but I recall the scowl on my mom's face in the rearview mirror– her lecturing me from the front seat of our minivan as we pulled into The Landing. She wouldn't let me play alone in the dunes for a quite a while. No one did. Then time went on, and we all forgot.

*Did they ever find that little girl?*

My dad interrupts my disturbing thoughts.

"You didn't walk Cadie to her bike last night and make sure she got home alright?" my dad asks while he stares at me, incredulous.

I just hang my head.

Dad strides out of my room.

"Get up and get dressed. We're heading into town."

I now feel like complete shit. Suddenly, I picture a fragment from last night: me yelling at Cadie.

*Why was I yelling at Cadie?*

*Who am I kidding? I know why.*

## CHAPTER 6

Jake Brennan sprinted out the cottage's side door and into the downpour. The spring rain pounded the driveway's brown brick pavers. Powerful winds besieged both men as they moved quickly to the gray and black Chevy Tahoe parked behind Nick's bright yellow Jeep Wrangler. The Tahoe had keyless entry, so Jake deftly clicked the key on his belt and quickly jumped in his SUV. Nick slid into the passenger seat.

"It's a gullywasher," dad said, profusely shaking the water off his police-issued duty rainshell. "My pants and shoes are already soaked."

"Dad, no one says gullywasher but you."

Nick quickly pulled his already wet track sweatshirt off over his head and dug around in the back seat of the Tahoe for one of his dad's hoodies as the SUV left the driveway. His heart continued to beat hard within his chest. When he sat back down, he looked at his phone. Still no messages from Cadie. A continued outpouring of messages about her, though.

"Any word from Cadie" Jake asked, looking over at his son's phone.

"No, nothing," Nick responded.

"Okay, let me know if you do. Hey, I noticed how dirty your Jeep was this morning. Good for you it's raining."

Jake tilted his head forward and brushed rain off his wavy brown hair. "What were you doing last night? Off roading? I told you if you keep doing that and your tires go bad, I'm not buying you new ones."

"I wasn't, dad. I just went to the party and went home."

Nick very rarely lied to his dad, but he had only a faint recollection of driving somewhere last night.

*But where?*

Nick wasn't sure at all what happened last night. He had a problem with blacking out lately.

24

With windshield wipers on high and the front window fogging up, the Tahoe headed down Laurel Lane, past the colorful, tidy cottages with green lawns all in a row. The street was littered with tree branches of varying sizes. At the first stop sign, they made a left and headed onto Broad Street and then into downtown Harbor Cove.

The winds made an eerie, whistling sound as they pushed against the vehicle.

"How long has Cadie worked at Scoops?" Jake asked sharply, like he was interrogating a perp. Nick could tell his dad was still mad at him. "I thought she was working at that winery in Traverse City?"

"Since October," Nick replied. "Cadie said she was spending too much money in gas driving all the way up there twice a week. She also wanted to work closer to home. Closer to Aunt Marie in case she ever needed her. Cadie always looks out for Marie."

As the police car drove through the windy, rainy town, both men were lost in thought. It was actually quite alarming to think of Cadie missing, especially during a storm. It blew in last night, right as the party was ending. What happened to the young woman? Where could she be?

Nick looked at his cell phone again. No messages from Cadie.

Now fully awake, Nick began recalling the night's events more clearly. One thing that bothered him immensely was Rod Koenig. That guy was bad news. Nick knew something had transpired between Cadie and Rod, but she would never tell him what it was. Nick always wondered why. He also remembered that as Cadie was leaving last night, taking the isolated trail that led to the bike rack, he thought he saw Rod leave that way a while earlier. He was a cocky, arrogant dude who flunked third grade and got held back. The guy always comes on strong. A rumor has it he sexually assaulted his own stepsister, but nothing came of it. There were other girls at school who also shared stories about Rod – things he said or the occasional grope, but is he dangerous? The thought of Rod Keonig hurting Cadie was making Nick physically sick.

Nick felt terrible about several things last night. He was drunk and just sat stupidly on a tree stump most of the night talking to Blake, who was badmouthing women and talking about how ugly he is. Nick thought Blake was basically a good dude when sober, but knew he got dark when he was drinking. Some people think Blake is weird, but Nick understood he'd gone through a lot in his life. He didn't know all the details, but Nick hated to write a guy off because he's had a tough life. His dad taught him to give people second chances.

A classmate was able to buy Blake a case of Solid Gold from Henley's liquor store in Empire, so Nick and Blake drained the cans, crumpled them, and began tossing them in the bonfire as the girls yelled at them to stop. Nick thought the three of them – Cadie, Nick, and Blake - were like a tragicomedy in Mr. Bradley's Shakespeare class. He and Blake were both probably in love with the same girl. (Although Blake insists his "crush" on Cadie is long over, Nick sees how he looks at her.) After drinking all the Solid Golds, Blake took off. Said he had things to do early the next morning. Nick was on his own for a while, just drunk and sitting near the dying fire.

Nick recalled some of his conversation with Cadie, but not much. He was angry about something, and he might have yelled at her. Then Cadie left. Nick was ashamed he didn't get up off that tree stump to walk Cadie to her bike and then follow her home. He was still a bit upset with her, which was unfair, he knew. Also, he was most likely shitfaced when she left. Earlier in the evening, Nick did five shots of Traverse City Whiskey with Glen Boer, a guy who runs the 400 and 200.

Now on his way to Scoops, Nick was disappointed with himself for throwing empty cans on the beach, for thinking bad thoughts about Blake, and for letting Cadie walk alone in the dark to her bike. What kind of man was he, anyway? Getting drunk, speaking harshly to the girl he adores? His dad would never act that way. (Yet, growing up, his dad had an intact family. Not to excuse his overdrinking and bad attitude as of late, but Nick felt that his mom leaving them was impacting him more than he was willing to admit. He felt a lot of anger lately. And sadness.) Nick remembered the many times he sat with Cadie - held her - while she talked or cried about her parents' deaths.

*Where was that man last night?*

Nick prayed he would see Cadie in a few minutes, her bright smile making everything all right.

*I know I can be an ass sometimes, but I know I can do better. I'm sorry, Cadie.*

The police car drove past the historic Foss Hardware, the newly renovated music park and gazebo, and Bell's Diner. In front of the fifty-year-old restaurant, a large twisted branch blocked the sidewalk, broken off a massive, ancient oak tree that towers over the business. Twigs were everywhere, and being swept up and tossed in the swirling winds.

"What a mess," Jake muttered, shaking his head. "This is going to be quite a cleanup."

As they slowly cruised past the diner, 98-year-old Frank Jansen, a fixture in Harbor Cove, shuffled over to the gnarled branch, surveyed it, and tried to pull it into a nearby alley. Frank raised a hand to wave, and Jake slowed and rolled down his window a bit.

"Hey, Frank, don't do that. You're going to hurt yourself. Just wait for tree service."

Frank smiled, nodded, and went on his way, his yellow hat pulled low as the rain picked up. Through the water-streaked windshield, Scoops soon came into view, and the Tahoe pulled into a parking spot directly in front of the charming, yellow shop with a large painting of a fuchsia pink ice cream scoop over the front door. Immediately, both men noticed that Scoops was dark and the usually cheerful neon open sign turned off.

There were a few cars in the dreary, overcast parking lot waiting for the shop to open. It was 9:25 am, and the doors promptly open at 9 am because, in addition to selling ice cream and frozen yogurt, Scoops also sells the area's best Traverse City coffee and homemade beignets. Thus, there are always morning customers waiting. Alcee Lagard, a New Orleans native, owns Scoops, and when she bought the decades-old ice cream shop, she decided to add a bakery counter. The town immediately lined up. This morning, some pastry faithfuls braved the rain and sat in their cars, engines running, windows fogging up under dark skies, waiting for some hot coffee and deep-fried goodness.

"There's Alisha's car," Nick said, pointing to the silver Chevy Malibu parked in the corner. "Alisha works with Cadie."

"I'll check the cars in the parking lot and then walk around the building," Jake said. "Why don't you talk to Alisha? See what she knows."

Jake got out of the car and walked around the parking lot, taking notice of the people in the cars. Nothing seemed to be out of the ordinary. He walked briskly through the rain to the shop's front door. Peering through the glass, he could see that the shop was empty and dark. No activity anywhere. Pulling his jacket up around his neck and leaning into the building to thwart the rain, Jake walked the perimeter of the small business, looking into windows and the back door. Nothing. No activity anywhere. Just a quiet little shop waiting for Cadie to throw open the front door, turn on the lights, and brighten the place with her Scottish charm. The business's dark interior spooked Brennan. His unease continued to grow.

Head down, Jake ran over to Alisha's car. He could see Nick leaned over, talking to the young woman through the partially rolled down window. Alisha was running her hand through her short hair. She looked upset.

"Hi, Alisha," Jake said. "How are you?"

"Not too good, Mr. Brennan," the girl answered.

"So, what's going on? Where's Cadie?"

"I have no idea, sir," the young woman responded. "She wasn't here when I showed up. The door was locked, and I banged on it, but she never answered. I went around back, but she wasn't there, either. So, I got back in my car, and I tried calling her. Her voicemail's full. I texted her, and she never texted back, and she always texts back. We were supposed to create a new display today. Cadie came up with some cute design. Now everyone is texting about her. People are already posting about it on Facebook. No one knows where Cadie is, and no one's heard from her since the party last night. This is just not like her," Alisha said, gripping her steering wheel firmly with both hands. "I'm really worried."

Nick turned to his dad.

"Alisha said that Cadie was excited for today because they also were planning on introducing a new ice cream."

"Okay," Jake said, his eyes squinting and his eyebrows low and knitted together. "Alisha, please text Nick if you hear anything. Do you have his phone number?"

"No," Alisha replied, but I can DM him."

Nick nodded in agreement.

"Whatever that means," Jake said. "As long as you let me know. Thanks, Alisha. And again, please contact us if you hear anything. You also can call the police station. They'll give me the message."

"Thank you, Mr. Brennan. Please find Cadie. We all love her."

Jake and Nick raced back to the Tahoe. It was raining even harder, and both men were soaked. Most of the cars had left by now. The empty parking lot just added to the heaviness of heart Jake and Nick felt as they got in the car and sat there quietly for a short while, neither saying anything. They were no closer to finding their sweet, spirited neighbor than when they got to Scoops.

"Where are we going now?" Nick nervously asked his dad as they pulled the Tahoe out onto the road.

"To the station. We have a lot to do. Something is wrong, Nick. Very, very wrong."

Nick felt he could throw up any minute. His mind swam with terrible thoughts. He looked at his phone: still no messages from Cadie.

As the men drove down Rodin Avenue, the rain picked up. Sheeting gusts of wind off Lake Michigan pushed the rain harder. Nick put his head on the cold, foggy window trying to quiet his brain. The rain was loud in the Tahoe, and the men had a time talking and hearing each other, so they just stayed silent. Jake also was having a hard time seeing out the windshield. He leaned forward in his seat to see better and turned the defrost on high, making the vehicle uncomfortably hot. The Tahoe sliced through the dark, rain-drenched streets, while both men inwardly felt rising terror about what might have happened to Cadie McLeod.

Jake's mind filled with dark images of Thomas, Aileen, the little girl who died in the bus fire, and now Cadie McLeod.

Nick's mind began to recall more of last night's party, and what he remembered he didn't like.

## CHAPTER 7

As they drove to the station, Jake Brennan was dreading the call he knew he had to make. With his left hand on the wheel and eyes darting front and down, Jake's right hand found the contact information and called. She answered in seconds.

"Hello?"

"Hi, Marie. It's Jake Brennan. I'm just checking in. Any news on Cadie?"

"No, Jake. Nothing," Marie said, her voice hoarse and shaky. "Did you go to Scoops?"

"Yes. Nick and I just drove over. She's not there."

Jake looked over at Nick. His eyes were closed, his head leaning on the window. Jake knew he was thinking about Cadie.

"I've called everyone I can think of," Marie cried. "No one's heard from her. I'm so worried! I looked all around the house. The yard. The garage. Her dad's Camaro. I even walked down the street. I was just trying to see if she was anywhere, but I didn't find her. And my bike is still gone. She rode it to the party last night."

"Hmm, okay," Jake said. "Listen, Marie, please don't get too worried. More than likely, she's at some friend's house and overslept."

Jake spoke the calming words, but he didn't believe a word of them. He didn't believe Cadie suddenly became irresponsible.

The windshield wiper dragged across the window, annoying Jake. His nerves were on edge. He took his hand off the wheel to twist the wiper knob back and forth somewhat angrily while still talking to Marie.

"I just pray Cadie is at a friend's house," Marie responded. "Except no one has seen her. I really can't think of a friend I haven't contacted. She's very conscientious about her job. She would never oversleep and not open the shop."

"Nick and I are on our way to the police station to meet up with my partner. We're going to drive over to The Landing to see if we can find anything. I'll call you after we check it out. Please contact me immediately if you hear from Cadie or get any information. Marie, how old is Cadie?"

"Eighteen."

After hanging up the phone with Marie, Jake got on his two-way radio and called his partner Craig Kitchen.

Just then, a tan Equinox swerved into his lane and swerved back.

"Shit!" Jake yelled out.

"What? What is it?" Nick yelled back, jumping up in his seat.

It was a teenage driver looking to avoid a large puddle. For a second, Jake and the teen's eyes met, and she stared at him, her eyes growing big. Jake had to swerve the Tahoe onto the shoulder to avoid her. The rain began to come down harder, and water pooled everywhere.

Jake called Craig on his two-way. His partner answered quickly.

"Hey, it's Jake. So, it looks like we might have a missing person."

"Oh, really? We haven't had one in a while."

"No one has seen this young woman or talked to her since last night. No texting, either. Can you meet me at the station? Nick and I are headed there now."

Nick heard Detective Kitchen say, "Absolutely" and, "Why is Nick with you?"

"The missing girl is a friend of Nick's. Cadie McLeod. Actually, she was our old neighbor. And Nick was at the seniors' bonfire last night where Cadie was last seen. It seems she just disappeared from the sand dunes last night."

"The Devil in the Dunes got her," Craig replied.

"What? What did you say?"

"The Devil in the Dunes," Craig responded.

"What does that mean?" Jake asked, nonplussed. "The Devil in the Dunes?"

"You haven't heard that before? Oh, it's just an old wives' tale. Years ago, when that little girl went missing from the sand dunes, some of the locals say it's the Devil in the Dunes that got her.'"

"Craig, I really wish you hadn't told me that," Jake said. "That's not helping."

"Sorry, I shouldn't have said anything. It just came to mind. It just seems weird to have another girl missing from the dunes. Anyway, I can be to the station in a bit. I'm over at the rec center with Kayla. She had a basketball game this morning. We're on our way home now."

Jake heard a faint, "We won!" from Kayla in the background.

"That's awesome, Kayla. Good for you," Jake said. "I'll see you soon, Craig. Then we're going to need to head up to The Landing, the last place Cadie was seen, so bring your rain gear. If we don't find her at The Landing, we'll have Marie make an official Missing Person Report. We'll also need to contact the Michigan State Police and enter her information in NamUs."

"What's NamUs?" Nick whispered.

"National Missing and Unidentified Persons System. It's a database of missing people."

Craig piped up, "What about an Amber Alert?"

"She's 18. As you know, if she was 17, we could issue one."

A sudden gust of strong wind shook the car. The winds were increasing.

"That's wild," Craig said. "She's closer to a kid than an adult."

"Not in the eyes of the government."

Jake looked over at his son.

"Nick, do you have a recent photo of Cadie?"

"I can find something on her Instagram."

"Okay, do that and send it to me."

The storm-filled clouds continued to dump rain on the Tahoe's windshield, and the metal wiper still dragged its cracked rubber blade across the glass. Jake felt a headache coming on and a painful knot forming in his shoulder blades.

Also, as he drove, Jake fought to keep a horrific memory buried – a memory that too often bubbled to the surface. He thought time would help, at least somewhat, but unfortunately the detective could recall that gruesome night six years ago like it happened yesterday. Despite his efforts, the memory began to play in his mind like a vicious horror movie.

It was a quiet June evening. Jake and Laura laid on their new, microfiber sectional watching a rerun of *Family Feud*. Nick was slouched in the oversized chair. His face glued to his PlayStation. Jake heard the name Peter Parker, so he knew Nick was playing Spider-Man. When the detective got home earlier, the windows were already pushed up, and an unseasonably warm June wind wafted through the screens and gently ruffled the soft, blue curtains. Jake found it relaxing.

Next door, Joe Webster had just finished mowing his back yard. He often got home late, so sometimes he mowed until it got too dark to see. Jake found the familiar sounds comforting. On TV, Steve Harvey was laughing at a contestant who scored only twenty points in the Bonus Round. Jake and Laura laid there, blissfully unaware - just a contented family spending time together in the seconds before their lives would change forever.

Suddenly, a cacophony of police sirens split the peaceful evening. Jake ran out to his front yard listening to one patrol car after another race through Harbor Cove, sirens blaring, heading north out of town. All the worried neighbors ran out simultaneously – as if on cue. Jake looked right and saw Joe standing frozen in his front yard. He nodded at Jake solemnly. Jake looked left, but he didn't see Thomas and Aileen, only Cadie and her babysitter standing on the front porch. Jake heard patrol car after patrol car racing north, and he immediately understood that the symphony of wailing sirens was either a mass shooting, house fire, or serious car accident.

He knew it was wrong to do so, but in that moment, he prayed the victim wasn't someone he knew. Unfortunately, for him and so many people in Harbor Cove, it was. It was two sweet souls known to many people in the small town, especially Jake, his neighbors, and, most of all, little Cadie McLeod. Jake jumped in his patrol car and raced through town following the sirens. He knew that what he was about to witness in the minutes to come would haunt him to his grave.

He wasn't wrong.

Thinking back to that horrendous night, Jake blinked back the tears. He tried to focus on the road. The two men were almost to the police station. Jake looked over at Nick who was on his phone.

"We're almost to the station," Jake said, his voice thick. "Get ready, son. This may be the toughest day of your life."

## CHAPTER 8
## Nick Brennan

We're almost there, and my hands are shaking - adrenaline coursing through me. I have so many messages on my phone. My friends, Cadie's friends, and people who were at the party. Still no word from or about Cadie. No one has seen her or talked to her. There's no posts on her Facebook or Instagram, either. The last Instagram post was Cadie and her teammates goofing around on the bus ride home from Ludington, but there are no recent posts. I remember Cadie and her friends taking selfies last night next to the bonfire. Cadie, Julie, and Tori, their faces all pressed together, laughing and pouting their lips.

I recall Cadie waving at me – "Aren't we cute, Nick?" - while they took the pictures. I'm sure Cadie would have posted those selfies to Instagram by now if she could. That fact makes me more alarmed than ever. It seems she disappeared right after she left the beach.

*Where in the hell is she?*

I'm feeling quite frightened now. Does the anniversary of her parents' death have anything to do with her being missing? Why did she take that strange walk on the beach by herself? Did she go back to the water later and something happened? Cadie is one of the toughest people I know. I mean, she endured her parents' deaths, right? She's also extremely intelligent (third in our class with a Mensa IQ), speaks Italian, and is super athletic. In the fall, she shot 145 over two days to set a school record in golf, won Regionals in the 100-meter hurdles, and earned the Harbor Cove Senior Female Athlete of the Year Award at last week's banquet. She even drove us to the banquet in her dad's '67 Camaro. There's no way a girl like Cadie McLeod waded into Lake Michigan and drowned herself. Cadie would never in a million years kill herself.

*Right?*

I remember when she was my new neighbor. Cadie was probably eleven or so, and she was skipping on the sidewalk in front of my house, just past our white picket fence. I ran up and made a lame joke about her pink and purple tennis shoes that lit up every time she took a step. She turned, her green eyes flashing, and stared me down.

"I'd challenge you to a battle of wits, sir, but you are clearly unarmed."

Then she flipped her red hair, turned back around, and skipped away. I just sat there, mouth hanging open. I was already captivated. At eleven. I didn't realize for years that she was quoting Shakespeare.

*I mean, how does an eleven-year-old even know Shakespeare let alone quote him?*

I can't comprehend someone like Cadie hurting herself or even coming close to killing herself. She also said several times she wanted to make her parents proud. No way she would do something to herself. But then the little unwelcome thought creeps in.

*Would she hurt herself?*

Or what if somebody grabbed her off the road? Last July, a girl about Cadie's age went missing as she walked along Lakeshore Drive by Barr Lake. The girl was never heard from again. I guess she was into heroin, so people assume it had to do with drugs. Like she took off for Chicago or something.

My brain is pounding, thinking about all these what ifs. What about weird Rod Koenig at the party? That dude's not right. He kept pulling his swim trunks down too low last night and walking up to girls. He doesn't get that girls don't like that. And what about that sex offender Karl Kessler from Leland who comes to stay at his grandma's house in Marie's sub? He's always walking around looking creepy, wearing a wife beater tee-shirt. Covered in black and red devil tattoos. People say he got caught outside Northern Lakes Middle School looking through the fence at the little kids during recess and trying to offer them candy if they came to the fence. I overheard my dad talking about how he was violating his parole, and Craig drove up to Leland and warned Kessler to stay away from the school.

*My brain is exploding with these crazy thoughts.*

That weird vein is throbbing again in my forehead. I massage it, trying to get it to stop. My ankle is hurting again.

*Ugh.*

And what about our conversation last night? I'm sure I didn't say or do anything that would cause her to take off. That's a crazy thought. I was just drunk. Surely, she knew that. Maybe she just wanted to be alone for a while and took an Uber to Traverse City or somewhere else.

Of course, she didn't. Cadie doesn't do things like that. She's responsible.

*God, I hope she's alright.*

I hate to let my mind go there, but if someone did kidnap Cadie, they'll have their hands full. That girl is tough. Three weeks ago, when she was running the 100-meter hurdles at Regionals in Remus, she exploded off the blocks and was in the lead. But at the ninth hurdle, her trailing leg got caught, and she faceplanted full speed. But in Cadie fashion, she jumped up, her knee and nose covered in blood, and finished the race. Then she jogged over, grinning, dried blood all over her face, and held up her second-place medal. We all busted up laughing. Who does that? *Cadie McLeod.*

I get a notification on my phone. Blake just left a text.

"Nick, get a hold of me. I want to know what's going on."

Then I get another notification – from Dirk.

"!!!!!!! Dude! What is going on? Have you heard from Cadie? Everyone is freeeeeeeaking out! Has she called you? I saw you having an argument with her last night before she left. What's going on? Call me!!!!!!!!!!!!!!"

Wait. An argument? No way. It definitely wasn't an argument. I know for a fact Dirk was drunk. But if he's told anyone we were arguing, what are people going to think? I'm probably the person around here who loves her most – except for Aunt Marie. I just wish I could remember everything that happened last night. It feels terrible not being able to piece it all together. I feel I'm letting Cadie down.

Then my anxious brain thinks about Senior Skip Day. That Mackinac Island trip two weeks ago. The day was perfect. Everything was going so good between us. Then I had to go and ruin it. I just had to go too far.

*She has every right to be mad at me.*

Then another little unwelcome thought creeps in: *Don't I also have every right to be mad at her?*

## CHAPTER 9

The rain finally ceased, and dark clouds masked the midday sun as the police SUV sped along the shore of the eight-mile-long Crystal Lake, one of deepest lakes in Michigan. The black Tahoe raced past thick, dark green forests – thousands of acres of woodlands comprised of birch, beech, pine and maple trees and forest floors blanketed in white Trillium flowers.

The two men, detectives Jake Brennan and Craig Kitchen of the Harbor Cove Police Department, were on their way to The Landing, a beach hangout just south of the Sleeping Bear Dunes National Park. They were looking for a young woman who was either drunk, sleeping, injured, missing, drowned, or dead in some other fashion. Both men knew any one of the scenarios was possible, but it was most likely Cadie was just somewhere else innocent and would turn up any minute. At least that's what the data says. Unfortunately, there are always terrible exceptions to every statistic.

The Tahoe travelled M-22 to Sutter Road to Hill Valley Road where the SUV turned left. After a few miles, the road dead-ended at the shores of Lake Michigan and a flat sandy spot surrounded by rising dunes. There is no formal parking lot, so people park up and down the sides of the dirt road bordered by clumps of leafy, spreading beach grass. Benzie County created a small visitor's area with large garbage cans, a water station, and a quaint aqua blue outhouse with white cedar trim maintained by the County. Across the dirt road, nestled in a small clearing, was a bike rack. There were just a few cars along the road this early afternoon. It was relatively quiet for a Saturday in June as the powerful storm had cooled the air considerably, and the rain continued to start and stop – not great beach weather.

Before they left that afternoon, Jake and Craig had Aunt Marie file a Missing Person's Report, and they agreed to wait to contact MSP and to enter Cadie McLeod's personal information and photo into the national missing person's database until after they had searched The Landing. They knew they had to be careful not to disturb any evidence at the beach. However, following the large storm that was now on its way to Michigan's Upper Peninsula and Canda, the detectives weren't sure there would be any evidence to find. Everything on the beach and dunes would be covered by new layer of sand and water. Jake also contacted the Benzie County Sheriff's Office. It was sending two deputies to The Landing.

Jake instructed Nick to stay back at the station and provide the officers everything he remembered about the bonfire last night as well as Cadie's family and friends. Nick also planned to mention Rod Koenig and maybe even that Kessler guy, although they probably knew all about Karl Kessler. Of course, Nick wanted to go with his dad and Detective Kitchen, but he knew his dad would say no. Nick knew his dad was protecting him from what they might find out there on the beach: Cadie's corpse in one form or another: laying bloated along the shore or sticking out of the windswept sands. They were gruesome thoughts, more than he could bear, so Nick fought hard to banish them from his mind.

As Jake and Craig drove into the sandy cul-de-sac with the sun straining to push through the leftover storm clouds, immediately Jake's eyes looked right and locked on the bike rack and the yellow Schwinn cruiser with bright red basket.

"Damnit!" he exclaimed.

"What?" Craig asked.

"That's Marie's bike. I've seen Cadie riding it for years. There's no way she would have left that bike."

Jake felt his stomach drop. Nausea took hold.

Jake knew the law. PA 102 says there must be evidence that a person did not "leave voluntarily," evidence Jake didn't have until now. He also knew that, by the book, he should've waited 24-72 hours before taking Aunt Marie's Missing Person's Report. He was skating on a bit of thin ice, but he was going to find Cadie and do what needed to be done. Jake pushed his hands through his thick brown hair while he processed what finding the abandoned bike might mean. He felt his stomach gurgle uncomfortably.

Jake and Craig got out of the Tahoe, the biting winds slinging sand into their faces. Both men instinctively pulled their jackets up around their necks to block the wind. As they got closer, they could see the bike lock was still in place. Jake leaned in and saw 'mcleod' etched into the yellow paint below the handlebars.

He groaned. It was becoming more and more clear that something bad had happened to his spunky little neighbor.

*I can't let another child die. I just can't.*

Suddenly, the familiar white Chevy Silverados with "Benzie County Sheriff's Department" in black letters on the sides came over the hill and headed their way.

With the frothy Lake Michigan shoreline churning close by and the day's temperature a chilly fifty degrees, Jake and Craig moved from foot to foot to stay warm and waited for the deputies to exit their cars.

"Hey, Jake. Hey, Craig," Sheriff's Deputy Will Ridenour said as he walked over to shake the men's hands. "Haven't had a missing person around here for a while. Heard it was a teen gone missing from a lake party. Maybe she took off?"

"Yeah, that's right," Jake said. "Actually, she was my old neighbor and a friend of my son Nick. Her name is Cadie McLeod. Nick was at the same party as Cadie last night. She hasn't been seen or heard from since. She's a good girl. No way she just took off."

Jake failed to mention that perhaps Cadie was depressed considering it was the anniversary of her parents' death. He couldn't bring himself to think she was suicidal. He kept this information to himself – for now.

"Oh, that's too bad," Ridenour said. "You always hope they'll just turn up. This is her bike?"

"It's her aunt's bike. Cadie rode it to the party last night. She wouldn't have left it. She also didn't show up this morning to open Scoops, the ice cream shop where she works."

"Yeah, I know that place," Deputy Deb Franko said. The petite second deputy, who had been on her cell phone in the truck, walked up to the group.

"So, you've taken all the preliminary steps?" Franko asked.

"I have," Jake said. "Cadie's Aunt Marie McLeod filed the Missing Person's Report a little while ago. We've got officers contacting all of Cadie's family and friends. We didn't enter her name in NamUs, though. We wanted to see what we would find out here today. Hopefully, nothing. I mean . . . well, you know what I mean."

"Yeah, let's hope we don't find a dead body out here today," Deputy Ridenour said.

Hearing that, Jake cringed.

Craig added, "We've got officers going through her socials."

"Socials?" Ridenour interrupted.

"Facebook, Instagram, TikTok, WhatsApp, even YouTube and Pinterest. If she has Snapchat on her phone with Location turned on, we might be able to track her last known location. Officers are working with her friends now on that."

"Good work," Franko said. Ridenour nodded.

"And depending on what we find this afternoon, we'll get a search warrant to obtain Cadie's cell phone and bank records," Jake said. "What about the K9 Unit?"

"Michigan State Police handle that," Ridenour said. "We'll wait to see if we need the dogs."

"Oh yeah, that's right," Jake replied, feeling foolish. It had been a while since he needed the K9 Unit.

"Again, depending on what we find, or don't find, we'll contact MSP when we get back."

"Sounds good," Ridenour said. "So, let's talk about our plan for searching the area. First, we'll conduct a preliminary search. Depending on the results of our search, we may need to call in Search and Rescue, the K9 Unit, the US Coast Guard, the MSP Marine Division, and even conduct a pedestrian search. This is a lot of land to cover. And with the storm last night, most of the evidence, if there is any, is buried by sand."

"I have a detailed map of this area," Franko added. "It's broken into grids. I'll be the main map holder. That means your report on today's findings will be turned into me. That way, I can compile the final report of all our findings. This will be necessary going forward if we have to call in SAR, the dogs, or everyone else."

Franko handed each of the men maps of the area with their grids highlighted in yellow. The maps were attached to Benzie County clipboards with red pens that said, "Benzie is Best!"

"Please make notes of anything you see that's out of the ordinary," Franko said. "Anything that seems suspicious or points to something amiss at last night's party. Anything can be a clue. I'm assuming we're going to see a lot of beer cans stuck in the sand. Just leave all evidence where it is, but take pictures and notes, detailing what and where you find anything out of the ordinary. If you find something, call me right away, and I'll head over with an evidence kit."

"Jake, tell us more," Ridenour said. "What did your son tell you that might be helpful? Did he see where she left the party last night? What she was wearing? You have his statement, I assume?"

Jake tried to ignore his painful stomach awash in acid.

"Yes, I do," Jake said." Let me pull up the pdf on my phone. Jake located the document and enlarged it, so he could read the small print on his cell phone.

"Cadie McLeod, age eighteen," Jake began.

Ridenour interrupted. "She's eighteen? I assumed she was seventeen or younger. Didn't you jump the gun on the Missing Person's Report? I mean, Cadie is an adult, and it hasn't even been 24 hours. She could be holed up at a hotel with some guy."

Jake's countenance immediately changed. His body stiffened, and he slowly looked up to meet Ridenour's eyes.

"Listen. I know this girl. I know Cadie McLeod very well. She was my next-door neighbor. I've known her since she was eleven. My son and Cadie played together. They're good friends. I know her. She's not holed up with some guy. She didn't run away. She didn't just take off. She's not at a friend's house. She's probably the most outstanding young person I know, and that includes my own son. Something happened to her, alright? So, I did what I thought best. And that's what I'll continue to do. If you don't like it, I don't give a shit, Will. Report me. Now let's not waste anymore time."

"Hey, I'm sorry," Ridenour said. "I didn't mean to touch a nerve. I probably shouldn't have phrased it that way. My bad. Yeah, let's get going. Finish what you were saying."

Just then, a massive gust of wind slammed the group, and the sand pelted their faces, stinging them. Three of them immediately reached up to wipe sand from their eyes, except Franko, who was wearing reflective black Ray Bans. The icy wind picked up, and the temperature dropped further. As they stood there, they saw two groups of people leave the beach and head toward their cars. A couple of people were slowly running, heads down to avoid the wind and sand. Even from where the officers stood, they could see angry whitecaps and large, powerful waves crash against the shore.

After wiping off his face, Jake again looked down at the document on his phone and continued reading out loud.

- "Cadie McLeod, age 18, missing since around midnight June 4 from The Landing on Mariner's Beach in Benzie County, Michigan.
- The missing person is Caucasian, with long red hair and green eyes. She's 5'10 . . ."

"Wow, that's tall," Ridenour interjected.

- "And about 140 pounds."
- "She was reported to be wearing a yellow, floral sundress and yellow flip flops. Her jewelry is a ring with a track shoe on it . . .

"A track shoe?" Franko asked.

"Cadie's a sprinter on the high school track team. And a hurdler," Jake said.

"That's impressive," Craig remarked. "My girlfriend in high school ran hurdles. She was constantly black and blue. She fell about every other meet."

"Yeah," Jake said. "Cadie's a fighter.

*God, I sure hope she's still alive and fighting.*

"And she's wearing a gold necklace. It's an unusual necklace. Only had half a heart."

"Half a heart?" Craig asked.

"Yeah. Half a heart," Jake replied. "The other half was on a necklace worn by her mother. It was very special to Cadie as both her parents were killed by a drunk driver six years ago."

"Wow, that's terrible," Franko said. "I hate coming upon those scenes. Mangled cars and mangled people."

"Only one car was involved," Jake responded, "Cadie's parents were hit by a driver as they crossed M-22. The driver's never been located."

Everyone stayed silent for moment. That was a lot to take in.

Finally, Craig spoke. "Was Nick able to provide any information about where Cadie was last seen?"

"Yes. Nick said that he was sitting on one of the tree stumps around the bonfire with some friends." Jake paused. He really didn't want to tell the group Nick was probably drunk. He had smelled the liquor on Nick in his bedroom this morning, and Nick's face was puffy with dark circles under his eyes.

"Nick had a couple of drinks, so we need to keep that in mind regarding his recollection of events. Anyway, Nick said he spoke with Cadie around 11:30 PM. He lost track after that. He says he vaguely remembers seeing her near the opening to Scenic Trail that leads back to the cul-de-sac. It's a shortcut to the bike rack. Also," Jake hesitated, "Nick said Cadie seemed a bit upset. I need to tell you something. Yesterday was the anniversary of the night Cadie's parents were killed."

Ridenour long whistled.

"Oh wow. Well, that information adds a lot. You should have told us that up front, Jake. Like first thing. Maybe Cadie was depressed. Or even suicidal."

Jake bristled.

"Anything's a possibility at this point. But what I do know is that Cadie is mentally resilient. She's handled her parents' death for years. There's nothing to suggest yesterday was any different."

"Yeah, but your son said she was upset," Franko said.

"There's a big difference between being upset and killing yourself," Jake said.

The rest of the group nodded, but still looked doubtful.

"Okay," Franko said. "Does everyone know the plan? You've got your maps with your grids. Observe closely. Take notes. Take pictures. And don't disturb anything. If you find something, call or text me, and I'll come over with the Forensics Kit. Understood?"

Again, a powerful wind gust pushed through the group, and a lone seagull flew over their heads. As it passed, it let out a screech and the strange "ha-ha-ha" seagulls are known for. The large bird seemed to mock them as they split apart and walked to their separate grids. Jake looked up at the creature and scowled.

"Stupid bird.

## CHAPTER 10
## Nick Brennan

After Detective LaCroix drove me home from the station, I laid on my bed. I curled up on my blue comforter for a long time feeling the saddest I have ever felt in my seventeen years of living on this blue ball. And I'm not afraid to admit it: I cried. A lot. I mean racking sobs. My ribs actually hurt. I never even cried this hard the night I found out that Aileen and Thomas were killed. Something is very, very wrong with Cadie. I know it.

I finally get up and wash my face. Then I take a seat and read numerous texts from friends looking for Cadie. Everyone is frantic. I scroll through Facebook and Instagram, looking for any clues or someone who might have posted something strange. Cadie's socials are full of smiling friends, track meets, poses with Tori's bunny, and, of course, me.

I decide to check Rod Koenig's socials.

I go to his Facebook first. Just lots of pictures of him posing with his truck. And bottles of whiskey sitting on the truck's hood and tailgate. Young people really don't use Facebook anymore, so I click on Instagram. I open the app and search for Rod Koenig. After a bit, I find him and am immediately disgusted. His account name is rodthebod, and his creepy bio says, "If you want a good bod, call Rod."

Geez, what a poet.

God, that dude's so wrong. I start looking through his Instagram posts. More pictures of, what else, trucks and booze. I click on his reels and see more of the same. I'm about to quit looking when I decide to see if Koenig was tagged in anything. I click on Tagged. Immediately, I see a freeze frame of a dark video: Rod's holding up a pair of women's pink panties.

I think I'm going to puke. I play the video.

Rod is swaying in the nighttime video; headlights illuminate his movements.

"Hey, boys and girls, looky, looky at what uncle Rod has."

He twirls the panties around in the air, waving them, having fun. Rod is clearly drunk: his eyes are red and watery, and he almost trips over a log. I can hear dudes snickering in the background as the camera jostles.

"Just don't ask me where I got 'em," Rod slurs. "That's my secret."

He then drops the underwear to the ground, steps on them with his work boot, and grinds them til they're black with dirt.

His final words: "and now you know what I think about that bitch."

The video stops. I look down to the right of the video, and there's three simple words: "1 Day Ago." The video was posted sometime last night.

I'm shaking. My heart is beating so hard, I swear I can feel it smacking my ribs.

*Oh my god, were those Cadie's underwear? Does Rod have Cadie?*

I'm starting to freak the fuck out.

Suddenly, I get a notification on my phone.

My locator app indicates dad just left Mariner's Beach. He's on his way to the police station.

*Did my dad find Cadie? Is she alive? What is happening?!*

My mind is all over the place. I'm sweating profusely and trying to calm myself.

I quickly download and forward the video of Rod to my dad's phone along with my highly alarmed thoughts and fight to control them. I can't bear to think about Rod Koenig hurting Cadie or my dad coming across her dead body out there on the beach. It's all too much.

I can't sit here any longer. I have to look for her. If dad found something, I'll know soon enough. I jump up, throw on my track jacket, run outside in the driving rain and down the driveway to my Jeep.

The streets are slick with rain. After ten minutes, I pull onto Hill Valley Road, the dark clouds throwing shadows over miles of dunes. Up the sandy road, I see yellow police tape and cones. As I drive closer, I see a patrol car parked behind a dune and feel myself suddenly feeling weak from the adrenaline drop and last night's alcohol. I drive up to the black and white car and roll down my window.

Officer Adams lowers his.

"Did they find Cadie?" I strain over the fierce wind, choking back my feelings.

"No, Nick, they didn't find her," Adams yells back. "They searched for quite a while. One of the deputies might have found something, though."

"What? What did they find?"

"I overheard one deputy talking to her partner about finding something on a trail, but I'm not sure what. If you're looking for your dad, he and the others headed to the station not too long ago. You can find him there."

"I'm not looking for my dad. I want to help. I want – I need – to look for Cadie. To help find her. I want to look around."

"Sorry, son, you know I can't let you look around," Adams says, scratching the top of his head. "Plus, they searched the area pretty thoroughly. I think they're also calling in the Michigan State Police and the Coast Guard. If there's something to be found here, they'll find it. And listen to me: If she's out here, you don't want to be the one to find her. You don't need to see that."

*Oh, man.*

I knew he was right, but it's unbearable to stand by while the person I love is missing.

"Could I at least walk down to the water's edge? To clear my mind? You can watch me. I won't go anywhere else. I promise."

Adams hesitates.

"Well, I guess that's alright. But you can't go down the beach. Just stay straight ahead where I can see you, okay?"

I nod okay and pull my Jeep to the end of the cul-de-sac closest to the path that leads to Lake Michigan. As I exit my Jeep, something catches my eye. I look right and see Cadie's yellow bike still locked to the bike rack.

"Oh, god no!"

I immediately run to the bike.

*Cadie would never leave her bike!*

I know in an instant it's Aunt Marie's bike. I've seen Cadie ride it a million times.

I stand there crying for quite some time. I'm hungover and exhausted. Also freezing from the cold, icy winds. Feeling dejected, I walk down the rolling path of speckled sand and come up over the hill that opens into the beach. Strong winds push against me. In all directions are miles of dark, powerful waves, one after another rushing the beach with their icy whitecaps.

"Ha-ha-ha!"

A long screech cuts through the wind.

I quickly look up to see a lone Herring Gull flying close to my head. It lands in the sand a few feet from me, watching me intently. The gull suddenly triggers a memory from last August: Cadie, looking adorable in her yellow bikini, stretched out beside me on her parents' quilt. We were playfully arguing over vintage cars. While Cadie tried to convince me that the Camaro is more muscle than the Corvette, a bird with faded pink legs suddenly landed right between us on the quilt. We both burst out laughing. It was so odd and unexpected. The bird cocked its head quizzically, looking back and forth at the both of us, completely unafraid. Like he simply dropped by to hang out for a while.

"Is this seagull a friend of yours?" I laughed. "If so, please introduce us."

Cadie laughed in return, while a gust of wind lifted her sparkling red hair off her shoulders.

"It's a Herring Gull," Cadie replied, watching the bird intently. She loved all manner of creatures. "Look at its yellow, hooked beak. The red splotch. Non è bellissimo?" she exclaimed.

"What?'

Isn't it beautiful?"

*You're beautiful, Cadie McLeod.*

"I don't know if I would use the word bellissimo, but I admire its confidence."

Finally, our new friend squawked several times and flew away. We laid back down on the quilt, and Cadie got quiet. She often went silent when thinking about her parents. Something would trigger a memory, and she would get lost in thoughts.

"My father loved old cars, as you know. But he also loved birds," Cadie finally spoke. "My parents both did. When I was younger, I couldn't imagine what they saw in birds, how they could sit out on our back deck watching them all evening. Do you know there are over 10,000 bird species in the world?"

"I didn't know that," I answered, just happy to be in her company. She was the most well-read person I knew.

"Each species has its own characteristics, from behavior, to bird songs, to even their colors and habitats. I think my parents were in awe of the natural world and appreciated its beauty and diversity. My father could look at any bird with wonder and joy, especially owls. My mother, too. She saw magic in everything."

Cadie was quiet again.

"I really miss them, Nick."

She began to cry softly.

"Come here."

I pulled her over to me and put my arms around her. We sat there for a long while.

*I wish I knew how to comfort her better. How do you comfort someone whose parents died when they were twelve?*

"You're just the best friend, Nick. I really love our friendship."

Friendship. I cringed. I felt so much more for this amazing person than friendship. Cadie was everything: intelligent, loyal, hardworking, clever - sometimes silly and always kind.

"I love it, too," I answered.

We spent the remainder of the afternoon talking about our upcoming senior year and our plans for the future. Cadie's plans on attending Michigan State to become a forensic scientist - to help people, which I so admired. And my plans to go to UM - to write books - and a novel hopefully about something meaningful. Neither of us, in any corner of our imaginations, could think that months later, I would be standing on the same beach, looking over the seemingly indifferent shoreline while the girl I love has gone missing. It was unimaginable. Horrific.

*Cadie, wherever you are, whoever has you, I will find you. I will bring you home.*

I leave the beach and spend the remainder of the afternoon driving around Harbor Cove. I go everywhere I can think of - looking for her or any sign of her. I even walk around the Harbor Cove Library, Cadie's favorite place, although I know it's ridiculous. Yet, somehow it gives me comfort and hope. I picture Cadie as a girl walking down the front steps with her red tote bag full of *Ranger Rick* magazines and a *Nancy Drew* mystery. Unfortunately, despite my efforts, I don't find a trace of Cadie McLeod.

The girl I love has simply vanished.

I suddenly remember Rod Keonig's video.

*Does Rod have Cadie?*

It's a simply unbearable thought.

## CHAPTER 11

After thoroughly searching The Landing, Jake, Craig, and Benzie County Sheriff Deputies Deb Franko and Will Ridenour met up at the Harbor Cove Police Station and were gathered around the conference room table. The police station was unique in that it was clad in slate blue vinyl siding with cedar shake accents and heavy white trim windows. Mayor Clark's agenda was to "cute everything up," and that included the police station.

The four officers were weary from battling powerful winds and deep dunes along Lake Michigan. Everyone's calves ached. Three of them found interesting, if unhelpful, items. Jake found a vintage Detroit Lions tee-shirt with a picture of lion cubs under the slogan, "Defend the Den."

Ridenour found a cloudy bottle of Boone's Farm Strawberry Hill that looked like it had been buried in the dunes for decades. It was half full. Not surprisingly, no one wanted a drink.

Craig's find was most interesting. Out of the zipper lock bag and wearing plastic gloves, Craig pulled the box of Trojan Bareskins and read its slogan, "Pleasure you want. Protection you trust." That elicited a few chuckles – except from Jake. He was in a dark place.

The discussion then became serious.

Jake first shared that he called Aunt Marie from The Landing. Marie told him she still hadn't heard anything from Cadie or any of her friends. He told Marie they found her bike still locked to the beach bike rack. Marie said that Cadie loved that bike because it belonged to her mom. Jake told the group he didn't realize the bike once belonged to Aileen McLeod. Marie said Cadie would never have left that bike voluntarily. He also shared the disturbing video of Rod that Nick had sent him, which caused raised eyebrows among the detectives. Craig said he would look into it.

The group then discussed the fact that Cadie didn't have Snapchat and its location feature or any location app on her phone. Also, from messaging with the station's other detectives, they learned none of Cadie's close friends reported hearing from her or seeing her since Friday night. There also were no pictures or posts on Cadie's socials. Last night, the young woman seemed to vanish into the incoming storm.

Now Jake and Craig awaited Deputy Franko's input and what she had to say.

"So, when I was searching Scenic Trail, I found something worthwhile," Franko said.

Jake and Craig quickly looked at each other, surprised. Franko hadn't said anything about finding something. As the Deputy began to share what she found, they could suddenly hear the detectives' sergeant, Dana Bakker, speaking loudly. She was in the adjacent room on the phone talking to a newspaper reporter from the *Benzie County Record Patriot*. The story about Cadie had already broken.

"Why don't we just wait until Bakker joins us?" Franko said. "I don't want to have to repeat it all again."

The men were slightly irritated at having to wait, but they knew Franko was not to be messed with, so they waited. Will and Craig pulled out their cell phones and scrolled through their messages. Jake, however, sat back, hands behind his head, and closed his eyes. Outwardly, it might have seemed he was resting. Yet, inwardly, his mind and stomach churned. He was thinking about that dreaded statistic: You need to locate your victim within 72 hours or their odds of survival drops considerably. Jake knew the clock was ticking. He just wanted to get going.

A few minutes later, Sergeant Bakker, her dark brown hair pulled back into a tight ponytail, entered the conference room. The late afternoon sun cast a shadow through the room from the western window, and the conference room became hazy with floating dust particles now visible in the air.

"Hello Jake and Craig. Good afternoon, Deputies Ridenour and Franko," Bakker said, taking her seat at the table. "I want to thank you for your quick response today and all the help you have provided so far. Detectives Brennan and Kitchen have already updated me on the most recent information and your actions at The Landing. Good work."

Ridenour and Franko nodded.

"It's my understanding from Deputy Franko's text earlier that an item possibly related to our missing person was discovered today. Can you fill me in?"

All eyes turned to Franko. Jake leaned in.

"Certainly," Franko said. "As you know, we conducted a preliminary grid search today of The Landing and Mariner's Beach. Within my grid location was a path known as Scenic Trail. People in the area know that it's a shortcut to the bike rack. It was reported that Cadie McLeod was seen near Scenic Trail close to midnight. She may have taken the trail to retrieve her bike, which, as of this afternoon, was still locked to the bike rack near the cul-de-sac at The Landing."

Franko continued. "While searching Scenic Trail, I found a pair of yellow flip flops."

"Flip flops?" The tired sergeant spoke loudly - agitated. "How can we know they belonged to Cadie McLeod?" Bakker asked. "The beach is a cemetery of flip flops."

"At the search, Jake relayed his son's report to us; it indicated Cadie was wearing a yellow dress. So, right after I discovered the yellow flip flops on the trail, I photographed them and sent the photo to our Trace Evidence Unit," Franko said. "When I get back to our post, I'll hand them over, and the Unit will analyze them. However, because time is of the essence, Deputy Lisa Stevens, a Trace tech, contacted Marie McLeod this afternoon. She messaged her the photo, and Marie indicated that the flip flops did – do – belong to Cadie."

"How can Marie be sure they belonged to her niece?" Bakker asked. "There's probably ten more yellow flip flops on the beach right now."

"Deputy Stevens conveyed that Cadie recently purchased unique flip flops to match a dress she wore to last night's party. Cadie showed them to Marie when they were delivered. In addition to being yellow, each flip flop has a daisy in the middle. Marie remembers the daisy distinctly because the daisy is Cadie's favorite flower. Marie said it also was her daughter-in-law's favorite flower."

At that bit of information, Sergeant Bakker cleared her throat and straightened a bit. She felt pain and burning in her gut. She was reminded that her investigative team never caught the driver who killed Aileen and Thomas McLeod six years prior. It was an utterly horrific and ghastly scene. Hardened cops puked and sobbed on the side the highway. One of the investigators even passed out. Bakker agonized for years about the lack of an arrest, and she had the bleeding stress ulcer to prove it.

Jake quietly sat in his chair imagining Cadie struggling with her abductor, kicking him, fighting for her life, and the flip flops being tossed off. He couldn't stop picturing that sweet girl happily walking the trail last night and coming upon an absolute monster. The imaginings of his mind were brutal. The stuff of nightmares. Cadie crying and pleading, begging her abductor to let her go.

*What is he doing to you, Cadie? Where are you?*

Jake fought to make the images stop.

"So," Franko concluded, "when you take everything into consideration, Cadie's abandoned flip flops, the bike still locked to the rack, the fact Cadie never showed up for work, that no one has seen her or spoken to her, and also that there's no activity on her social media, I believe Cadie McLeod is not missing voluntarily."

The fifty-year-old sergeant listened carefully, collected her thoughts, and then spoke slowly and matter-of-factly, leaning into the officers across the table while trying to ignore the pulsating pain in her upper abdomen.

"I agree with your conclusions, and I appreciate your work so far – all of you. Thank you. After hearing your information, I agree Cadie McLeod is a missing person, so I am launching a full investigation. After our meeting, I'll contact the Michigan State Police and ask that they conduct a thorough Search and Rescue of the area as soon as they can. I'll ask them to employ their K9 Unit. Depending on what they have to say, we may need to coordinate a pedestrian search. I'll also contact the US Coast Guard and have the MSP employ its Marine Division to search Lake Michigan and the three inland lakes close to The Landing."

Jake listened intently to Bakker, but his mind continued to wander. He fought to keep his emotions in check.

*I'm going to find you, Cadie. I promise you I will.*

Bakker continued.

"Then I'll contact Special Agent Dority at the Traverse City FBI office. He'll activate the FBI's Child Abduction Rapid Deployment Team and get in contact with the National Centre for Child Exploitation and Violent Crimes Against Children. Now, have we recovered Cadie's cell phone?"

"No, we haven't," Jake replied.

"Okay. I'll get warrants to get Cadie's bank records and cell tower records from AT&T. If Cadie has her phone with her, we may be able to get some information about her location and anyone who might be with her as well as others in the area that night. It's a longshot, but we need to cover every base. Jake, will you upload Cadie's information and a recent photo into NamUs? Also, I would like you to create a list of Cadie's family, friends, acquaintances, coworkers, friends from church, teachers, principals, and peers at school from sports she plays to any other extracurriculars. I would like that report as soon as possible."

"You got it," Jake said. "Nick has already provided some of that."

"Yes, I read through his notes. I expect a complete list as soon as possible. Nick's list as someone who knew Cadie and attended the party as well as everyone else in Cadie's sphere."

The officers in the room nodded.

"What time are we meeting tomorrow?" Jake asked.

"We'll meet here in the conference room at 7 AM," Bakker said. "We'll go through the list, make any additions, start contacting people, and schedule interviews of people who require interrogation. I'll enlist officers Dan Zielinski and Rebecca LaCroix to help with the interviews. Having read over Nick's information, I'm going to have Jake interview Rod Koenig. I'll have Detective Brooke Field interview Blake Van der Velt and Glen Boer. Jake, you also need to reach out to our local pedophile Karl Kessler and make a list of other known sex offenders in the area. We're probably going to have to coordinate interviews with the MSP Missing Persons Unit. We have a lot of ground to cover. Now, next question, was Cadie seeing anyone? Did she have a boyfriend?"

"Not that I know of," Jake said. "I'll look into it. I'll also talk to Nick. But Blake Van der Velt was her ex. I remember Nick once saying Blake was obsessed with Cadie."

"Really?" Sergeant Bakker said, her eyes opening wider and seeming a bit taken aback.

"Well, we need to learn all about all the men in her life: boyfriends, lovers, stalkers, admirers – anyone who may have wanted to hurt or kill Cadie or have her to himself. No one is looked over, even if they are rich."

"Craig, I want you to contact Marie McLeod. Jake, do you think Marie will be okay with a complete search of her home and property?"

"Absolutely. She is heartbroken right now and will do anything she can to find her niece. She said she's already searched everywhere, but she may have missed something."

"Okay, good. So, Craig, arrange to have her house, Cadie's bedroom, the garage, her dad's old Camaro, the grounds – everything - searched. You also need to contact Harbor Cove High School to see if Cadie left any items in a school locker, gym locker, or elsewhere in the school. Arrange a meeting with Superintendent Hastings. Make sure the principal, assistant principal, and dean of students attend as well as Cadie's school counselor. Have them also talk to Cadie's teachers."

"Will do, Sergeant," Craig replied.

"Jake, do you know if Cadie is in therapy?"

"I don't, but I'll talk to Marie."

"Good. See what you can find out. Also see if Cadie kept a diary."

"Deputies Ridenour and Franko, would you be able to coordinate a door-to-door search of Cadie's neighborhood?"

"Yes, we can do that," Ridenour replied.

"That would be great," Sergeant Bakker said. "We would appreciate it."

"Jake, where does Marie live?"

"She lives in Waters Edge Subdivision. I've got the address in my phone. I'll forward the contact to the group."

"Thank you. Everyone, we clearly have a lot to do and not a lot of time to do it. As we all know, time is of the essence. If Cadie is hurt, dying, incapacitated in some way, or being held against her will, time is against us – and her. We need to do everything in our power to find this young lady and bring her home. We are also aware that yesterday was the anniversary of her parents' murder. However, we don't how that impacts the situation."

The Sergeant was quiet for a brief moment as if collecting herself. She then put both hands on the conference table and purposefully pushed herself up until she was standing. Jake thought he could see tears in her eyes.

"We never found the killer of Cadie's parents," Bakker said, looking around the room at the officers, her voice thick with emotion but also conviction. "But we can sure as hell find their daughter."

As she spoke the words, Bakker dearly hoped they would come true. It was horrifying enough not to have caught the killer of Aileen and Thomas McLeod. But not being able to locate their daughter? That was simply unthinkable. In fact, Bakker thought she might leave police work altogether if she failed again. As she walked back into her office, she also wondered about Jake's son, Nick. Someone at the party saw him yelling at Cadie last night. Bakker didn't want to say anything in front of the group – or Jake - yet.

She needed more answers.

## CHAPTER 12
## Nick Brennan

*What else can I do, Cadie? How can I find you? I'm just so sorry I'm not there with you.*

For a long while, I stare out our kitchen window into the cloudy, darkening sky – just thinking. Feeling the deepest pain I've ever experienced. And rising anger.

*Who took you, Cadie? I promise I'll find you and the bastard that has you.*

I'm literally shaking. Just then, I hear Jake's V8 pull up into the driveway. I look out the window, and through the rain I see the Tahoe.

*Thank god.*

I've texted him but heard nothing back. I know he's busy trying to find Cadie, but I'm in anguish. No one I know has seen her or heard from her. She's really gone. This is like something you see on TV. I'm having a hard time believing it's real.

"Hey, dad," I say as he walks in through the cottage's side door. I stare at him intently, studying his face, trying to gauge the signs, trying not to panic. Dad quietly undoes his utility belt and places it on the counter.

"So?"

He looks over at me wearily.

"Nothing, son. I'm sorry. I don't have any news about Cadie – good or bad."

I'm shocked by how bad he looks. His normally wavy brown hair is flat and limp; his broad shoulders are slumping; and his typically tanned face is paler - his eyes a duller shade of blue. It seems like he's aged five years in a day.

"And you haven't heard anything?"

"No, I haven't heard anything. I can't believe this is happening, dad. I really can't. It's unreal."

I start to cry, and he walks over and puts his big arms around me. He hugs me tight. We stay like that for a few minutes, and I feel like I'm ten years old again, safe in his presence.

"Let's sit down," my father says.

We take a seat at the kitchen table.

"The news is all around town, dad. Everyone is talking about it. Trying to figure out where Cadie is. I've gone through her socials over and over again. Just nothing. No pictures, no posts. It's like she just vanished. And everyone is sending me messages. But none of it is helpful. People are just worried. I got a text from Dirk a little while ago. He said he saw Aunt Marie come into the station when he was driving by."

"Yes, she did. She was bringing in an item of Cadie's clothing for tomorrow morning's search. MSP is bringing in its dogs."

He sees the red and white pizza box on the table, opens it, and takes a bite of cold pizza. Talking while chewing, dad says, "You need to get me that list."

His directness rattles me a bit. It's like he's talking to a suspect rather than his son.

"Okay, sure. Let me go grab it."

I run to my bedroom and grab the list off my bed and run back to the kitchen. "Here you go. I wrote down everyone I could think of."

He silently takes the list and sets it on the table. His head drops for a moment, and then he looks up. He looks me squarely in eye.

"I found something concerning, and a sheriff's deputy searching The Landing today also found something on Scenic Trail."

I'm thoroughly panicked. I immediately pull my chair closer to the table.

"What did you find?"

*This can't be happening.*

"Well, I found Cadie's bike still locked to the bike rack."

I shake my head solemnly. Silently.

I don't mention I went to The Landing and already discovered Cadie's bike.

"And a deputy found something we know belongs to Cadie."

*I'm terrified of what he will say.*

"What? What did they find?"

"A pair of yellow flip flops. She was wearing them at last night's party."

"I remember she was wearing a yellow dress last night, but how do you know the flip flops are hers?"

"MSP texted a photo to Marie, and she identified them. She said Cadie just ordered the flip flops from Amazon to match her dress. They had daisies on them."

"Her favorite flower. Her mom's favorite flower, too."

"How did you know that?" Dad looks up at me, incredulous I would know this information.

"I don't know. I just remember when they lived next door to us. They had all those tall daisies everywhere. Along the porch and the steps leading to the sidewalk. Aileen was always picking a daisy bouquet for mom. It just seems like everything Aileen loved, Cadie loves, too. Maybe it's a way to stay close to her mom?"

"Wow, son, when did you get so insightful?" Jake softly smiles. "You're pretty observant. And perceptive. You sure you don't want to be a cop?"

"Dad, there's no way Cadie would just leave her new flip flops with daisies on them on the trail."

I'm starting to feel sick again. I begin imagining Cadie struggling in the dunes against an attacker.

"No, not likely. Finding the flip flips along with Marie's bike and the fact that no was has seen her or had any contact with her is enough to consider this a Missing Person's case," dad says, his face dropping even more. "So, tonight, we entered Cadie's name, photo, and personal information into the nationwide database. We also contacted the Michigan State Police, US Coast Guard, the Marine Division, and the MSP is conducting a Search and Rescue tomorrow and bringing in the K9 Unit."

*Wow, this is really happening.*

"There's another thing. Something else was found at the start of the trail. A whiskey bottle. Maybe you know something about that?"

I'm immediately uneasy.

"Why would I know about a whiskey bottle?" I ask. (I really don't want dad to know I was drinking last night, let alone whiskey. He's been lecturing me a lot lately. I've blacked out twice from drinking whiskey this past year, and my dad knows it.)

"Some of your classmates at the party came forward today to share what they saw last night," dad explains. "Craig took down their statements. One of the girls who came forward mentioned she saw you drinking whiskey at the party with that big guy who runs sprints on your team."

"Glen Boer."

"Yes, Glen Boer. She said she doesn't recall anyone else with the whiskey. Just you and Glen and Blake. She said you and Glen seemed pretty drunk. Plus, I could smell it on you this morning. The bottle Deputy Franko found was a bottle of Traverse City Whiskey - that company we toured last Labor Day weekend, remember?"

I remember drinking that brand of whiskey with Glen last night. But why was the whiskey bottle at the trailhead? Glen wouldn't take Scenic Trail to get to the car lot.

*Did Glen do something to Cadie?*

My mind starts racing down various pathways. Yeah, the guy is strangely quiet, but he seems harmless (although, so did Ted Bundy for that matter). But I suddenly recall Glen passing the whiskey bottle around to a few other guys last night.

"Yeah, that whisky was on the beach last night. But other guys were drinking it, too, dad. I don't know why the girls targeted me, Glen, and Blake. I have no idea who ended up with the bottle."

"Well, I'm not happy you drank whiskey last night. You know how it affects you. Jesus, Nick, you've blacked out twice this year."

"I know. I'm sorry! I didn't really intend to drink it. It was being passed around. I should've known better. I promise I'll do better."

There is an awkward silence between us. My father looks down at the table. He's thinking. He knows it's the fact that my mother, his wife, abandoned us and moved away that has damaged me emotionally. It's hard for my dad to get truly angry at me when he knows I've been affected by his disintegrated marriage. He just cares about me, that's all.

Trying to change the subject, I say, "Dad, can Blake come over? He wants to find out what's happening with Cadie. How things are going. He also mentioned the idea of holding a candlelight vigil tomorrow or Monday at the marina's pavilion if we can't find her by then. What do you think?"

My dad rubs his stubbly face.

"I guess so. Just don't tell him any of the things I told you, all right? Keep it vague. Tell him we are doing everything we can to find Cadie but nothing else. Regarding the vigil, it's not my place to tell the community what to do. Whoever organizes it will need an event permit, though. But it actually might not be a bad idea. We can have detectives present to see who turns up, who is acting strangely."

"Nick."

"Yes?"

"Was Blake drunk last night?"

I hesitate.

God, I don't want to rat on my friend. But I'm not really sure how much he drank.

"I really don't know, dad."

"And Blake and Cadie used to go out, right? She broke it off with him?"

"Yeah. That's right."

I'm feeling anxious talking about Blake in this way with my dad. No way Blake hurt Cadie.

"How did he take the break up?

"Well, like any guy who gets dumped. Not good. He gets angry sometimes. Mostly when he's drinking, though. He said he's sworn off women. I think he's got low self-esteem."

"Blake is going to be interviewed at the station tomorrow."

I'm super uncomfortable now. I change the subject again.

"Blake's uncle said his foundation could offer money for a reward. Dirk's father also said his company would donate. Do you think that's a good idea?"

"That's very kind of Robert and Luuk. I'm sure Marie would appreciate that. And I don't think it could hurt. When is Blake coming over?"

"In a little bit. I just wanted to make sure it was good with you first."

"Yeah, it's okay," dad says. "Just remember not to tell Blake what we've talked about tonight. I hate to say it, but at this point Nick, everyone is a suspect. Everyone."

Dad stands up and strides across our strangely lit kitchen. One of the bulbs in the overhead light must have burned out while we were talking, creating an eerie vibe. Suddenly, he stops and turns. Dad is looking down at his work boots. There is a silence in the room as I wait on his words. He slowly looks up at me, his brown eyes wet.

"I didn't want to tell you this, son, but I have a feeling in my gut that someone abducted Cadie. I think someone kidnapped her off that beach last night."

I just stare at him. Absorbing the words. Even though I've been thinking this very thing, hearing it out loud is like a hard slap to the face. It just makes it more real.

Dad then leaves the room, and I decide to text Blake. My fingers are trembling. I clench and unclench my fists, trying to get the shaking to stop. As I message him, my friend, a guy I thought I knew, I feel a growing unease. My mind begins to wander. Like dad said, everyone's a suspect.

  Even me, I suppose.

## CHAPTER 13
## Cadie McLeod

The unconscious young woman lay naked on the hard dirt floor. Suddenly, she began to stir and gingerly lifted her groggy head. She was shivering profusely from the damp cold.

*Where am I? What's going on?*

Her green eyes opened slowly, lazily. It took them a moment to adjust to the barest of morning light that dappled the walls from the vent above. She sluggishly looked around the rustic room, trying to process where she was. What was going on. A thought began steadily taking shape in her foggy mind.

*Have I been kidnapped?*

Slowly pushing herself to sit upright on a thin piece of carpet, she felt the cuts in her wrists burning from the zip tie lying on the floor beside her. Cadie wrapped her arms around herself, trying to stay warm. She saw her sundress lying crumpled a few feet away on floor. She leaned over, picked it up, and put her hand in its pocket. Nothing. Of course, her cell phone had fallen out – or been taken. She gradually pulled the yellow dress on over her aching head and neck. She immediately felt warmer. She wondered where her panties were.

*Where am I? How long have I been out?*

She vaguely recalled waking up earlier, but she couldn't be sure.

*Was there a man in here with me?*

It was a strange room. Narrow, long, and mostly dark. Slightly damp and musty. Once her eyes adjusted, from the light above she could make out wooden shelves lining the walls and filled with mason jars of varying sizes. A root cellar? She could hear no human voices, only the soft, sweet trills of nearby Warblers. She ran her hands across the pebbly dirt floor and studied the decaying walls of concrete and stone. Bits of sunlight peeked through here and there where mortar had pulled away slightly from stones. Decades-old dust particles floated through the air, illuminated by the sliver of light above her head. Cadie almost retched. The air was putrid.

*Is that vinegar and rotting potatoes?*

AP Science class had taught her about pathogens, and she knew somewhere in this room, potatoes were liquefying. The soft rot smell gagged her. She crawled away from the carpet and vomited in the corner on the floor.

Suddenly, the enormity of the situation crashed down on her. She felt overwhelming terror. Cadie tried to stand and run for the large wooden door to break free, but she lurched forward in the darkened room, almost falling headlong into a stone wall. The effects of the drug made movement difficult. She reached out instinctively and grabbed a protruding stone with her left hand, breaking a nail, but she steadied herself. The movements caused her to feel a deep pain in her neck.

*Was I choked?*

Cadie gently moved her hand where her chin and neck met, trying to determine if there were fractures to her hyoid bone. She didn't feel any sharp pains or hear grinding or crackling. She seemed to have no problems swallowing or intaking air. She determined nothing was broken. Cadie could just feel the intense soreness where her kidnapper had powerfully pressed against her neck. Then she realized.

*My half a heart necklace is gone.*

A deep sadness washed over her. That necklace was given to her by her parents, and her mother always wore her half of the heart around her neck – until she was killed. Cadie's half of the heart was a way to stay connected to her mom – to her beautiful parents - and now it was gone. She got down on her knees, her hands moving over the rough dirt floor, trying to locate the necklace in the dark, but it was no use. She sat down dejected.

She strained to think, to remember, to recall anything about time before this room. Nothing. Just a hazy recollection of bizarre thoughts and images. Hallucinations, she surmised.

*Who took me? And why? What are they going to do with me?*

The questions were cloudy in her drugged brain. Then Cadie noticed something.

*I'm terrified, but my heart isn't racing; Why am I breathing normally?*

She thought for a moment. Then she knew.

*I was poisoned.*

Cadie struggled to recall the dangerous drugs she studied last summer in a class at MSU and became acquainted with through so many crime shows, trying to determine the chemical that was currently coursing through her vascular system.

*Halothane? Pentothal? Maybe Propofol? No. Most likely Ketamine.*

Not only could she taste the bitterness ketamine was known for in her mouth, she felt oddly detached and dreamlike. Weirdly relaxed for her predicament. And there were the hallucinations. All hallmarks of the dissociative anesthetic.

She glanced down and studied her arms. From the faint light above, Cadie could make out small puncture wounds. She ran her finger over the fledgling scabs - the sites of injection.

A terrifying thought suddenly exploded into her mind, and she frantically shoved her hand between her legs and felt for semen. There was no sign of ejaculate. No vaginal pain. Cadie felt she hadn't been raped. She let out a small groan.

"Oh, thank god."

She got up and cautiously moved to the oversized door and twisted the rusted, metal handle. Of course, the door was locked. She pulled the handle back and forth, but the solid door didn't budge an inch. She could make out faint light coming from under the door. The door didn't lead to the outside. It led to an exterior room.

"Hello! Hello! Is there anybody there? she called out shakily. "Please help me if you can hear me."

No response. From the lack of noise – no voices, cars, or human activity, just bird sounds – she knew she was being held captive somewhere remote. She tried to remember time before this room but couldn't. The drug's amnesic effect wouldn't allow her to remember the party.

Cadie made her way back to the carpet.

Another awareness entered her mind.

*Aunt Marie! She's going to be so worried!*

With agonizing empathy and loneliness, heartsickness overcame her, and Cadie collapsed on the ground sobbing. She tried to be strong. She thought of Nick.

How she wished he was here next to her, holding her. He always made her feel better. God, how she wished things had gone better on Mackinac Island. Cadie hoped she lived through this so she could see Nick again, talk to him, but she was afraid she might not.

The young woman wanted to be brave like her childhood hero Nancy Drew, but at the present moment, she could not. Her mind filled with terrible imaginings of what lay ahead for her in this room.

*Dear god, what am I in for? What's going to happen to me in this room?*

Cadie shivered even harder.

*I just need to be brave like Nancy.*

Nancy Drew was just a character in a childhood book when she was imprisoned in *The Secret of the Old Clock*, Cadie knew, of course. Yet, thinking about the brave protagonist gave her comfort.

"Unfortunately," Cadie smiled weakly, "I'm not a character in a book right now. I'm in a real, live nightmare. But I'll be brave soon, Nancy. I just need some sleep."

*Someone, please find me.*

*Or give me the strength and wisdom to save myself.*

Cadie laid down on the carpet, curled up, and cried for a while. She then wiped her eyes and tried to think about how she could escape tomorrow. However, fully exhausted she quickly fell back into a chemically-aided sleep. As she slept, she never heard the thick, excited breathing. She never spotted the jagged little hole in the wall across the room and the darting eye pressed up against it. The smiling person on the other side. The Weirdo surveilling its captured prey.

# *SUNDAY*
## *48 HOURS MISSING*
## *CHAPTER 14*

As Harbor Cove sprang to life Sunday morning, its residents were greeted by a cheerful sun tucked into clear blue skies – a welcome aftermath from yesterday's storm. The slight breeze was refreshing, and the waters of Lake Michigan calmer and peaceful. However, the radiant day was overcast for many: Cadie McLeod had been missing over thirty hours.

While Detective Jake Brennan drove toward the police station, thoughts of Rod Keonig and Karl Kessler on his mind, MSP Search and Rescue, its Marine Division and K9 Unit, and the US Coast Guard were busy searching land and sea for the missing young woman. The tourists who had awakened early and driven to Mariner's Beach were sad to find yellow cones and police tape and a sheriff's deputy next to a white Chevy Silverado blocking the entrance to Hill Valley Road. Car after car was turned away.

Meanwhile, under the bright sun rising slowly overhead, twenty uniformed men and women and two police dogs combed Mariner's Beach. They also searched The Landing and the nearby dunes - diverse formations due to the westerly winds that blow across the Great Lake.

Karik and Kiki, muscular black and tan German Shepherds from the Leelanau County Sheriff's Department, had been given Cadie's track jacket by Aunt Marie. After thoroughly smelling the coat, the dogs began to track. The dog's handlers, sheriff's deputies from Leelanau, held the leashes as Karik and Kiki sniffed various locations. The large, agile dogs were both trained in tracking, and their extreme intelligence made them perfect for this task. From a distance, a group of people huddled together down the beach watched the dogs with their square muzzles and bushy tails carefully inspect the surroundings. Their handlers took the dogs into the sloping Sleeping Bear Sand Dunes National Lakeshore and later headed into the beach dunes adjacent to the low-lying beach with their clusters of Cottonwood trees as well as Aspen, Alder, and Dogwoods.

Around 9 AM, Karik, who was trained in Volgograd, Russia, and his handler were tracking in the southern end of Scenic Trail, about sixty yards from the dirt road that led to the rustic parking lot. His handler, Sheriff's Deputy Scott

McDougall, watched as Karik suddenly seemed to hit a brick wall and abruptly change course. Taking a few steps, Karik snapped his head and looked down, detecting the target odor source. The dog began breathing louder and faster. Almost frantically.

"Hey, we've got a positive indication," McDougall yelled loudly to the MSP Sergeant who was talking to some troopers on the road. McDougall knelt down and saw just a hint of a cell phone poking up in the sand. As he peered closer, all he could make out regarding color or design was a small yellow daisy on the phone's rounded pink corner.

McDougall closed his eyes. He then quickly sent up a prayer. He prayed that this was Cadie McLeod's phone and somehow its discovery would save her life.

## CHAPTER 15

One hot, humid summer at the Happy Camper Campground near Platte River, Rod Koenig felt up his stepsister Sharon in the back of the family's dingy RV. His mom Marla and her negligent boyfriend had driven their dune buggy to the party store in Empire to buy more beer, leaving Rod to babysit Ken's daughter Sharon. Even at the age of eight, Sharon knew Rod was weird.

Once, when Rod was at baseball practice, Sharon and her best friend Missy rummaged around the back shed on the corner of Marla's weedy property, looking for Sharon's rarely-used pink pogo stick. Instead, they found some folded papers along with a baseball magazine tucked away behind a loose board. The papers contained pictures of little girls, some cut out of magazines but some that appeared to be printed photos. A few of the girls didn't have shirts on. One child was naked. Sharon recognized the child as a neighbor girl Marla sometimes babysat.

Both girls immediately knew the pictures belonged to Rod.

"Creeper," Missy yelled, and they cracked up laughing, even though both girls felt thoroughly uncomfortable and a little scared of Rod. Later, Sharon told her dad about the pictures, but Ken said they probably belonged to someone else. More specifically, Ken, drinking his fifth beer, slurred, "How the fuck should I know who those pictures belong to? Leave them the hell alone, Sharon."

Days later, when Sharon went back into the shed, the papers and magazine were gone.

Sharon knew her dad didn't like to upset Marla. She and her alcoholic ex-husband tried to kill each other once, firing guns across the yard at each other in a drunken stupor. Fortunately for them, each was terrible shot.

Marla had a temper and often yelled at her father for the littlest things. One time, Marla whipped a full bottle of Bud Light at her dad's head because he changed the channel. Luckily, the bottle missed Ken's head, but it did leave a gouge in the living room wall and a spray of brown beer on the ceiling that neither bothered to clean. The sticky ceiling still resembled a crime scene.

At a sleepover a week later, Sharon and Missy told their girlfriends about the naughty pictures. The seven little girls had placed their pink and purple sleeping bags into a circle and were sharing scary stories. When it was Sharon's time, she turned off the light and put a metal flashlight under her chin for dramatic effect. She told the unsettling tale of Rod and his nasty stash of little girl porn. Missy, in the background, added the occasional "gross" and "sick" to heighten the drama.

The next day, the girls exited the sleepover with a piece of their childhoods gone forever and a new fear of Rod Koenig. Soon, a rumor about the town miscreant spread around Harbor Cove, but, like most smalltown deviancy, nothing came of it. As time went by, another story of deviancy simply took its place. Just more weirdos in town to keep an eye on.

The lack of action was unfortunate because Rod Keonig, who had never had success with women his own age, continued his taste for little girls unchecked. Little girls didn't look at him like he was a weirdo. Instead, little girls were nice to him. Some even seemed to like him. But they were little girls. They didn't know Rob was a monster.

## CHAPTER 16

Detective Jake Brennan walked into the foyer and pushed through the thick, double glass doors of Harbor Cove Police Station. He passed by the gray receptionist's desk made of quartz that resembled marble, said hi to Debbie Brown who was drinking her morning black tea, and walked briskly to Sergeant Bakker's office four doors down.

He stood in the doorway while Bakker furiously typed something into her computer. From the already tall pile of notes on her desk and empty coffee mug, it looked like Bakker got in earlier than usual. Jake looked up and pondered Sergeant's large poster: "I'm a cop. What's your superpower?"

*That might actually be true. Bakker is next level.*

Then on her credenza, he noticed the photo of the Sergeant's daughter Lila - her middle school track picture ("Cheer for Cove" underneath Lila carrying a gold baton). The picture immediately made Jake think of Cadie and all the track meets since middle school he'd attended watching Nick and Cadie run sprints, relays, and the hurdles. The two grew from children into strong, confident, and winning athletes.

"Mind if I come in?" Jake asked. Bakker waved him in, her head continuing to stare at the screen while she finished typing.

"You have the list?" she said, not looking over.

"I do," Jake said, taking out of his pocket the list Nick and he comprised of people who were connected to Cadie one way or another. He leaned over and handed it to Bakker. She set it down on her expansive mahogany desk covered with a layer of protective glass.

"As you know, we interviewed numerous people yesterday, including most of the sixteen girls and twelve guys who were at the bonfire, which I'll get to in a minute. Unfortunately, no one had much substantial to offer. Right now, the MSP and the K9 unit are out conducting the search and rescue. The Coast Guard and Marine Division haven't turned up anything. I'm getting search warrants for bank records and pings off local cell phone towers. I should have those within hours. Nothing yet from NamUs."

"It's like she dropped off the earth," Jake said.

"Or the devil in the dunes got her," Bakker said under her breath, but Jake caught it.

"That's what Craig said. I don't appreciate the joke."

"I'm not really joking," Bakker said. "A girl went missing from that area. Granted it was years ago, but it still gives me pause."

Jake just shook his head.

"Mind if I sit?"

"Oh, sorry. Yeah, of course."

It took Jake a moment to pull out the heavy mahogany chair as it dragged on the Berber carpet. He took a seat in the oversized chair.

"I called Aunt Marie last night. She still hasn't heard from Cadie. And she said, as far as she knew, Cadie wasn't in therapy. And no diary. Have we had any luck with her school? Her teachers? Classmates?" Jake asked.

"We were able to talk to a few officials, but not all. I'm hoping to get to the rest today," Bakker said, tightening her ponytail. "Principal Marks did mention a few guys at the school that seem odd. And a couple that have already graduated. Now what I'm about to tell you has to stay on the down low – for now. I want to learn a bit more."

"Of course," Jake replied. "I'm guessing one of the guys was Rod Keonig?"

"Yes, it was. Marks said that when Koenig was in school, he was suspended twice for inappropriately touching girls and was almost expelled. He once grabbed a freshman girl by her shirt and tried to pull her into an empty bathroom. The girl broke free and ran screaming down the hallway. Koenig was almost kicked out of school for that, but the school board voted 4-3 to give him another chance. Marks also said Koenig was warned numerous times about his language. 'Whore' and 'bitch' being his favorites."

"So, Rod is no longer in school? He already graduated? I thought he was a senior."

"Yeah, he graduated last year, but the principal said Rod still hangs out with the younger crowd. I believe he works at Lou's Chicken Shack in Buckley."

"Nick didn't have much good to say about Rod. He told me that something happened between Rod and Cadie, but he doesn't know what. Cadie didn't want to tell him. Nick also said Rod is strange and can be aggressive toward women. Nick called him an incel – the new word for weirdos."

"Oh, he's definitely involuntarily celibate," Bakker said. "And that's pretty concerning, knowing something went down between Cadie and Rod."

Bakker stood up and walked to her white filing cabinet. She grabbed a paper off the top and read Detective Dan Zielinski's notes:

"Kara Schumaker and Candice Griffin were at the party. Kara reported that Rod walked up to Candice and grabbed his 'junk' in her face. Kara also said Rod kept brushing against women's breasts saying, 'Excuse me.' Kara said when she and a few friends were down by the water, Rod walked by and flipped them off, calling them 'a bunch of whores.' He said something strange about 'getting even.' Of course, the young ladies were not happy about any of that nonsense," Bakker said.

"That sounds about right. Nick said Rod has never had a girlfriend and never has anything good to say about women."

"You need to track down Mr. Koenig pronto. If he's got Cadie, we really don't know what that guy's capable of. I've pulled his address."

Bakker moved a few papers around and found a slip of paper and handed it to Jake.

"I'm having Detective Field interview two other guys Principal Marks mentioned. One is actually a teacher with a less than stellar reputation. Name's Edward Dawson. Marks said Cadie complained about him recently to the dean of students. I guess he says creepy stuff to the girls at school. The other guy's name is Chad Katz. Marks said he's a loner and gets caught jacking off about once a week somewhere on school grounds to porn magazines. Bondage stuff. Not your typical teen porn. Sounds like the kid has some issues. I haven't heard that he's dangerous, but you just never know."

"No, you don't," Jake said, shifting in his seat and watching Bakker continue to stress tighten her ponytail. "If we could tell who the bad guys are by looking at them, it would make our lives a lot easier," Jake said.

"Ditto that. I also wanted to let you know that there's going to be a candlelight vigil tonight at Van der Velt Marina. You know they've got that pavilion down by the water. I'd like you to attend and observe. I'll have a few other officers go as well. Who knows, our perp might show up. You know the drill."

"Of course," Jake said. "I'll be there. So, who is interviewing Blake Van der Velt? As I mentioned, he got dumped by Cadie and didn't take it well. Blake is a friend of Nick's, so Nick told me about it."

"Craig is taking care of that. Kind of a dicey situation with the Van der Velt status in town. Let me know what you find out about Keonig. And I'll call you when I hear something from MSP."

Bakker looked down at her cell phone. "I swear I've got a million texts."

Her finger starting swiping faster and faster.

Suddenly, Bakker stopped. Her entire demeanor changed, and she brought the phone close to her face, reading the text intently - her lips quietly reading the words out loud while color drained from her face.

"Oh shit, SAR found something. Looks like it might be Cadie's cell phone."

Jake quickly sat more upright.

"Why do they think that?"

"There's a daisy on the phone," Bakker said. "They found the cell phone on Scenic Trail. MSP is sending it for analysis by its Computer Crimes Unit. They're also contacting the Michigan Missing Persons Unit. This shit just got really real. You need to go see what that loser Keonig is up to right now."

## CHAPTER 17

Jake strode across the small police station parking lot headed toward his Tahoe, the bright morning sun warming his face. He was already sweating, and his heart raced. Cadie has been missing since Friday night, and Jake wondered what he might find today when he visited the Keonig home. From years of police work, Jake knew there was no preparing for the horrors a cop might witness on any given day.

Two years ago, on a routine child welfare visit, he found an asphyxiated toddler in a garbage bag in a garage. He opened the black bag and immediately smelled death and saw tiny, bulging eyes staring up at him. He puked right then and there on the garage floor. In this job, no one can prepare you for the evil you might encounter at any time.

As he thought about Cadie, and what he might find today, Jake's hands trembled. He gripped the warm steering wheel tighter and headed the Tahoe towards Pilgrim Highway. He prayed he didn't find Cadie dead in a garbage bag.

*Where are you, Cadie? Who has you? What have they done to you?*

He tried to push his dark thoughts out the window and into the Lake Michigan breeze as he drove into rural Benzie County.

Located in Michigan's northern tip, Benzie County, the smallest county in Michigan and comprised of just 316 square miles, is a tourist's dream. Deriving its name from the French "la riviere aux Bec-Scies," or "River of the Sawbills," the County is home to twenty-five miles of Lake Michigan shoreline, quaint towns like Honor and Beulah, thirty hiking trails, wineries, breweries, rivers, forests, farms, and fifty-seven lakes and state and federally-protected sand dunes created by long-ago glaciers.

The Tahoe turned onto Sutter Road and began driving North Scenic Highway to Little Platte Lake, where Rod lived with his mother Marla and her boyfriend Ken. Marla owned a house and several acres on a private, sparsely-populated dirt road off Dune Eagle Drive.

Jake knew the area well. As a young boy, Jake's dad took him fishing for Walleye and Bluegill on the quiet lake surrounded by towering Pines and fast-growing Aspen-Birch trees. On the way to the lake, with open forests on both sides of the road, Jake would hang his head out window of his dad's Ford truck. With the wind in his face, he'd keep a steady eye out for deer, an overhead eagle, or maybe even a rare Black bear looking back at him through the trees.

Once they got to the lake, dad always spotted the Loons first. The black-headed birds would float serenely on the warm water's surface, and sometimes Jake and his dad would hear their eerie wailing, "oo-loo-lee." Thinking about his father caused a sadness Jake hadn't felt in a while. He remembered how they would look over the side of the boat at their reflections, laughing, and marvel that the clear, sandy lake was only eight feet deep. His dad was a good father. Jake hoped he was half the dad his father was.

Turning off Dune Eagle Drive and onto Koenig's dirt road, Jake began to feel the usual fear rise up. A nervous, panicky feeling. Would he find Cadie on the Koenig's property? Would she be dead? If she was, what would she look like? Jake steeled himself for the immediate future.

The detective pulled his car up the bumpy dirt driveway to the farmhouse. Dirty pink and yellow toys were scattered around the poorly-tended yard filled with weeds and dirt spots. Just then, two massive, heavy-boned black Mastiffs tore from behind the house, galloping towards the Tahoe.

*Oh, hell no.*

Jake sat in his SUV, waiting for someone to do something about the agitated, pacing dogs with their broad heads drooling on the side of his car. Finally, a middle-aged woman came to the front door, dressed in a light blue housecoat and smoking a cigarette. She yelled at the dogs in a gravelly smoker's voice.

"Batman! Joker! Get over here!"

After more pacing and growling, the dogs ran onto the uneven porch and into the house while the wooden screen door slammed behind them. The branches of an enormous Red Oak Tree created a canopy over the Tahoe, and already the yellowish string-like clusters were blanketing Jake's windshield. He liked a clean car, so his mood continued to sour.

"Can I help you?" the woman called out. Jake assumed it was Marla Koenig. She was standing on the edge of porch now, her cigarette hanging unattractively off her lower lip.

"Hello, ma'am. I'm detective Jake Brennan from the Harbor Cove Police Department," Jake said, walking up to the aging porch. "I'm here . . . "

"It's about Rod, isn't it?" Marla said, cutting Jake off. He could smell the beer on her breath.

Jake thought she looked old for her probable age. Lots of hard living, he figured.

"Yes, it is," Jake replied. "As you might know, a senior – Cadie McLeod - at Harbor Cove High School has been missing from a lake party that took place Friday night, a party that Rod attended. We're questioning everyone who was at the party. So, who are you?"

"I'm Marla Koenig. I'm Rod's mom."

Just then a young girl stepped through the squeaky screen door. "Rod is a big loser. No one likes him."

"Shut up, Sharon. No one likes you, either," Marla yelled, motioning her hand toward the door. "Get your skinny ass back in the house."

"Is Rod home?" Jake asked.

Marla laughed and took another drag off her cigarette.

"That kid is never home. He does what he wants."

A breeze blew yellow clusters off the porch roof and onto Jake's head and shirt, causing him to cough. Clouds were moving in.

"When's the last time you saw him?"

"I don't keep track of Rod's comings and goings. But if I had to guess, I probably saw him Thursday."

"You haven't seen him since Thursday? And he lives at home" Jake asked, surprised. "Well, where is he?" Jake could see Sharon peeking at him through faded lace window curtains.

"Hell, if I know. I'm his mother not his prison guard," Marla spit out, now annoyed. She crossed her arms over her chest and leaned against a rotting porch post.
"The kid loves to party. Especially weed. He's probably drinking and smoking at our camper right now."

"Camper? Where is that?"

"We have a camper parked out on an old farmstead that belonged to my opa – my grandpap. It's about a mile down Hill Valley Road. On the south side. The RV sits a ways off the road near some other old buildings on the property. Rod and his friends like it because it's close to the beach, and they can do whatever they want there."

"Ms. Keonig, does Rod know Cadie McLeod? Did he ever speak of her?"

Marla flicked her smoldering stub of a cigarette out into the yard next to a pile of beer cans. A tight smile formed on her thin lips that were surrounded by smoker's wrinkles.

"I've never heard Rod mention Cadie; he's not good with women. He's never even had a girlfriend. Just lots of girl trouble. Honestly, and I hate to say this, my son is a dick. He's strange and mean and arrogant – even to me - and he never has anything nice to say about anybody, especially women. If he did say something about Cadie, I'm sure it wasn't good," she laughed strangely.

Jake just looked at her, shocked by her words. Not trusting her.

"Did he say something, though? About Cadie?" Jake stared at Marla intensely.

Marla's posture suddenly shifted, like she had said too much. Spoken too freely. That third beer had gotten the best of her.

"No, I'm not saying he said anything. Hey, I gotta get back in the house. Start making lunch."

Sharon was still watching from the window, her little nose pressed against the filmy window.

Jake eyed Marla warily.

"I'm going to drive over to your property after I leave here. Do I have your permission to look around the grounds and the camper?"

Marla looked nervous. She began to fidget.

"It's just routine. We're just ruling people out. Everyone who was at the party."

"Uh, I guess so," Marla said.

"As I said, it's no big deal. I just want to find Rod and ask him a few basic questions. Same questions I'm asking of all the kids who were at the bonfire Friday night."

"Well, okay. I guess that's alright."

"Does Rod have a car?"

"Yeah. A Pontiac. Thinks it's called an Acadian."

"I didn't know those existed anymore."

"Ken found it online. Some guy who moved here from Toronto."

"Okay. Thank you. If you see or hear from Rod, tell him to contact me right away."

He handed Marla his business card.

"One more question, Mrs. Koenig. Does Rod have access to guns?"

Marla chortled like it was the most ridiculous question she'd ever been asked.

"Who doesn't? Right now, I've got a loaded Glock by the front door."

Marla turned and headed back into the aging house. She bent over and picked up an old heater off the porch and carried it indoors, shutting the door behind her. Meanwhile, Jake briskly walked back to his Tahoe, glad to be leaving the depressing house and property. In minutes, he was driving quickly down Dune Eagle Drive. About a mile in, he stopped short. In front of his Tahoe, a momma Loon and her six brown-black loonlets stepped out and marched across the road. Jake smiled. He got a kick out of the little family. He loved animals and remembered as a kid watching loonlets ride on their mother's back when first born. It was nice to observe something heartwarming after talking to a soulless woman like Marla Koenig.

He got out his phone and called Detective Craig Kitchen.

"Hi Jake," Craig said, answering after two rings.

"What are you up to?" Jake asked.

"I've been working my way down the list. Talking to some students, parents, teachers - you name it. I've got Blake Van der Velt coming in later this afternoon for an interview. I tried to meet up with him last night, but he said he had plans. Kind of a weird response when we're trying to find a missing person, someone he even dated. One of the kids at the party said he saw Blake grab Cadie by the arm, and she pulled away. Don't know what that means, but we need to talk to him. Just a bit awkward on account of his uncle's reputation in town. I guess he makes a big donation to The Thin Blue Line every year."

Jake thought about the young man who had visited his house several times over the past year. Jake never knew the full story as to why Blake came to live with his uncle, and Jake had always found the young man and his over-the-top vocabulary somewhat off-putting.

"So, what's up?" Craig asked.

"I just left the Keonigs out by Little Platte Lake. Rod Keonig's mother Marla said Rod and his friends like to hang out on an old farmstead they own on Hill Valley Drive. It's probably half a mile from The Landing. They have a camper on the property. I'm driving over there to check it out right now."

"Marla Koenig gave you permission?"

"She did. And I have a bad feeling about this guy Rod. Can you head over and meet me at that pull off on Pilgrim Highway? The one near the bait and tackle shop? Then we can check out the Koenig property together. Her son is bad news."

"Sure. I'll meet you at the pull off in about fifteen minutes."

"Great," Jake said. "See you then."

Jake had a little bit of time before meeting Craig, so he called Sergeant Bakker.

"Hey, Sergeant, just checking in."

"Thanks, detective," Bakker said. "Where you at?"

"I just left the Koenigs. Rod's mother Marla Koenig said she hasn't seen Rod since Thursday. Craig and I are going to check out some other property the Koenigs own on Hill Valley Drive. I guess they have a camper on it that Rod and his friends like to party at."

"That reminds me," Bakker said, "a partygoer we interviewed today mentioned Keonig. He said Rod talked about Cadie sometimes."

"Really? What did he say?"

"Stuff in today's slang," Bakker laughed. "Like she was sic or snatched."

"He's a weird one, for sure. His mother gave me permission to search their farmstead, so that means several old buildings. And there's a camper on the property. A lot to look through. Marla said Rod and his boys like to party on the property."

"Oh great," Bakker said. "None of that sounds good. A bunch of delinquents with no supervision."

"Yeah, I don't have a good feeling."

"I'm concerned that we don't have a search warrant," Bakker said.

"I recorded her."

"What?"

"I recorded Marla Keonig giving us permission to search the grounds. When I was talking to her, I had my phone recorder turned on."

"Oh, that again. Up to your old tricks. Well, if you see anything truly incriminating, we'll get a search warrant," Bakker said. "But in the future, please try to follow procedure, Brennan. We don't need to mess this up."

"Yeah, I know you're right," Jake replied. "We just don't have a lot of time. I'll let you know ASAP if we find anything."

"On another note," Bakker said, "Digital Analysis found something. First, the cell phone the K9 Unit located this morning on Scenic Trail does belong to Cadie. The lab analyzed it, and they're reporting no helpful information from its apps, photos, text messages, etc. However, they did find one thing."

The way Bakker said "one thing" made Jake uneasy.

"What? What'd they find?"

"Cadie was taking selfies and pictures of her friends right before she entered Scenic Trail Friday night. Two partygoers now confirm that. On the phone, there are pictures of her friends waving at Cadie from around the bonfire."

"Okay, how is that helpful?"

"Just wait. So, there was a three-second video on Cadie's phone. It appears the phone inadvertently took the quick video when it dropped or there was a struggle."

Jake, now extremely interested, barked out, "So what's on the video?"

"It's blurry, but basically it records the dark form of a person bending over. From the size and outline of the form, it looks to be a man. The moon is behind the head, so the face is dark. The lab can't make out the face – yet - but the person is wearing a hat with some sort of fringe or frayed fabric along the top of the bill."

"Oh, Jesus," Jake said. "That's creepy."

"Yes, it is," Bakker said. "The lab is trying to enhance the video to see if they can make out a face or any helpful details. But the phone definitely captured someone that night who appears to be the last person near Cadie's phone."

"Can you send me the video?"

"I will when I get off the phone," Bakker said. "Examine the hat. As I said, it has a unique feature with that trim. Let me know if it rings a bell. So, you're headed to the Koenig's farmstead now?"

"Yeah, I'm meeting up with Craig, and we're going to check it out together."

"Good idea," Bakker said. "Be careful, Jake. If Rod or his friends have Cadie at that property, no telling what they are capable of. Text me as soon as you can and let me know how it goes and if you need back up. You're going to the vigil later, right?"

"Yeah, I'll be there. I'm going to call Nick to find out more details and see if he's heard anything."

"Before I let you go, I got an address for Karl Kessler. He's been living with his brother in Leland and occasionally a relative in Marie's sub. He works part-time at a bread company just outside Harbor Cove and helps with his brother's dairy farm. Track him down tomorrow and interview him. It seems he's still up to no good. Always trying to hook up with teenage girls."

"Another loser."

"Actually, the guy is pretty smart. He graduated from Kalamazoo College. I guess he was diagnosed as schizoaffective – mania and delusions. In one of his college classes, he threatened some female students. His high school records also indicate he's on the spectrum and has trouble relating to his classmates. Anyway, just because he likes teenage girls doesn't make him dumb. Just criminal. So be careful."

Okay, will do," Jake said. "I'll look up the bread company. If I can't find him there, I'll head up to Leland."

After hanging up, Jake rolled down his window to let in some fresh air as the interior of the SUV had warmed. Clouds continued to roll in, creating a discomforting pall over the landscape. Jake pulled the Tahoe back out on the road and headed toward Pilgrim Highway. His mind swirled with thoughts of Rod Koenig, Blake Van der Velt, Karl Kessler, and all the other local creeps lurking around town and elsewhere. He wondered if he would find Cadie McLeod, and if he did, would it be in time? He pushed the image of the baby in the garbage bag far back in his mind where it always lurked.

Jake turned the SUV out onto the paved North Scenic Highway and drove to the pull off to meet Craig and whatever lay ahead at the Koenig compound.

## CHAPTER 18

## The Weirdo

*What are you up to right now, Cadie McLeod?*

I laugh to myself imagining her crying her eyes out and stumbling around that filthy, little room – still weak from the Special K. Sorry. Not sorry. The image of her sobbing and praying brings a smile to my face. I'm feeling so much happier. I placed a zip tie around my rearview mirror to remind myself how great it felt to drag her limp body to my truck. The complete control was honestly exhilarating. It's hard to put into words the thrill I felt when I shoved her unresponsive body in the truck bed and zip tied her tight. I feel like I understand serial killers a bit better now.

Late last night, I watched her sleeping through the peep hole. Then I quietly opened the door and put three water bottles and three granola bars for her next to the wall – not too many, though. Just enough. I also brought in a bucket and toilet paper. I'm not a monster.

She must have awakened earlier and put her sundress back on. No mind. I didn't take her clothes off because I'm some kind of pervert and want to watch her naked. Her boobs are too little for my taste, anyway. No, it's about getting even. I want her to feel humiliation, isolation, and pain – and a deep loss of control. Girls have always had the power. Now it's my time to be in control, to give payback. I want to grind down this person's spirit and utter life to dust just like what was done to me.

*Revenge.*

I think back.

Every morning, I'd open my eyes and picture her beautiful, sun-kissed face looking down at me. Her soft hair falling all about her tanned shoulders while a playful smile formed at the corner of her kissable mouth. We'd have tender sex and then lay next to each other for hours, talking and listening to music. My mind was consumed by fantasies of her luminous green eyes staring right into me, the confident way she walked, her silly laugh. She was the first and only girl who really got to know me, who seemed to care about me. With her, I felt like I would have a normal life – a good life - like other people. For as much as I was capable, I loved her.

We were friends at first. But I'd catch her watching me. Peeking at me through long, brown eyelashes. She'd twirl her hair and slightly tilt her head. That's how I knew she loved me. She was giving me clues.

Saturday night couldn't come fast enough. I was dressed in new khakis and a blue crewneck sweater that matched my eyes. My mom always said blue was my color.

*Where are you mom? Where did you go?*

I sprayed on some cologne and made a final check in the mirror. I almost didn't recognize myself. When I walked out the door that evening, I felt confident for the first time. By the end of the night, I'd have a girlfriend. In a few years, a wife.

The party was in town, just a mile away. Steve's parents were on a Caribbean cruise, so he put out word he was having a party. As the sun set over the lake, I rode my mountain bike through the crisp autumn air, feeling exhilarated as the fall leaves swirled across the street in front of me. My mind kept playing over and over the night's big reveal: when I would tell her I loved her and ask her to be my girlfriend. She would throw her arms around me, kiss me deeply, and tell me she loved me above all others. It was going to be perfect. I took my right hand off the handlebar and felt the ring in my pocket.

Minutes later, I got to Steve's, and the driveway was wall to wall cars. In fact, cars were lined up and down the tree-covered street on both sides. When I made it to the cottage's front door, I literally had to push it open with my shoulder. That's how many people were crammed into the tiny living room. I finally got the heavy wood door open and was met by a roar of pounding music, loud conversations, and laughter from a mass of humans pressed tight - squirming against each other. A haze of weed and cigarette smoke wafted above their sea of heads.

I began looking for her. She loves parties, so I knew she would be there. I again touched the ring in my pocket – a pink ice rhinestone that belonged to my grandmother. Dad gave it to me when Nana died. I was surprised. He never gave me anything.

I didn't see her in the front room. My head throbbed from smoke and stress. Feeling a strange urgency, I fought my way to an opening and squeezed myself down the packed narrow hallway – a gauntlet of loud, drunk partygoers - their garish voices ricocheting off aggressive yellow walls. I eventually emerged in the kitchen. I looked around the 1950's-style room. Still, no sign of her. I began to get a little irritated.

"Hey, Marissa!"

I saw her friend sitting open legged on the kitchen counter talking to some guy with a beard. I worked my way over. People were playing a beer drinking game at a red vintage kitchen table. Over in the corner, by the window, I saw Tim Matthews chugging a beer bong and spitting up while a group cheered him on.

"Where is she?"

She knew who I meant. People said I was obsessed.

"Sheeeze wit TJ," Marissa slurred. "Innn the back."

TJ was a friend of mine. Of ours.

"She's with TJ?"

"That's whuuut I said, din't I?"

Marissa was drunk - a sloppy bitch. Her thin, unattractive mouth was stained red, and then I saw the bottle of Sloe Gin in her hand.

"Fine. Whatever. I'll head to the back yard."

I pushed through the kitchen crowd and could feel the refreshing outside air pouring in through the screen door. Grateful for an escape and a cool breeze, I stepped through the door and out onto the back deck, ready to find my soulmate and profess my love.

The sun was almost gone. Just an orange and red blur on the horizon. Little bugs were buzzing by my head; I swatted them away.

I glanced around the small backyard, a rectangle of deep green grass bordered by well-kept Yews. Lawn chairs were placed sporadically, and people pulled their jackets a bit closer as the air cooled. They spoke animatedly while the alcohol took effect. A small propane-fueled fire cast light around the yard. I searched the faces of the people sitting in the chairs, but I didn't see hers. More vigorously now, I walked to the side of the house, but no one was there. Just a riding lawn mower and a tangle of green garden hoses.

*Why was my heart beating so fast?*

I decided to walk around the entire house. Passing the front window, I glanced in and saw the same squirming mass of loud people. I walked past the front steps to the small, one-car garage. Four guys stood in a group, enthralled, while Phil Grant gave a spirited play by play of his heroics in last night's win over Manistee. I moved quickly to the north side of the house. It was an empty stretch of grass. I did notice, however, that someone, most likely Steve, didn't mow this side of the house. Everyone knows he's a lazy ass. The tall grass was turning into weeds and covered by 'helicopters' that fell from the neighbor's maple. I hastily rounded the corner and was back where I started.

She wasn't there. My face flushed hot.

They say the opposite of love is hate. I now know that to be true. It's shocking how quickly one's emotions can turn that dangerous corner. I was now breathing hard, dripping sweat in my new sweater, and becoming furious.

WHERE? WAS? SHE?

Just then Annabel, Marissa's best friend, walked over.

"Did you find her?" she smiled coyly.

"No. I looked everywhere," I spat. I could hardly contain my rage. My hands were shaking.

"No wonder. She left with TJ. They were holding hands."

*Holding hands?*

Suddenly, my brain stopped. My mouth quit working. It seemed like a century passed before I was able to form words.

"'WHAT? WHEN?"

"Jesus. Calm down. I saw them about fifteen minutes ago.

'WHERE DID THEY GO?"

"I saw them in the road by TJ's car. They make a cute couple, don't you think?"

Without a word, I turned away from her. She came within an inch of being throat punched. For a split second, I pictured my fist opening a bloody gash in her neck. I felt like I was going to be sick. My body trembled. My hands were clenched so tight, the nails cut into my skin.

In Biology class, Clark Freeman had told me TJ had a crush on her.

"You're full of it," I told him.

No way TJ would do that to me.

He wouldn't dare.

Besides, she *loves* me.

I stomped up the driveway, the stones crunching under my heavy steps. It was dark now, but the moon was out, and most of the cottages had streetlamps on, casting uneven shadows over the road and cars. A group of people from the party were leaving, and their laughter floated over, distracting me. One of the guys looked at me, nodded his head, and said, "Hey."

The group turned left on Sandhill Lane. After they were a ways down the street, I turned right and slowly walked, hands still clenched, adrenaline coursing through my every vein. My narrowed eyes scanned the long rows of cars as I hunted for TJ's vintage Marina Blue Camaro – his eighteenth birthday present.

*That guy gets everything. He's got it so good.*

I walked to the end of the street, and that's when I saw it: TJ's shiny blue Camaro parked on Piper Lane, visible under a streetlamp. I walked closer to the car. Then I heard it. The sound of two people laughing. Enjoying themselves.

I dug my nails further into my hands.

A car slowly made its way up the street, its lights almost landing on me as I stepped back into the shadows of a tree. I waited for the car to pass and stepped back out.

Then, in the dark, with a cool fall breeze blowing across my flushed face, I approached the car slowly. I walked carefully, so as not to be detected. Then I stood very still, just off the corner of the Camaro, and oh so gradually bent over and strained my neck. I peered into the small back window of the car that was just beginning to fog. And that's when I saw them. In the backseat. She was straddling him, her floral skirt hiked up around her hips, while she kissed his neck passionately. His head was leaned back on the leather seat with eyes closed while he moaned with pleasure. It was hard to see everything that was taking place, but I had seen enough.

These were not my friends.

They didn't care about me.

She probably never even loved me.

That's when my brain exploded.

I felt violent shards of envy and rage pierce my heart. I grabbed the cold metal door handle, and, as I did, a deep primal scream erupted from my mouth into the cool night air – the culmination of all the pain, sadness, loneliness, and indifference I had endured for as long as I could remember. When I opened the door, TJ lurched forward, and I wrenched him. With a strength based on years of hate and despair, I pulled the shocked young man from his car. He stumbled out onto the grass. That's when my life of vengeance began.

Later, when the police officer who cuffed me asked me why I did it, I just stared at him dumbfounded. I was incredulous.

*Is he serious?*

"Because," I said while TJ's fresh blood dripped from my broken fist, "they betrayed me."

## CHAPTER 19

Jake drove down North Scenic Trail silently, endless trees rushing by, on his way to the pull off to meet Craig Kitchen. He couldn't bear to listen to music. He needed to focus, and he needed to call Nick. The detective glanced at his phone and saw that his son had left him a voicemail.

"Hey, dad, it's me. Did you find out anything about Cadie? I really can't believe this is happening. I'm freaking out. It's like the worst nightmare. I keep thinking all these terrible thoughts, but I'm trying to be brave like you. And I wanted to make sure you remembered about the vigil tonight. It's 9 pm at the Van der Velt pavilion. A lot of people are going. Cadie's Aunt will be there. They have a program planned, and people are putting up reward money. Derrick's dad, Blake's uncle, the guy who owns Scoops, and something called the Netherland Society. Derrick's dad is going to speak about it tonight at the vigil.

I also wanted to share something weird I heard today. A couple girls in my class texted me about our science teacher, Mr. Dawson. He's the teacher that sometimes helps out with track. Sheila and Amanda texted that a few girls have had issues with Dawson. Sheila said he keeps girls after class, makes them clean his blackboard while he watches, rubs girls' shoulders at track practice – creepy stuff like that. Sheila also said she heard that Mr. Dawson was sexting a student last year. Who knows if that's true. Anyway, Sheila said she saw Cadie in Dawson's classroom a few times after school the past couple months. Just for the heck, I decided to Google the dude and found out he used to teach at a school in Alpena but was let go for nondisclosed reasons. The news article said there was a closed school board session about it. It's probably nothing, but I thought you should know. Like you said, everyone's a suspect. Well, I hope you're okay. I'll see you later at the vigil."

A minute later, Jake turned into the pull off bordered by large white oak trees. Craig was sitting in his SUV on the phone. He waved as he saw Jake pull up next to him. There was a picnic table in the grass next to the small dirt lot, so Jake sat down while he waited for Craig to get off the phone. As he studied the picnic table, Jake saw all manner of messages carved into the rotting wood: Paul loves Tiffany; Fuck Off & Die; and Don't Stop Believing. A lifelong Journey fan, Jake chose to focus on the latter's positive message. He had to for Cadie's sake.

As Jake waited for Craig to finish his call, he smelled the nearby row of Japanese Barberry, and it triggered a memory. He recalled a spring day when Laura was in their front yard digging a hole for planting. Aileen, her long red hair lifting in the breeze (god, she was a beautiful woman) wandered over to warn Laura about the shrub and how invasive it could be. Of course, his soon-to-be-ex-wife didn't listen, and now the invasive species has taken over his front lawn.

*How strange life is – recalling this memory of Aileen while trying to save her daughter's life.*

"Sorry about that," Craig said, walking over and taking a seat. "I was talking to Kayla, trying to get her a ride home from basketball practice."

"No worries," Jake said. "First, let me bring you up to speed on Cadie's cell phone."

Jake explained that Digital Analysis positively ID'd the phone as belonging to Cadie and discovered a blurry video. Bakker had texted it to him, so both men studied the three-second clip.

"There's something about the hat that is familiar," Jake said, "but I can't quite place it."

"I know what you mean," Craig agreed. "I feel sure I've seen it. Hopefully, it will come to us sooner rather than later. So, how do you want to approach the Koenig property?"

"Marla said there's a RV on the property. It's an old farmstead, so we can anticipate some ancient buildings. If Rod is there, some of his buddies may also be there. Hopefully, they're all smoking weed. That will make our job a lot easier," Jake smiled.

"That would be some luck," Craig laughed. "So much better than Meth."

Jake continued, "Let's walk up to the RV casually, like it's no big deal. We're just checking names off our list. Like we're bored and going through the motions. Then let's try to access the RV and search it the best we can. After, we'll search the grounds. With the older buildings, there might be a lot to cover. If there's anything out of the ordinary, or we see we're over our heads with the amount to cover, we'll call for backup. Sound good?"

"Sounds like a plan," Craig said.

"Oh, and Marla said Rod has access to guns."

"Who doesn't?"

"That's what Marla said."

"Do you want to drive together or bring both SUVs?" Craig asked.

"Let's both drive," Jake responded. "Let's rattle them a bit with increased presence."

"Okay, I'll follow."

Within seconds, both men were on their way to the Koenig's property, adrenaline flowing, not sure what or who they would encounter. This was an exciting part of a cop's job – heading toward the unknown. It was also the most deadly.

Two miles down the road, about a half mile from Lake Michigan, was the Koenig's property. There was no proper driveway, just a narrow dirt rut between large pines that opened up into a clearing. On one of the tree branches hung a faded blue, rotting sign with a big letter K. Jake thought the trees looked like imposing sentries, keeping guard over what devious activities took place behind their line. The detectives maneuvered their Tahoes down the narrow drive and then parked where the property opened back up. Both men exited and stood for a moment surveying the property.

In front of them, they saw what was once the small farmhouse – now just decaying wood floor boards covered in moss and weeds, shards of jagged glass, an old metal latch, and stone piers that were part of the home's foundation. A few remnants of the rotted vertical columns remained. Jake had seen this construction in other 1800's homes in the area due to the unstable ground that accompanies living near a coast.

They walked closer. Along the house was part of a rotted fence, and next to that, lying in the thick, long grass was a rusted red lawnmower and an old boat motor. Some vintage farm implements were scattered in the grass. To the left and behind the house - closer to a row of thinning pines - were a decaying wood shed, granary, and what appeared to be a sugar shack made from rough sawn lumber. Further back to the right was the RV. So, far, no human activity.

Craig and Jake then began walking toward the white and blue RV.

"Smell the weed?" Craig said.

"Oh yeah. The boys have been partying."

They slowly approached the RV, the embers in the fire pit out front still smoldering. A few ashtrays with mostly smoked blunts were on a rusted table. Faded and ripped fabric lawn chairs encircled the fire pit, which was full of beer cans, their identifying characteristics burned away. As the detectives drew closer, they suddenly smelled something putrid. They leaned into the firepit and spotted a charred animal with a rope around its neck. It appeared to be a cat. They just looked at each other in disgust and shook their heads.

Jake and Craig didn't see anyone. The place was deserted. No cars anywhere. The men headed to the side of the RV, and Jake walked up the metal steps and peered in the small window in the door. The wind blew eerily through the surrounding trees. It was unnervingly quiet.

"I don't see anybody," Jake said. "Let's go in. We have Marla's permission."

"We don't have a warrant, though," Craig answered.

"I was recording her."

"What?"

"While I was talking to Marla, I was taping her on my phone. So, I recorded her giving me permission to search the RV, buildings, and property."

"Wow, you're my hero," Craig laughed. "Just hope it holds up."

Jake slowly and carefully pushed in the metal door. He had to duck considerably to squeeze his large frame through the smallish opening. Craig, at 5'8" and a crewcut, easily made it through the doorway and stepped onto the dirty green carpet. Jake steeled himself for what he might find in the ensuing minutes.

*Dear god, please don't let Cadie be in here dead.*

He tried not to picture the joyful young woman tied up in a closet in the back of the RV. Then the image of the dead baby in the trashcan flashed in his mind.

The RV was sweaty warm and awash in hazy sunlight. A dirty film covered the windows, making the outdoors a blur. Dust particles floated lazily, settling on the dated brown faux leather interior that abutted wood paneling. Both men quickly smelled the stench and gagged. A noxious mix of sweat, smoke, mold, and urine. Your basic filth, Jake thought. He had smelled it many times in his career. People who had given up or didn't care. Craig covered his mouth and nose with his sleeve.

"Why don't you start up front," Jake said. "I'll head to the back. Check the bathroom and bedroom."

"Thank god," Craig laughed through his sleeve. "I really don't want to see the bathroom."

Craig began looking around the kitchenette while Jake headed down the narrow hallway.

After searching the bathroom and finding nothing but more filth – a moldy toilet and a sink ringed in a hard water orange stain - Jake made his way to the back bedroom. He stepped over a pile of shoes and dirt-encrusted work boots. He noticed that the full-size bed was not made – no surprise – and that the exposed, dingy sheet looked like it hadn't been washed in, well, maybe never. The yellow comforter with white stars lay wadded up to the side of the bed, a visible stain on top. His nose immediately registered the stale smell of mold – like wet socks – and he saw grayish stains where the ceiling met the walls. He, too, covered his nose with his sleeve to blot out the musty fungi that would eventually engulf the entire structure.

Jake went through the drawers in the small built-in dresser and found nothing out of the ordinary except a *Maxim* magazine in the bottom drawer. Next to the dresser was a narrow closet with a sliding door. When Jake slid it back, he was shocked. The closet was crammed with various overstuffed clear storage bags that appeared to contain clothing.

"Strange way to store your clothes."

He grabbed one large bag off the upper shelf. In black marker, a small bag was labeled "panties." A second bag was labeled "tube tops," and a third, slightly larger bag was labeled "daisy dukes and dresses." It also looked like it contained a blonde wig.

"Hey, Craig, come take a look at this," Jake yelled out the bedroom door.

Craig quickly made his way down the hallway, entered the small room, and looked at the bag Jake was holding in his hand.

"What's that?"

"Clothes porn."

"Huh?"

"Look at the labels: daisy dukes, panties, bras. Why is there such a large and labeled inventory of women's clothing? Like clothes for a photo shoot. Or fetish. Something is definitely not right about this."

"Whoever stashed this clothing definitely objectifies women," Craig added.

"Objectifies women?"

"Yeah, like not seeing women as human beings but only sex objects. Men who do that don't relate to women as people but only objects to fulfill fantasies," Craig said.

"That's pretty good, Craig."

"When I attended the Academy at Grand Valley, we had to take courses in criminology and psychology. The classes gave me a better understanding of the male criminal mind."

"I agree," Jake said, "whoever is hoarding this stuff is definitely fantasizing. Hopefully, they're not using it on women without their consent."

As he said that, he noticed one more bag tucked back in the closet corner. Jake pulled it out and turned over the bag filled with pinks and yellows. Its label read "little girls."

"What the hell?" Jake said, his voice gruff.

"Oh man, that is messed up," Craig said. "I sure hope it's just clothes for someone's child. Let's keep looking and see what else we find."

The men searched the remainder of the dark paneled closet looking for any other incriminating items like rope, zip ties, handcuffs, duct tape, dark porn, etc. Not finding anything else in the closet, they finished searching the rest of the humid RV. Nothing else was worrisome, just an abundance of empty booze bottles, cigarette butts, smoked weed, and, of course, mold. They were just about to leave when Craig looked down and saw something on the carpet to the right of the door. It was a zip tie.

"Hey, look at this."

The men bent down and inspected the clear plastic tie sometimes used by perps to control women. Craig reached in his pocket and pulled out a pair of gloves and bag. Putting on the gloves, he placed the zip tie in the evidence bag.

"Never good news to find a zip tie," Jake said.

Jake and Craig exited the RV. The sky was now complete cloud cover – dark and overcast – matching Jake's mood. The winds picked up, thrusting yellow pollen into the air that swirled above their heads. The tall, surrounding trees shook as if angry, and the lake gusts that moved through them created an intense buzzing. Jake pulled his coat closer as he felt an eeriness settle in. He also felt the day slipping away, and they weren't any closer to finding Cadie.

"Let's take a look at those buildings," he said, and they headed for the sugar shack first. As the men approached the small wooden shed with a stove pipe, they read the faded quote carved into the wood: "Men can take your life, but only the Lord can take your soul."

Jake found the quote unsettling. His pulsed quickened.

*Are you in one of these buildings, Cadie? Please don't let me find you dead.*

For several hours, the two detectives searched the buildings and property. They peered in grimy windows and searched the rotting sugar shack, another wooden shed, and a square granary with a thatched roof but to no avail. No sign of Cadie McLeod. Just rotted wood floors, rusted metal, dust, mold, dead rodents, and mice droppings. All they found were decaying buildings that no longer mattered to anyone.

After searching the buildings, Jake and Craig separated and searched amongst the overgrown trees that lined the property. They then headed to the back three acres, knowing the two of them would not be able to adequately search the remaining land full of rolling, sandy hills covered in tall grasses and occasional tree groves. They would need to bring in a search team, but could they get a warrant? They were already walking a fine line by even searching the property using only Jake's recording of Marla as permission.

"Let's head back to the station," Jake yelled out to Craig who was barely visible in a small valley between two large hills. Jake turned to head back, his shirt soaked through with sweat from activity and anxiety. He slowed his walk and waited for the jogging Craig to catch up.

"There's a lot more property to search," Craig said, slightly out of breath. "Too much for us, though."

"Yeah, I'll talk to Bakker when we get back. See if she thinks we could get a warrant."

The detectives were walking toward their vehicles when they suddenly heard a noise.

The men stopped.

All was silent but the warm wind working its way through pines. They listened intently. Then they heard it again! A faint, deep moaning. It seemed to be coming from the bowels of the farmhouse. The men locked eyes for a second and took off running. They quickly reached the old home's remains and began frantically searching the foundation.

"Cadie! Cadie McLeod! Is that you? Are you down there?" Jake yelled repeatedly.

They desperately searched the perimeter of the foundation, conscious that an injured Cadie McLeod could be dying just feet away. Finally, Craig spotted it: a barely visible, moss and sticks-covered wooden door flush with the ground. Most likely the small entrance to a historic Michigan basement.

"There it is!" Craig yelled.

They ran over. Jake reached down and pulled on the rusted metal door handle. It held tight. Craig grabbed onto the handle next to Jake's hand, and both pulled furiously on the stuck door. Suddenly, from deep under the old floorboards, the men heard the sound again.

They stopped and locked eyes wide with terror.

"Oh god!" Jake yelled out.

It was a woman moaning in agony.

## CHAPTER 20

As the sun slipped below the horizon, Cadie McCleod had been missing 45 hours. The sky was now filled briefly with hazy sunshine and muted lines of red. The afternoon's playful waves were hushed, and the marina's nearby occupants – fishing boats and charters, sports cruisers, motor yachts, houseboats, and jet skis – all bobbed silently in their protected slips. Within minutes, the sun quickly slid behind the horizon, and the sky darkened. The light pedestals throughout sprawling Van der Velt Marina quivered on, casting mysterious shadows over the murky water. Evening had arrived.

As he walked past the marina and made his way to its nearby pavilion, Nick heard low conversations and an occasional laugh. Some carefree boat owners were enjoying a lovely Sunday in June drinking glasses of Dolcetto Rosé from the Ciccone Winery in Suttons Bay. The rest settled in their boat cabins for the night. Blackish waves lapped at their expensive yachts, while a throng of people poured into the nearby pavilion.

Nick walked over the neatly trimmed grass to the vigil. The cooling breeze blowing through the whispering maple trees was no comfort for the misery he felt within. The girl he loved was missing. Maybe even dead. And there didn't seem to be a damn thing he could do about it. But he would do something in the next hour. He could observe the people attending the vigil. Maybe he could get lucky and spot someone acting suspiciously.

*God, I hope dad found something today. Anything.*

Nick hadn't heard from his father all day. He left him a voicemail hours ago but had not heard back. Nick wondered why – where was his dad? Was he alright? Had he found something? Had he found Cadie? Nick pulled out his phone and looked again. Nothing from Jake. Just numerous texts from friends worried about Cadie. He looked up and scanned the pavilion.

*I pray I spot the bastard who took Cadie.*

Up ahead was the growing crowd. It buzzed with talk of the missing woman. Even with the overhead lights, it was a challenge to see. Still, Nick could tell the octagonal Van der Velt Pavilion was packed. People squeezed together next to the wooden platform that had been erected for the service. Others pressed together outside the cedar pavilion and began lighting their white, hand-held candles. The flames flickered over the people's faces, revealing solemnity but also strength and solidarity.

Nick worked his way through the crowd to a wooden column inside the pavilion and leaned against it. While the crowd continued to grow both inside and outside, Nick felt a buzzing from his phone and looked down at the text. It was finally his father.

"Sorry, son, no news about Cadie, and I'm not going to make it to the vigil. I had a crazy afternoon at the Keonigs' property near Lake Michigan. We found some disturbing items," dad texted. "We're trying to locate Rod right now. I also gained more information about Karl Kessler and Mr. Dawson. So, I'm in my office doing some research. I need to track down Kessler tomorrow. I'll explain when I see you. Have you spoken to Blake?"

Nick messaged back.

"Glad you're okay. I was concerned when I didn't hear from you. Then I started getting worried that you found Cadie. No, I haven't heard from Blake. I spent the afternoon looking for Cadie. I drove everywhere I could think of where Cadie could be. Why are you asking about Blake?"

"After Koenigs, I went to the station. Spoke to Detective Brooke Field. She interviewed Blake today," Jake texted.

"How did it go?" Nick messaged back.

"Not good. Let's meet up after the vigil at Ted's. We can get a bite to eat and talk. I'll text you when I'm leaving the station."

Nick slowly put his phone in his pocket and closed his eyes, his mind in chaos. He tried to breath normally to stay calm.

*What did my dad mean by 'not good?' Is Blake somehow involved? Did he take Cadie? This is absolutely crazy.*

When he opened his eyes and looked around, his mind suddenly recalled a happier time. A July afternoon when he and Cadie playfully walked this very pavilion looking over wooden tables of turquoise jewelry, sculptures, local paintings, and pottery. It was the West Michigan Artisan Fair. Cadie loved art like her mother Aileen, and Nick loved the fact that Cadie had invited him. The two young people walked arm in arm around the cheerful fair flirting and sparring while Cadie at times rested her lovely head on his shoulder. When they took an ice cream break and sat outside the pavilion in the grass, Cadie kept trying to lick his ice cream.

"Your ice cream is better," she laughed.

"Well, why didn't you get your own Mint Chocolate Chip? Nick retorted, laughing.

"Because yours is always better," Cadie grinned.

How could he help himself? She was so cute. He would let her lick his ice cream all she wanted. It brought her breathtaking smile and glowing face closer to his.

A little while later, Cadie bought Nick a tiny watercolor painting of Mariner's Beach with a red umbrella and Lake Michigan painted in vivid blues. She looked at it carefully and said it reminded her of mother's paintings hanging throughout Aunt Marie's house.

"I want you to have this," Cadie said. "You knew my mom. When you look at it, you'll think of her."

Cadie looked soulfully at Nick. When their eyes met this way, Nick couldn't deny his undeniable longing.

Then, possibly to escape Nick's gaze, Cadie would become impish.

"Don't you just love art?" she would smile and make a silly face. How could he resist those luminous green eyes? They were capturing his heart.

*I think I love you, Cadie McLeod.*

As he came back to the present, Nick felt powerful pain clench his heart: What if I never see her again? What if everything I dreamed of for my future with Cadie is gone? The thought of it almost crippled him, and he bent over. The elderly woman standing next to him touched his arm, smiled warmly, and handed him a candle. He stood there, despondent, thinking of his beautiful girl and hoping for a miracle as the service for Cadie McLeod began.

People took their seats on stage, and Nick saw detectives Brooke Field and Dan Zielinski slowly maneuvering through the crowd, watching and observing - looking closely at faces and body language for anything out of the ordinary. They also scanned the mass of people for Rod Koenig, Karl Kessler, and a short list of other concerning individuals.

Nick, too, watched the crowd. As he did, he suddenly saw Blake Van der Velt in blue slacks and a white Polo golf shirt walk up on stage and take a seat at the far edge. He seemed nervous, tapping his expensive boat shoes on the stage and moving his head constantly.

*Why is Blake on stage?*

Nick didn't know what to think or feel at the moment. He considered Blake a friend. Yet, Blake dated Cadie, and he claimed she broke his heart, which she denied. As Cadie put it, "Blake is more in love with the idea of me than me." Now Blake was under investigation. Nick couldn't imagine what his dad had to tell him later at Ted's.

Up on the platform, to the left of Blake sat his uncle Robert, then Dirk's father Luuk, Police Chief Debbie Markum, Benzie County Sheriff Todd Foster, Sergeant Dana Bakker, Cadie's Aunt Marie, and Pastor Todd Turner from First Presbyterian. The podium was surrounded by earthen pots of pink and white begonias, and someone had enlarged Cadie's graduation photo and placed it on an easel to the left of the podium. It was a casual picture of Cadie sitting on the pier. The crowd grew silent as Pastor Todd walked forward to speak. He opened with the Lord's Prayer, and most of the crowd recited along, while Nick's eyes scanned the people's faces.

*Is Cadie's abductor here?*

Off to his left, Nick saw movement. A balding man pressed forward, moving sideways to push ahead in the crowd to get closer to the stage.

It was Chuck, the creepy janitor from Scoop's.

Nick's eyes narrowed as he watched the weird man, his deeply etched wrinkles prominent in the flickering candlelight. Chuck finally stopped and was now staring transfixed at the service taking place – not eyes closed and reciting like everyone around him. For anyone watching nonchalantly, Chuck appeared like any other member of the vigil. However, Nick saw something that disturbed him: a subtle smile crossing the janitor's face? He seemed to be – enjoying this? Then Chuck put his hand over his mouth and actually seemed to laugh. Nick shuddered.

*What if that bastard kidnapped Cadie?*

The man pushed through the crowd and out of Nick's sight. As he did so, Nick also spotted Mr. Dawson, the science teacher. Nick never liked that guy. He was one of those male teachers who thought he was still eighteen and flirted with students. A weirdo, basically. Dawson was staring at his phone, seemingly uninterested in the activities surrounding him.

*So why are you here?*

Luuk de Vries, once a standout quarterback for Central Michigan, now strode across the platform to the podium. His still lithe 6'6" frame commanded attention.

"Good evening, everyone," de Vries said, leaning in, his hands on the podium. "I'm here tonight, along with several others, to not only show support for Cadie McLeod and her Aunt Marie but to announce a significant reward for any information that will lead us to Cadie."

The crowd murmured.

"My family, along with several others, have come together to create this reward. I'd like to take a moment to mention them: the Missing in Michigan organization, the FBI in Traverse City, my good friend Jonas Meijer who was a classmate of Thomas McLeod at Alma College, The Netherland Society, Annie Janson, president of Janson Industries, Robert Van der Velt, owner of Van der Velt Marina, and Charles Winsome, a custodian at Scoops where Cadie worked, uh, works."

Hearing Chuck's name, Nick automatically stepped forward.

"We've all come together to offer $300,000 for the safe return of Cadie McLeod. If anyone knows anything, please contact the Harbor Cove Police Department, Police Chief Markum, or Sheriff Foster. Any information might prove helpful, so please come forward with what you know. We need to bring Cadie home."

De Vries stepped away from the podium, while the people in attendance clapped enthusiastically.

One of Cadie's friends read a poem about butterflies, another a prayer.

Police Chief Markum then gave an update on what information she could release to the public, all of the resources being applied, and everything being done to find Cadie.

The crowd talked quietly in response to her remarks.

Then Aunt Marie came forward.

The last two days had visibly taken a toll on Cadie's Aunt. Marie's glowing chestnut hair, normally styled in a precise bun at the nape of her neck, now hung drab and limp around her face. Deep, dark circles were visible from the candle she held in her hand, which was shaking. Her voice was rough and scratchy as she spoke.

"Hello, I'm Cadie's Aunt."

Marie's raspy voice immediately began to quiver; she was on the verge of crying.

"I want to thank all of you for coming here tonight for Cadie. Something happened to our precious girl. We don't know what exactly, but we have to find out, and we have to find her. As many of you know, Cadie's parents died years ago, and I feel the presence of my brother and sister-in-law here with us tonight. I feel sure they are looking over us and want their daughter returned to us more than anything."

Then a visible change came over Marie. She paused for several seconds. She stood up straighter and slowly turned her head left to right as if to acknowledge every single person in the silent crowd.

"Someone took Cadie. Maybe even someone in this crowd. And when we find that person, which we certainly intend to, it will not go well for them. God willing, there will be justice. And they can be sure we will not stop looking for Cadie until we find her – one way or another. So, whoever you are, be warned. We are coming for you!"

Marie abruptly turned around and purposefully walked to the edge of the stage, down the stairs, and out into the crowd.

Her fighting words animated the gathered, and it bustled with energy. Then, over the loud speakers hanging in the roof's four corners, Cadie's favorite song by the Beatles began to play. The whole crowd joined in, gently swaying and singing with renewed hope.

"Here comes the sun."

"Here comes the sun."

"And I say, it's alright."

As the mood shifted to optimism, and people warmly patted each other on the back, The Weirdo smiled. He felt optimistic for reasons all his own. He knew that in the days to come, all these happy people would feel nothing but confusion and deep pain while Cadie's body rotted away in that dark, lonely place. As the days turned into weeks and the weeks dragged into months, the weary people with childish attention spans would have no choice but to forget about Cadie and turn their attention to the next new tragedy.

The Weirdo would finally claim victory.

That's how revenge works. Eye for eye. Pain for pain.

The Weirdo contentedly walked among the crowd and put his hand in his pocket, fingering the heart necklace. A broad smile crossed his face as he recalled ripping the necklace from Cadie's neck and rolling her unresponsive body into his truck. His smile continued as he pictured the odorless carbon monoxide that would soon be pouring into the cellar. He imagined Cadie, unaware, breathing in the poison and suddenly becoming confused, then dizzy, maybe even a headache beginning to form. Then chest pains and vomiting. Terror taking hold. Screams for help. The utter despair of knowing she would die alone in that forsaken crypt. Finally, unconsciousness – then death.

Now that was something to be happy about.

*Here comes the sun.*

Nick watched the crowd sing Cadie's favorite song, but he wasn't feeling uplifted. Finding Cadie wouldn't come from humming a Beatles' tune. It would come from his dad's efforts and the efforts of a great many people. It might even come from Cadie herself. Nick prayed that somewhere out there the feisty love of his life was working towards her freedom. Nick knew that whoever abducted Cadie messed with the wrong girl. If there was a way out, his budding forensic genius would find it.

The pavilion lights turned on, and the crowd began to disperse. Nick saw Blake and his uncle talking to Dirk and Luuk by the stage. He made his way over. He felt nervous as he approached Blake. Would his words and demeanor betray the doubts he was entertaining about his friend?

"Hey Nick," Blake yelled out, his always boyish grin taking over his face. "I've been looking for you. Wasn't this a great vigil for Cadie?"

Nick walked over and gave his friend half a hug.

"Yes, it was. I wasn't expecting them to play her song at the end."

"That was my doing," Blake said. "I knew Cadie would get a kick out of it."

*That's a weird thing to say.*

"Yeah, I guess so," Nick replied.

*Should he bring up Blake's interview at the police station?*

"Hey, so are we still going out for my birthday" Blake said. "You know I despise being alone on my birthday."

"What?"

"My birthday on Tuesday. On the boat. You remember."

From Nick's blank look, Blake could tell that his friend did not.

"At the party. I told you I wanted to celebrate my eighteenth birthday on my uncle's boat Tuesday. You, me, Dirk, and the dads. Just some fishing and partaking of spirits. You know - the tradition. I'm hoping you'll grace me with your presence."

"Oh yeah, that's right," Nick replied. "But honestly, Blake, with Cadie missing, do you really want to go out on your boat?"

Nick thought he saw Blake's mouth turn down – just for a second. Then the smile took over.

"I'm sure she's going to turn up any minute. Honestly, I don't even think she's missing. I heard that Lester guy who owns Happy Taxi picked up a girl near The Landing Friday night and drove her to Saugatuck. I'm sure that's where she is. Probably just wanted to get away because of her parents' death. I bet we hear from her any time now."

Blake flashed a big smile and perfect white teeth.

"Well, I hope you're right," Nick said, "but I'm not sure I believe that."

Nick knew he couldn't reveal to Blake anything his father had told him about the evidence that pointed to Cadie's abduction.

"So, are you going?" Blake asked. "We don't have to stay out long. Just long enough for me to catch a fish, get inebriated, and vomit," Blake laughed. "Another birthday tradition."

"I'll talk to my dad and get back to you," Nick said. "I guess we can probably go. At least for a while."

Nick thought it could give him opportunity to talk to Blake and learn why the police suspect him.

*Sure, I'll go to your birthday party, Blake. But I'll be there to get the truth.*

"Oh, that's stellar," Blake grinned. "My uncle said he has some Glenlivet, an expensive Scotch he's been saving. He's bringing it on the boat. I need my boys there to drink it with me. It's not every day a young man turns eighteen!"

Nick wondered how Blake could be so enthusiastic when the girl he supposedly loved was missing. Could even be dead. He studied Blake's face.

*Is this guy a psychopath? Has he been a psycho all along?*

Blake suddenly spotted someone in the crowd and darted off, giving Nick a quick wave goodbye. His uncle Robert and Dirk's dad Luuk saw Blake leave and turned to address Nick.

"Oh, Nick. I am so sorry about Cadie," Robert said. "This is a terrible situation. I met her once at the marina. I do hope the reward money does some good."

"Me, too," Nick replied. "At this point, I think everything helps."

"I'm sure it will," Luuk said. "It's got to encourage someone to come forward with what they know."

"I overheard Blake mention the boat trip planned for Tuesday," Robert said. "I hope it doesn't seem insensitive – going out on the boat. It's hard to know what to put on hold in a situation like this. And despite his outwardly happy demeanor, I imagine he's really suffering inside over Cadie, don't you think? Time with his friends might help."

"We're planning on going," Luuk added.

"Yeah, I told Blake that my dad and I could probably go. At least for a while. Of course, it depends on what's going on with him. I don't know if my dad can take even an hour off while they are looking for Cadie. But I'll see what he thinks."

"Thank you, Nick. I appreciate that. Maybe we can just make it a short trip. Head over to the Manitou Islands."

"That sounds good," Luuk said. "I've heard the fishing is good by the islands right now. I'm looking to catch some Big King Salmon."

"I'll talk to dad," Nick said. "Would you say goodbye to Blake for me? He took off somewhere."

"I will," Robert said. "Thank you again. Please let us know if you hear anything."

"Yeah, let us know," Luuk said.

"I will."

Robert and Luuk walked away, and Nick scanned the crowd looking for Blake. He saw him talking to Lisa Haan, smiling and laughing and gesturing in the air.

Seemingly not a care in the world.

## CHAPTER 21

"Welcome to the witching hour.
Isn't it marvelous to be up and about when others are still asleep?"
*Nancy Drew – The Treasure in the Royal Tower*

After the good cry and Ketamine-assisted sleep, Cadie awoke. The room was mostly dark; however, through the vent above, Cadie could see moonlight. She calculated the time was 3 am.

The young woman thought about Nick and Aunt Marie. She ached to see them both again, the people who loved her best. She would give anything to be with them. Cadie was devastated to find herself in this predicament - imprisoned and laying on an old piece of carpet in a root cellar. She also felt she let herself down by crying. She didn't like to cry – to show weakness even to herself. She wanted to stay strong for her parents - in her fight for their justice. Yet, Cadie knew crying releases the endorphins oxytocin and endogenous opioids, which help ease pain – both emotional and the soft tissues of her neck that were damaged from being choked. Plus, oxytocin calms you and makes you feel a bit better.

"Maybe I got it all wrong: maybe I just need to cry more," Cadie laughed, her halfhearted chuckle echoing down the long, narrow cellar. She had found a wrinkled potato laying on the cellar floor that resembled a little old man. She was reminded of Tom Hanks in the movie *Castaway* when his volleyball Wilson became a friend.

"Should I name you Wilson, little potato head?"

Talking to the potato made her feel a bit better – less alone. She more fully understood Tom Hank's non-human connection to Wilson that served as a coping mechanism.

Cadie knew that if she wanted to make it out of this predicament alive – which she most certainly planned to do – she would need to keep calm and her wits about her. She stretched out her long, slender, but muscular legs and thought of the many Nancy Drew books she read in middle school. She pondered how her fellow 18-year-old would handle this perplexing situation. Cadie knew the young sleuth would remain unruffled, logical, and call upon all her crime-solving acumen to free herself.

She smiled wryly, aware of the irony of her and Aunt Marie watching countless crimes shows only to find herself now the victim of a crime. With a candle always burning on the coffee table, the two women would snuggle on the couch and watch numerous episodes of *Dateline, 20/20, Forensic Files, 48 Hours, Deadline,* and *Investigation Discovery*. While Marie was partial to Josh Mankiewicz, of all the hosts, from Keith Morrison, Lester Holt, Chris Hansen, Kate Snow, and Elizabeth Vargas and more, Cadie's favorite was Tamron Hall. Hall's sister had been murdered, and even though everyone suspected her domestic partner, no one was ever charged. So, as they say in the crime business, the case remains unsolved. For Tamron, solving crimes was personal. It was a way to obtain the justice her sister never received.

Cadie often thought the reason she was hooked on crime shows was her own parents' murder. Could she solve their hit and run some day? She was sure going to try. Since her parents' deaths, she had spent countless hours poring over online news stories, trying to find a connection between other car crashes and her parents' murder - but to no avail. Finding justice for her mom and dad was the driving force behind her plans to study at Michigan State in the fall and ultimately pursue a PhD in Forensic Science. To solve their deaths but also obtain truth and justice for other grieving families. Someday, she would discover who ran over Thomas and Aileen McCleod six years ago and simply drove away. She wondered if she could ever forgive them.

Suddenly, Cadie's thoughts were interrupted by a noise.

"Hoo-hoo-hoo-hoo."

It came from outside the cellar. Then there was another soft hoot but in a higher pitch. The calls went back and forth.

"Oh, my goodness!" Cadie exclaimed. "Owls!"

Cadie knew her parents loved owls, especially her father. He had several figurines in his office. A watercolor painting by her mother of a Great Horned Owl with a reddish-brown face and endearing white patch on its throat had once hung in their living room over her dad's favorite leather chair.

She heard their hooting outside the root cellar again. Cadie suddenly felt feelings of hope flood through her. In that moment, she felt she might survive.

She sensed her parents might be there with her, watching over her. Even though her right brain knew it was illogical to think the owls were her parents protecting her, Cadie also knew that a scientist must keep their mind open. She recalled the poster hanging in AP Environment: "Science at its best is an open-minded method of inquiry." Healthy skepticism, of course, but open to possibility. And right now, Cadie needed all the possibility she could get.

Cadie heard a fluttering sound and looked up. One of the owls had landed on the vent overhead. In the moonlight, Cadie could make out the two prominent feathered tufts. The bird cocked its head, and with an inflated throat let out a long and deep, "Hoooooooooot."

"Hello, dad!" Cadie yelled up.

She thought she could almost make out its yellow eyes staring down at her. Encouraging her. It rested for a second and then flew away. Cadie could hear the male and female birds' duet - their alternating calls - in the distance.

A sense of strength and determination surged into Cadie.

"I will not let this situation get the best of me. I will not let this person win."

Cadie stood up, walked across the room and devoured a granola bar. She drank half a bottle of water, mindful of her dwindling supply. She did some stretches to get blood flowing throughout her body and her brain. Then she walked back to the carpet and sat down - cross legged. She closed her eyes and began to think deeply, engaging her critical thinking and deductive reasoning. Her favorite quote by Nancy Drew came to mind: "I'm a ready for anything kind of girl."

*Time to get ready.*

It was time to create a battle plan. She just hoped it would be in time to save her life.

## CHAPTER 22

Like everyone else in Harbor Cove, Jake loved Ted's – the 1950's-era tavern situated down a dirt road on Crystal Lake. The historic restaurant was nestled in a grove of white Birch trees near the beach. The small cedar chalet had a wooden deck that wrapped around the structure and overlooked the pristine, seventeen-mile-long lake (ninth largest in Michigan). Ted's was popular among the locals for its stunning sunset views, extensive Michigan beer selection, proximity to the beach, and, of course, the two-patty Benzie Burger with a dash of honey and paprika in its sauce.

Tuesdays were Burger and Brew Nights, and the place became packed to overflow. People who couldn't get into the cozy tavern called in their orders, and Melinda, the owner's niece, delivered hot burgers and cold brews to the parking lot in a big wicker laundry basket.

The cops loved Ted's because its owner Harry Harper was a retired police captain from Grand Rapids, and the walls of the tavern were covered with medals, plaques, photographs, and newspaper clippings about decorated Michigan police officers and their success stories. One of the biggest framed articles was, of course, about Harry. He was off duty at the Ludington State Park Beach with his wife and stepson when a ten-year-old boy got stuck in a rip current on Lake Michigan.

While a crowd formed, Harry, who swam for Ann Arbor Pioneer and still owns the Michigan State High School 200-yard Freestyle record, dove into the water and swam through the powerful waves. He entered the current, grabbed the exhausted boy, and swam parallel to the shore until he could angle back – fighting the entire way to keep the child afloat. Sometimes referred to as "High-Speed Harry," the owner is famous up and down the west coast and never has to buy his own beer. When Harry retired from the force, he bought the aging tavern, fixed it up, and renamed it Ted's after swimming hall of famer Ted Erikson, the first person to swim across Lake Michigan – 43 miles – in 1961.

Sunday is the only night Ted's slows down a bit, and Jake, starving and craving a Benzie Burger, texted Nick around 10 pm to let him know he was leaving the station and headed to the restaurant. Jake is a Ted's regular because, like Harry, ever since he rescued those students from the burning bus, Jake, too, is a local hero. At Ted's, his beer is always on the house.

Twenty minutes later, Jake walked in, nodded to Melinda who was drying a glass behind the bar, and took a seat. A few minutes later, Nick joined him in a deep green leather booth, a dim metal light hanging overhead. Jake saw two real estate salesmen he knew from Manistee sitting at the bar. Other than that, the place was empty. The lights were low, and "Turn the Page" played quietly on the blue and silver Seeberg in the corner. Always a Seger fan, Jake smiled. In the distance, he could hear the waves of Crystal Lake lapping the shore.

Jake looked at his son. Nick looked terrible, especially in the muted light. His face was washed out, and his eyes red and inflamed – signs he had been crying and not getting much sleep.

"How are you doing, son?" Jake said quietly, touching Nick's arm that was stretched out on the table.

"Not very good," Nick replied.

"I'm so sorry you're going through this. I want you to know we are doing everything we can to find Cadie. The good news is there's nothing to suggest she's not alive. I hate to be so direct, but no one, not the Coast Guard, Michigan State Police, Search and Rescue, K9 unit, or FBI has found her body. So, we have to stay hopeful, and we will find her. We are looking hard and investigating every possible suspect."

"Can you tell me what you know? I really need to know, dad."

"If I tell you, you absolutely cannot share this information. It could jeopardize the case. You must promise."

"I promise, dad. I won't tell anyone. But is Blake involved?"

Before Jake could answer, Melinda walked up to the booth and gave Jake his free favorite beer – a frosty Solid Gold from the tap.

"Hi fellas. Nick, can I get you something to drink? And do you boys know what you want to eat? The kitchen is closing soon."

After Jake and Nick ordered, Jake took small notepad out of his coat pocket.

"Let me go through the list of suspects, and I'll tell you what I know."

Nick pushed a hand through his thick brown hair, wavy like his dad's, and leaned back into his seat, ready to absorb what his dad was about to tell him. His blue eyes studied his father.

Just then, the two men got up from the bar, smiled over at Jake, and left the tavern. Now it was just Jake and Nick.

"I'll start with Edward Dawson. You were right: Dawson was let go from a school in Alpena. The story is he groomed and had sex with a 14-year-old girl. The girl was in his biology class. Dawson convinced the teen to go back to his apartment where they reportedly had sex. My sources say it happened on several occasions as well as sex acts in his classroom closet after school. The girl finally told her dad. However, when it came to charging him, the girl recanted. Said she made the whole thing up. So, they didn't have the evidence. But Dawson agreed to resign.

Unfortunately, he moved across the state and became our problem. They 'passed the trash,' as teachers say. Principal Marks said Dawson is on thin ice at Harbor Cove High School for suggestive comments and touching girls - stuff like that. We know that he had been talking to Cadie recently, keeping her back after class, touching her at track practices and meets."

"Yeah," I saw him doing that a couple times, Nick said. "I thought it was weird. The guy always comes across as aggressively friendly. It's hard to know who is just weird and who is trying to get with your girl. I wish I would've done something to that asshole," Nick said, leaning forward and tightening his jaw. "Maybe this whole situation never would've happened."

"We can't know if Dawson is our guy," Jake said, taking a drink of beer. "But he doesn't have an alibi for Friday night. Says he was at home watching TV. But that's not evidence he took Cadie. However, Dawson's neighbor, a fellow teacher, said she saw him leave his house late that night. She was walking her dog and saw his truck drive past her house. Dawson said he just ran up to the BP to buy smokes. But no one at BP remembers him that night, and his truck doesn't show up on their tape. So, we have to keep Dawson in the mix. Craig is reinterviewing him tomorrow. He and Brooke are pulling the good cop/ bad cop."

"Which cop is Craig?" Nick smiled, already knowing the answer.

"Good cop, of course. That guy's too nice to pretend to be bad," Jake laughed. "He's not a good actor. But he's a helluva cop."

Melinda walked up and put the two baskets of steaming Benzie burgers and seasoned fries down on the table.

"Let me know if you need anything else. Also, the two guys who were at the bar bought your dinner."

"That was very nice of them," Jake said. "Thanks, Melinda. This should do it."

"No problem. Take your time."

The men ate their burgers in silence for a bit, thinking, the old Seeberg now playing "You Belong to the City" by Glen Frey. Harry stocked the vintage jukebox with as many Michigan singers as he could. On any given night, customers would hear Seger, Frey, Stevie Wonder, Marvin Gaye, or Alice Cooper. Harry's musical tastes ran the gamut. He loved everything Michigan, and people loved him for it. Unexpectedly for a tough, former cop, Harry's favorite was Anita Baker, so the Ted's crowd got to hear its fair share of Harry's singing "You're my angel" from behind the bar. Her signed *Rapture* album was framed and hanging on the wall not far from the article about Jake's heroism.

"Next on the suspect list is Rod Keonig," Jake continued. "As you know, this afternoon Craig and I investigated the property his family owns on Hill Valley Road. First, I gotta tell you. The craziest thing happened."

"What?" Nick said, looking concerned.

"Craig and I were about done. We had searched the RV, the old farm buildings, and most of the back property when we heard a woman moaning. Like she was crying out in pain."

"Wait? What?! A woman moaning?! You're just now telling me this?!"

"Hold on. We ran over to where the old house had been. We could tell the sound was coming from its basement. It took forever, but we finally pried open the old metal door. Craig kept yelling to 'hold on. We'll be right there.' Honestly, we did think it might be Cadie down there. We thought we found her. We were both losing it."

"Oh my god, dad! Tell me! Who was it? Was it Cadie?!"

"We turned on our flashlights and slowly made our way to the back corner where the noise was coming from. It was terrible down there. Mold and spiders everywhere."

"Dad, tell me!"

"We were coughing the whole time and just trying to stay calm."

"Dad, get to the point!"

"Okay. Okay. We finally made it to the back of the basement, and I froze. I was almost too scared to shine my light at the noise. I didn't know what I was going to see. But we shined our lights, and suddenly we saw eyes glowing back at us."

Nick became completely still.

"Yeah, deep red eyes. It was a momma Bobcat and her kittens."

"Oh my god! Dad, really?! You were freaking me out!"

Nick let out a half laugh and shook his head.

"I've never seen a Bobcat before, but she had black-tipped ears and was just standing there motionless, staring at us, protecting her litter. I could see the crack in the foundation where she got in. Must have thought the basement made a good place to den."

"So, what happened?"

"Nothing. We slowly backed up. Didn't want to spook her. Typically, Bobcats are not dangerous. But you don't want to provoke a momma Bobcat protecting her young."

"That's crazy. But thank god you didn't find Cadie down there hurt or dying. You really had me spooked, dad."

"Yes. That's the good news. But we did find some concerning stuff in the Keonigs' RV and on the property, including a strangled, burnt up cat in the firepit. We haven't been able to locate Rod, but we've got officers trying to find him."

"What was in the RV?" Nick asked.

"We found women's and little girls' clothing in marked bags. Weird stuff like a wig and daisy duke shorts and tube tops. Just creepy male fantasy stuff. We called Marla Keonig, Rod's mom, and she said the stuff doesn't belong to her or her boyfriend's daughter. We also looked for bondage porn, zip ties, rope, duct tape."

"A rape kit," Nick said.

"Yeah, but we didn't find one. But as we were leaving the RV, we did find a zip tie laying on the carpet. That bothers me. Why a random zip tie laying by the door? And who dropped it there? As you know, Rod hangs out with some strange guys. We'll have to take a look at them as well."

"What about Blake?" Nick asked. "You said things didn't go well in the interview today."

Jake shifted uneasily in the seat.

"Craig interviewed him this afternoon. So, what do you know about Blake's background?"

"I don't know. Not much. I know he had issues with his parents, so his uncle took him in. Mom was a drinker. Something like that."

"Blake has quite a dysfunctional family. His relationship with his father was never good. His parents split up, and then he passed away later. His mother is an alcoholic who was called in to Social Services a few times for neglect. She's not winning mother of the year. According to our sources, Blake became a very angry young man. There was an incident when he hurt a classmate. That didn't go over well at the school, so his mom decided to move them over to the west side of the state for a fresh start."

"Yeah, I remember Blake saying they lived in a town across state but then moved here. I never knew why they moved. So, wow, Blake hurt somebody?"

"Yes, he did. According to our source, Blake suffers from some mental health issues."

Jake took out his phone and scrolled through his emails until he found a document. He read it out loud.

"'Blake can be charming and often wears a mask to cover his anger and mental health problems like a need to control and a poor sense of self. He also occasionally engages in delusional thinking, so he can act out his thoughts and feelings.' This report says his behavior may be part of an undiagnosed Bipolar I Disorder. It also says Blake suffers from relationship challenges and difficulty regulating his emotions."

"I knew Blake had some issues, but wow. You know, though, I can tell he's wearing a mask sometimes. He'll have a smile on his face, but you can tell he's thinking something else. His smile and his actions don't always match up. Why isn't Blake with his mom anymore? She was that bad?"

"Blake's mom Cindy, Robert Van der Velt's sister-in-law, went from an addiction to Vodka to an addiction to cocaine."

"Oh, wow," Nick exclaimed.

"Yeah, our source says she was pretty messed up. Sometimes violent. I guess she hit Blake. Social Services was called, and Cindy took off. No one knows where she is. Everyone decided the best thing was for Blake to go live with his uncle."

"It's just hard to believe Blake could kidnap Cadie. I really hope he's not involved, and honestly, I don't think he is, dad. I also wanted to tell you something from earlier. This strange guy, Chuck – Charles Winsome – was at the vigil."

"Who's Charles Winsome?"

"He's a super weird janitor that works at Scoop's. Cadie mentioned him a few times. The dude creeps her out. He stares at her, follows her out to the dumpster, makes sex comments. Anyway, he was at the vigil tonight."

"Go on."

"It was just so strange. I saw him for a moment in the crowd. It looked like he was smiling. Even laughing. Everything about his vibe was totally off for a vigil about Cadie. And then later, he was up on the platform with Blake's uncle and Dirk's dad donating reward money. I mean, the guy's a janitor. How much money could he even have to donate? And why of all people was he donating? I just feel like there's something suspicious about that guy."

"He donated reward money? Jake said. "I'll mention Winsome to Sergeant Bakker. We'll take a look at him."

Just then Melinda walked over. "You want another beer, Jake?"

"No, thanks, Melinda. I need to keep my head clear."

"I bet. I heard about that girl missing from Harbor Cove," Melinda said.

"Yeah, she was our old neighbor and a good friend of Nick's. We're trying to find her."

Melinda suddenly stopped and looked around the empty bar as if someone might be listening. She leaned in.

"A guy was here last night," Melinda said quietly. "Was talking about a girl. At first, I didn't think nothing of it because he was pretty drunk. Drunk people say all sorts of things. 'Specially young dudes trying to impress people."

"Who was the guy?" Jake asked, studying Melinda. "What did he say?"

"I don't know him, but he was with another guy. Maybe his brother? They looked alike. They were sitting in that booth over there."

Melinda pointed to a green booth with a large tear covered by a piece of duct tape. "When I brought them their bill, I overhead the guy talking. He was laughing and saying 'that bitch deserved it. How she had wronged him and got what was coming to her.'"

"Did they mention Cadie by name?"

"No, they didn't. That's another reason I hesitated to tell you," Melinda said. "But I thought I heard the one guy say he grabbed her."

"Do you have their bill," Jake asked. "Can you get it for me?"

"Yeah, I have it."

Melinda walked back to the bar and went through the prior evening's receipts. She stopped and pulled out the two men's bill. She walked back over and handed the bill to Jake.

The detective looked down at the piece of paper and froze. He immediately recognized the name scrawled on the bottom of the wrinkled paper: the convicted pedophile.

"Oh shit," Jake snapped and looked up at his startled son.

"It's Karl Kessler."

# *MISSING 72 HOURS*
## *CHAPTER 23*

The next morning, Jake awoke early to light rain pinging against his bedroom window. With bloodshot eyes, he glanced at his bedside clock in the still-dark room: 4:59 am in red, glowing numbers. It had been a rough night as evidenced by his sweat-soaked sheet. Jake had dreamt of Cadie – her red hair and bloated body floating in the Lake Michigan waves. He could still see her green eyes - lifeless and swollen - staring up at him.

His nightmare also included Thomas and Aileen. The two parents were on their old front porch, sitting in the wicker and wood swing Aileen's father made for their wedding present. In happier times, the McLeod family – all three of them - would squeeze together in the white swing under a yellow quilt listening to Motown and reading books to Cadie. Then Aileen would jump up and pull Thomas from the swing, and suddenly the two of them would be laughing and dancing with little Cadie twirling around beside them. In Jake's nightmare, however, Thomas and Aileen swung back and forth in the swing maniacally, "My Girl" playing loudly on their vintage Kenwood stereo. In his dream, neither of the McLeods had a face. It was a terrifying image – one he hoped to forget.

Now 5 am, Jake's cellphone ringtone startled the quiet room.

Jake extricated himself from the lumpy waterbed his soon-to-be ex just had to have. The mattress sadly reminded him of his past life, of all the times he lay in that bed with his back turned to Laura. He was pretty sure he had PTSD. For several years after the bus fire, when he closed his eyes at night, all he could picture was nine-year-old Clara Anderson. The child was unconscious on the floor of the bus, but Jake never saw her. Jake Brennan saved several children that day, but he didn't save Clara.

The guilt and horror of that moment were absolutely crushing. For months and even years later, in an attempt to cope, Jake shoved all his thoughts and feelings deep down inside himself where he hoped he could shut the door on them forever. Unfortunately, he also shut the door on his ability to communicate with his loved ones. To be vulnerable. To be intimate. Laura stayed as long as she could, but in the end, the cold, quiet nights were torture for her as well.

*I miss you, Laura. I hope you're doing well.*

Jake quietly opened the door to Nick's room. His son was still asleep – or at least Jake thought so.

"Hey, dad," Nick said groggily, slightly lifting his sleepy head off the pillow.

"Hey, son. I wanted to tell you to have a good last day of school. I know it's a terrible time right now, but try to enjoy your last day of high school."

"I don't know how that's possible," Nick said, now sitting up. "Have you heard anything this morning?"

"No. Nothing."

Nick's head drooped in response.

"And no news about Rod?"

"No. Officers are still looking for him. I got a text that he might be at a friend's apartment in Ohio. Police down there are keeping an eye out. I'm getting ready to go over to where Karl Kessler works to search his office. Then I'm heading up to Leland where his brother owns a farm. I'm hoping I'll find Karl there. I'll let you know what happens."

"Okay, but be careful."

"I will."

"Dad?"

"Yeah?"

"I'm starting to feel like Cadie's dead. I mean it's been two days with no word from her," Nick said, his voice cracking. "No one has seen her. I just feel like she must be dead."

Nick began to cry and buried his head in his hands.

Jake walked over to his son, sat down on the bed, and hugged him tightly.

"Hey, there. It's okay. I know you feel awful, son. But we just have to stay optimistic. She most definitely could be alive, and we can't give up. She needs us to remain hopeful, and we're doing everything we can to find her. Do you remember a girl named Elizabeth Smart?"

"No. Who's that?"

"Elizabeth Smart was a fourteen-year-old girl who was actually kidnapped right out of her own home. She was missing nine months, and most people had given up hope. They thought for sure she must be dead. But someone spotted her with her kidnappers, and she was rescued. It just shows that anything can happen. And in Cadie's case, it's only been two days. I know it seems like forever, but we just have to keep trying and not give up hope. We also know Cadie – what she's capable of. She's out there fighting for her life."

"I know. I try not to think dark thoughts. Can I tell you something? I've been meaning to tell you, but it's hard."

Jake sat up a bit straighter on the bed. He was wondering what his son was going to say.

"What is it, Nick? You can tell me anything."

Nick paused then took a deep breath.

"I'm in love with Cadie."

Jake sat on the bed, shocked. Silence took hold of the dark bedroom. Finally, he responded.

"You're in love with Cadie? Really?"

"I am, dad. I think I've been in love with her all my life. Or least since when I met her," Nick smiled. "She is an amazing person – probably the most amazing person I've ever known - and she makes me happy. I just hope I didn't ruin things between us on Mackinac Island - what I did."

Jake winced slightly.

"What happened on Mackinac Island? What did you do, son?"

"I really don't want to talk about it right now, if that's okay."

"Sure. That's fine," Jake replied, wondering what his son did to Cadie. He felt a wave of trepidation.

"Well, you've certainly chosen a great person to love. Cadie is an exceptional woman. I promise I will do everything in my power to get her back. Everyone is looking for her: our police force, the Michigan State Police, even the FBI is looking for her. We're going to find her."

"I know you're doing all you can."

Suddenly, Nick hugged his father. Jake was taken by surprise. It had been a while since his teenage son initiated a hug. Both men embraced fiercely – the moment encapsulating all their feelings.

"Dad," Nick said in a voice thick with emotion.

"Yes, son?"

"I love you."

"I love you, too, buddy. I love you very much."

Then Jake stood up.

"It's still early. Why don't you try to get some more sleep?"

Nick laid back down, and Jake shut the door and headed for the kitchen. After a quick cup of coffee and bagel, Jake left the cottage and was soon behind the wheel of his Tahoe. He drove through the cool, misty rain and the dark streets of Harbor Cove thinking about the words Nick had just spoken: "I'm in love with Cadie" and "What I did."

His son's admissions troubled him.

As the sleepy little town awakened, Jake continued on – his mind now swimming with ugly thoughts of Karl Kessler hurting Cadie McLeod.

"I'm coming for you, Karl," Jake growled as he headed north on M-22. He gripped the steering wheel tighter. "I'm coming for you, you son of a bitch."

Fifteen minutes later, Jake pulled his SUV into the industrial park parking lot. He drove past Watt's Blue Waters Swim Club and observed some dedicated athletes already making their way into the large building at this early hour. He then maneuvered his way to the back of the lot to the Great Lakes Bread Company. Even though it was early, Jake had reached the owner, Finlay Stewart, yesterday evening and arranged the morning meeting – this before he even saw the receipt Melinda showed him last night. With the overheard conversation Melinda shared and the image of Karl Kessler's name scrawled on that receipt, Jake began to feel more strongly Karl was involved in Cadie's disappearance. Karl's boss had told Jake that Kessler didn't work on Mondays. He was probably up in Leland at his brother's, so Jake asked if he could look through Kessler's office.

"What's he done now?" the owner had asked over the phone when Jake called.

Stewart believed in helping young men get back on track. He often hired ex-convicts through the Michigan Department of Corrections Offender Success Reentry Program. A violent, alcoholic father led Stewart to become a chronic youthful offender himself. To assuage his own pain, when Stewart was young, he took out his anger on other children. Back in the day, he beat up his fair share of boys. Spectrum - a Michigan program for juveniles - helped turn his life around. Now he was paying it forward.

"As far as I know, he hasn't done anything," Jake replied. "But as you've probably heard, a local girl is missing, and Karl has a taste for young women and a rap sheet to prove it. So, I have to check him out."

As Jake pulled into the parking lot, he could see a light on in a front room of the building and the shadow of someone moving about. A minute later, Stewart let him in the front entrance and guided him down a dark, aging hallway to Karl's office, which seemed to be a glorified closet with a small, black metal desk and an old computer and printer. A wooden mid-century floor lamp illuminated the office. The men stood outside Karl Kessler's office talking.

"What all does Karl do for you?" Jake asked.

"Mostly, he just makes deliveries. Uses my truck to fill bread orders up and down the coast."

"So, he's out and about on a daily basis?"

"Well, he works part time, but yeah, he's always on the go. And I realize that gives him a lot of freedom. But I'm here to give him the chance to turn his life around, not imprison him again. Karl has to go out into the world and be able to handle his bad impulses."

"You said on the phone you saw Karl Friday and that he was in Harbor Cove that day. What did you see?"

"He seemed pretty normal that morning. Nothing out of the ordinary," Stewart said. "The only thing I noticed he was on his cell phone a lot more than normal.

Just texting a lot. Every time I walked by his office, he was either reading a text or sending one. That's not usually Karl."

"Why not? Most people are on their phones constantly."

"Karl just has an old flip phone. He can't afford a data plan. So, I don't see him using his phone much. But Friday, he was glued to his phone. I just thought it was odd."

"Is it okay I take a look around his office? Go through the drawers?"

"Sure. Go ahead. I'll leave you to it," Stewart said and walked away down the dimly-lit hallway to his office. Once he got to his office door, Stewart stopped and turned around.

"I just thought of something else a bit strange."

"What?"

"Friday morning, I looked out my office window and saw Karl cleaning out the back of his truck. He was taking stuff to the dumpster by the road. It surprised me."

"Why is that?"

"Karl is pretty messy. And I've never seen him take anything from his truck and put it in the dumpster. So, I just wondered why he was cleaning it all of a sudden."

"Is the stuff still in there?" Jake asked.

"No. Unfortunately, garbage pickup is Friday afternoon," Stewart responded.

The owner walked into his office, and Jake sat down at Kessler's small desk and began looking through its drawers. Strangely, everything was in perfect order - like Karl decided to do some spring cleaning and throw most everything out; it certainly wasn't messy. Jake didn't find any old receipts or incriminating messages. Not even a stick of gum or Chapstick. The desk was as clean as if Friday was his first – or last - day on the job. Or like he committed a crime and was getting rid of evidence and his fingerprints.

Jake pulled up the heavily scratched plastic floor protector under the office chair, but there was nothing but a smashed Stink Bug. Jake hated Stink Bugs. They were everywhere, and just like their name says – they stink.

Then Jake remembered something. One time he was searching a desk and found a piece of paper stuck inside, shoved down in the drawer runner. Jake got down on his knees and pulled out the bottom drawer of Karl's desk. Using the Stinger flashlight from his holster, he examined the cavity it left behind. Nothing.

The second drawer was the same. But when he took out the top drawer, his light landed on a piece of paper that seemed purposefully crumpled. Jake reached into his coat pocket and took out a pair of sterile nitrile gloves. He carefully removed the paper so as not to tear it. He sat down in the chair and straightened the paper on the desk in front of him. It was a receipt from Home Depot dated last Thursday evening. For a shovel.

Jake just sat in the chair staring at the paper.

*A shovel. That bastard bought a shovel.*

Of course, Jake understood immediately the implications of Karl's purchase, and it terrified him. Jake knew he had to find Cadie before Karl had a chance to put that shovel to use. He placed the receipt in a breathable evidence bag for safe keeping and quickly left the building, jumped in his Tahoe, and headed north, more determined than ever to find Karl Kessler and Cadie McLeod.

He felt he had only hours – maybe minutes – to find Cadie alive.

## CHAPTER 24

The sun was beginning its ascent into the blue sky as the detective and his Tahoe headed up the various coastal roads and highways that would take him to Leland. He drove north past grain and bean farms, charming towns, cornfields, pens with chickens, cows, and pigs, horses grazing in fields, the Sleeping Bear Sand Dunes, Glen Lake, Little Traverse Lake, glimpses of the big, blue Lake Michigan, and finally Lake Leelanau. Jake's route took him up Scenic highway, Northland Highway, Leelanau Highway, Glen Lake Road, Harbor Highway, and South Manitou Trail before he entered Leland that is situated on a sliver of land between Lake Leelanau and Lake Michigan. Popular with tourists, the coastal town – also known as historic Fishtown - is bisected by the Leland River and as quaint as they come.

As a kid, Jake spent weekends in the then sleepy, close-knit town of Leland playing with his cousins at the colorful fishing shanties in Shanty Village on the wharf along Leland Harbor. He also did a fair amount of fishing by the North Manitou and South Fox Islands with his dad and grandad Paul on his 36-foot, carver-built Mackinac Boat *The Brennan Brothers*. His daideó docked the family fishing boat at a marina on Lake Leelanau. Paul and his brothers were commercial fishermen who fished spring to Christmas for Whitefish, Lake Trout, Bass, Walleye, and Sturgeon that they sold locally and also shipped on ice by rail to Chicago, New York, and Detroit.

On early Saturday mornings, Jake joined the boisterous men as they navigated the red, white, and blue boat through the Leland River, past Fishtown, and into Leland Harbor and then Lake Michigan. His hard working but playful uncles taught Jake to catch fish by line and net and to fillet, gut, and pinbone. The tough men never complained about wind or cold; they taught Jake by example how to endure. The picturesque town held good memories for Jake. In many ways, he grew to be a man in Leland.

As he drove up the tree-lined Main Street past its colorful cottages, hip boutiques, wine and art shops, The Dairy Barn, and a bakery that served up Michigan's best cherry pie, his memories were tempered by the serious task at hand. By day's end, Jake hoped to locate a possibly dangerous, even murderous, pedophile with a newly-purchased shovel and rescue Cadie McLeod.

The sun was now higher in the sky as Jake slowly made his way north of town. In his rearview window, he could see a few business owners bustling up and down the street, getting ready for tourists headed their way. He turned his attention to the road ahead, driving further north into what people call "Michigan's Little Finger" because the somewhat triangular peninsula extends about thirty miles from the west coast of Michigan into Lake Michigan.

Karl's brother Richard owned a small dairy farm – Kessler's Crooked Creek Dairy - in the county just east of St. Wenceslaus Catholic Church. Jake drove north on M-22 or North Manitou Trail. As he passed the 200-foot-high Clay Cliffs – an accumulation of rocks and earth deposited by glaciers - he glanced over his left shoulder and was reminded once again of his childhood adventures in Leelanau County.

Many times, he and his dad visited the 105-acre preserve and made the steep climb up the wild lakeshore's cliff. Upon reaching the top, they would stare in awe at the surreal, panoramic views of mighty Lake Michigan stretched out before them. Off in the distance, past miles of shimmering teal-blue water, he could see the Sleeping Bear's steep and massive lakeside dune Pyramid Point and the Manitou and Fox Islands. Jake loved the towering Clay Cliffs; they were simultaneously frightening and magical.

Later, he and his dad would pick raspberries and blackberries growing wild throughout the park and keep an eye out for eagles. Before they left, they'd hike a trail that opened into a gentle meadow of native grasses and yellow wildflowers. The peaceful meadow overlooked the rolling North Lake Leelanau that was over 120 feet deep. It made Jake feel good picturing his young father in that meadow picking flowers and animatedly educating Jake about plant characteristics. He was a unique man. Dad died when Jake was twenty-two, but his intelligence, wit, kindness, and deep empathy made a lasting impression on his son.

Jake's thoughts turned to Karl Kessler. What was his childhood like? His father? What happened to turn a boy into a menacing predator? A man who sexually assaults little girls? It was confounding. Throughout his career, Jake had encountered many sexual deviants, but he never got satisfactory answers to what drove them to commit their heinous acts. Jake wondered if he'd find any answers to his questions at Richard's farm. Were there dark family secrets on the grounds? Incriminating evidence to be uncovered? Cadie's body? The thoughts unsettled him.

Over the years, he had found his share of disturbing materials at homes he was called to investigate: corpses with syringes in their arms, butchered animals, all manner of weapons and drugs, dirty, forlorn, and neglected children, dark pornography, and soulless individuals with black eyes and blank stares. Jake also wondered about Karl's older brother Richard. Was he damaged goods as well? Another predator?

Driving by farm after farm and numerous orchards, the now radiant sun shining on rows of young crops and apple trees, Jake thought about the studies he'd read. He knew that criminal characteristics are often shared by siblings. He'd read research that suggested a brother of a man convicted of a sex crime was five times more likely than average to also commit the same sex crime. The study suggested that genetic factors were the biggest influence. That surprised Jake. He thought sons learned deviant behaviors from fathers and uncles. But the study said genetics played the larger part. Jake thought it might be a mixture of both: nature and nurture, but it's hard to say what factor has the upper hand.

So, was Karl doomed from the start? Was Richard? Did Richard assist Karl in kidnapping Cadie? Was Cadie on their property somewhere suffering? Even dead? Jake wondered what a world would be like without the Karl Kesslers, a world in which people – especially little girls and women like Cadie – felt safe and were actually safe. Where females could travel freely without having to look over their shoulders, always keeping an eye out for trouble.

*Unfortunately, that world will not exist in my lifetime. Maybe not in several lifetimes. Maybe not ever.*

Jake suddenly got a notification on his phone and saw it was from Sergeant Bakker. He pulled his SUV over to the side of the road. The quiet countryside still sleepy. There wasn't another car – or human being – in sight. Just sunny, rolling farmland for miles. Jake saw that Bakker had left him a voicemail.

"Hi Jake. I don't have any good news to report. There's still no helpful information about Cadie. Nothing from the State Police, FBI, or NamUs. However, and sorry to be blunt, no one has found her body, so that's good news. I did want to update you on Rod Keonig. A little while ago, Ken Bronson and his daughter Sharon came into the station to report Rod for molesting Sharon. They provided a detailed account of what Rod did to Sharon and one of her friends. Judge Nolan just issued a bench warrant for Rod, and new information places Rod in Detroit. Craig is on his way down there to Rod's relative in

Corktown. Call me when you can. I need to hear what's going on with Kessler. And be careful. Talk to you soon."

Jake sat there for a bit, processing what Bakker had just told him. He sent her a quick text and mentioned the shovel that Karl had purchased Thursday.

"That Koenig guy is something else," Jake said, shaking his head, revulsed at the idea of that man abusing little Sharon. Was it Rod who was responsible for Cadie's disappearance and not Karl Kessler or someone else? His resolve regarding Karl was now slightly altered. Yet, he recalled the shovel Karl purchased Thursday. He had to get to the bottom of Karl's whereabouts Friday night and any possible involvement he had with Cadie. Hopefully, he would locate the convicted sex offender in a matter of minutes.

Jake rolled down his SUV's window; it was getting warm and stuffy as the sun climbed higher in the sky. He finally reached East Kolarik Road and drove past large farmsteads and decaying historic houses that had once been the pride of the County. He was just a few miles from the Kessler property when suddenly, like a panic attack, a familiar and unwelcome fear flared up inside. He gripped the steering wheel and tried to control his breathing. He had to mentally prepare himself for what he might encounter. Jake looked over at his 9mm handgun in his leather duty holster on the seat beside him. The holster also held an extra full magazine, a can of pepper spray, and flexi handcuffs. All of the items might be used within the hour.

Suddenly, up ahead on his left, he saw it. A leaning, rusted, and oversized metal mailbox with one word sloppily painted on the side in faded red: *Kessler.*

Jake slowed and turned in the drive.

## CHAPTER 25

After his father left, Nick went back to an uneasy sleep. He didn't see the numerous texts from Blake ("Dude, are you coming out on the boat with us? You'd better!"). Nick was exhausted in every way and needed to replenish his reserves. He was in agony over missing Cadie and also worried about what might happen to his dad at the Kessler property. Also, it was terrifying thinking your friend might've kidnapped or even killed the girl you love. The young man tossed and kicked off his blankets numerous times, but he finally fell asleep. After ninety minutes or so, his brain reached its final state of sleep - REM - and Nick began to dream about Mackinac Island - that warm June day two weeks ago when things took a bad turn.

Senior Skip Day.

Last year on Senior Skip Day, Brad Mueller and his cousin Mike got drunk and drove their grandpa's vintage Jeep onto the sand dunes and straight into a nest of Piper Plover Shorebirds – an endangered species - destroying it. They were arrested while still joyriding over the dunes and also suspended from Harbor Cove High School for three days. Several other seniors high on weed spraypainted foul language like, "Principal Warner sucks the big one" on the side of the high school's utility shed.

School officials were not happy – especially Principal Warner. So, this year, the class sponsor, a beloved but wacky art teacher, came up with a new, somewhat lame concept: *Senior 'Be Hip' Day*. Apparently being hip could mean just about anything, so the inaugural being hip meant bussing forty-four soon-to-be-graduates to Mackinac City, loading them on a boat at 7:30 am in the morning, and letting the Shepler's crew ferry the group through the Straights of Mackinac and over choppy Lake Huron waters to Mackinac Island for a day of fun.

Even though it was now only 7:46 am – the ride takes a mere sixteen minutes - the seniors sprang from Miss Margy, a steel ferry boat named after the founder's wife Margaret, like wild dogs set free from a cage. The young men and women poured out of the boat and ran down the expansive wooden dock willy nilly into the old-fashioned, historic town. Immediately, the island's fudge shops were swarmed with talkative teens. The poor horses (there are no cars allowed on the Island) were forced to navigate the groups of students who were drunk with freedom.

Nick's group was comprised of Dirk, Mike, Blake, Layne, and Glen Boer. Cadie was hanging out with her best friends Tori and Julie. The boys immediately ran north up Main Street headed for Fort Mackinac, a fortress that sits up 150 feet on a bluff overlooking the harbor, and raced up the steep hill to see who came in first (Glen Boer). The group was excited to tour the fortress and witness the first cannon firing of the day at 8:45 am. They raced through building after building going from the Post Guardhouse to the North Blockhouse and finally plopping down on the wooden benches for a minute in the Soldier's Barracks to watch the twenty-minute film, "Heritage of Mackinac."

The early hour was finally catching up with the young men.

The entire time Nick rode the ferry to Mackinac Island, he was thinking about Cadie. She was gathered with her friends at the bow, wind blowing through her lovely red hair, while Nick and his group sat in the back. They often caught each other's eyes and smiled. When he looked at the beautiful, fresh-faced girl, Nick flushed with sexual desire but also feelings of love for his childhood playmate who had grown into an amazing woman. Now, sitting with his sometimes-juvenile pack of sweaty friends on a wooden bench watching a movie about military drills, Nick decided it was time to sneak away and find Cadie. He had a lot on his mind that he wanted to share.

He walked back down Main Street and peeked in a few shops but didn't see her. He peered in the large plate glass window of The Pink Pony restaurant in the four-story, Victorian Chippewa Hotel that overlooks the harbor and Straits of Mackinac, but no Cadie. Spotting the black and white-striped awning, he walked across the street and popped into Murdick's for a free sampling of fudge and then continued south past the brightly-colored dollhouse and Gothic Revival buildings that housed a variety of modern boutique shops and restaurants. As he pushed through the growing throng of tourists, the clip-clop of horse hooves echoing through the street, he looked for Cadie up and down.

When he reached the south end, he turned west on French Lane to Market Street. He wondered if Cadie and her friends had gone to the crown jewel of Mackinac Island: Grand Hotel. Cadie always spoke about the Grand Hotel with such affection because her parents were married in the Mission Church on the Island and spent one night at the historic hotel that sits like a stately queen atop a long hill and looks majestically over the Island.

He was so excited to talk to her. He had done a lot of thinking lately, and he wanted to share his thoughts and feelings and his plans – *their* plans – for the future. His mind brimmed with ideas, excitement, and hopefulness. Nick turned right off Market Street onto Cadotte Avenue and walked confidently up the bumpy stone street. He smelled the thick, towering Lilac trees for which the island was famous. He passed the long, white, and wooden two-story Astor Grand 'cottage' with its verandas, cupola, and deep green shutters.

In the distance, he spied The Gatehouse and its orange doors and large black and orange sign. Past it, on the opposite side of the street was the historic Little Stone Church made of glacial fieldstone and colorful Gothic stained-glass windows. He reached The Gatehouse, the Grand Hotel's casual restaurant at the foot of a long, sloping hill, and walked onto its outdoor patio. Seated underneath a black and white umbrella were Cadie, Tori, and Julie. They were laughing and sipping lemonade through black-striped paper straws. When he saw her, his heart surged.

Cadie saw Nick walking toward her, and her entire face smiled.

"Hey, ladies," Nick said, trying to control his beating heart. "How are you this fine morning?"

"Isn't it breathtaking?" Tori said. "I've never been here before, and I absolutely love it."

"There's no other place like it," Nick agreed. "So, Cadie," he said a bit dryly, the words getting caught in his throat, "would you like to walk up to the Grand Hotel with me? I know you've always wanted to see it up close."

Cadie looked at Tori and Julie. "Would you guys mind?"

"Of course not," Julie said. "Go ahead. Maybe we can meet up later at Murdick's for fudge." Tori nodded in agreement, sipping her lemonade.

"Oh great. Thanks for being cool about it."

Within minutes, Nick and Cadie were climbing the hill, the street flanked on each side by lush grass, and the large, luxurious Grand Hotel adorned in sunny white and yellow awnings and the world's largest front porch up ahead, waiting for them. They could hear laughter from children swimming, splashing, and occasionally shrieking in the nearby hourglass-shaped Esther Williams pool. They looked at each other and laughed.

"Someone's having fun," Nick grinned.

His mind flashed with the many times he and Cadie swam together off Mariner's Beach under sunny skies in Lake Michigan.

When they reached the east entrance of the expansive hotel, they saw Sadie's Ice Cream Parlor with its red and black striped awnings.

"Oh, we definitely need some ice cream," Cadie laughed, running ahead and yanking the door. The young couple eagerly went inside. They saw on the menu that the old-fashioned ice cream parlor offered 24-flavors of Hudsonville ice cream, so it took Nick and Cadie a bit to make a decision. Cadie was eyeing the Strawberry Shortcake.

"What about a famous Grand Hotel Pecan Ball?" Nick asked.

"What? A big ball of pecans?" Cadie laughed. "Of all the flavors, that's what you want?"

"It's not a big ball of pecans," Nick laughed, "but a big ball of ice cream rolled in pecans."

They settled on the medium Pecan Ball and soon were walking the hotel's outstretched front porch lined with red geraniums in earthen pots and amazing views of the Straights of Mackinac, Mackinac Bridge, and the garden down below. Nick and Cadie found two white wooden rocking chairs and settled in to share their treat and watch a line of horse-drawn black carriages drop off hotel guests – the mighty Mackinac Bridge off in the distance.

However, to Nick, Cadie was the most amazing sight. He couldn't stop looking at the vibrant young woman who looked stunning in her pink crop top and white shorts. With her Aviator Ray Bans and long red hair blowing in the lake breeze, Cadie looked like a celebrity sitting in the back of a wooden Riva speedboat on the French Riviera.

The morning was perfect – at least for the moment.

## CHAPTER 26
## The Weirdo

Tomorrow is the day! She must've run out of granola bars and water anyway. I'm not looking to make her suffer endlessly. Now that this story has reached its conclusion, I'm closing the book. I got what I came for.

Revenge is sweeter than I imagined. Anyone who says it isn't has never achieved it. Never tasted it. And they've never had the love of their life – their soulmate – ripped away by their supposed friend. So, Cadie has to suffer. As my asshole of a father often told me, "When the bill comes due, people have to pay."

I pull into the home supply store and wonder: Was my dad simply a mean drunk? Or was he a bona fide sociopath? He did strangle my cat - the one creature in this world that seemed to care about me. *Of course, there was that time he tried to kill me.*

It was a late November night. The traffic on West Bay Shore Road was bumper to bumper, so we didn't reach our cabin in Omena that overlooks Suttons Bay until 10 pm. The entire ride my father was quiet, looking straight ahead, which was unlike him. Usually, he spent the car ride complaining about my mediocre grades, my lack of friends, my introverted personality, and on and on. But tonight – nothing.

The silence made me uneasy.

Dad wanted to winterize the family's decades-old gathering spot before the heavy snows came. It was a cozy log cabin at the end of a forested road that got less and less use as my dad's drinking increased. Even though I was wearing a wool jacket, the cabin was freezing. My dad quietly went outside and brought in a red can of kerosene from his truck and placed it on the living room floor. In a few minutes, he had the wick on the portable heater lit, and its open flame created dancing shadows on the knotty pine walls.

I thought they looked pretty, but I was only ten. I didn't realize you shouldn't burn a kerosene heater inside a house. The cabin began to warm, and dad grew fidgety.

After about thirty minutes, I was slumping over – I felt so tired. I forced myself to stand and walk to the sink for water. My dad, who had been out in the shed since he lit the heater, entered the kitchen and announced he was going to Home Depot.

I groggily murmured, "I think Home Depot closes at 10."

Dad barreled across the room and stopped short - right in front of me, glaring.

"How the fuck do you know when Home Depot closes?" he said, leaning in so close that flecks of his spit landed on my nose and lower lip.

He turned and walked out the side door, and I heard his truck tires crunching on the stones as he drove away. I was now even sleepier, so I groggily walked into the living room and laid down on the oversized couch on top of my grandma's crocheted blanket.

I didn't know how much time had passed, but I awoke because my heart was racing. Beating intensely. It felt like I had sprinted 400 meters. My shirt and jeans were drenched in sweat – so were the blue couch cushions and blanket. I yelled out weakly for my dad, but got no response. My body felt so heavy. In seconds, I went back to sleep.

A little while later, I woke up because I couldn't breathe. It seemed like I was at the bottom of a deep well – my brain growing dark and foggy. Then I started having a hard time seeing; my vision was closing in and becoming black. I freaked out and flailed around, trying to suck in air, but in seconds, I was unconscious.

The next thing I remember was our neighbor, Mr. Kent, shaking me. He was walking his dog, and the dog started barking maniacally at our cabin; he smelled the kerosene. In my stupor, I heard the elderly man say 'carbon monoxide' as he jostled me awake. At that point, I was in a complete fog. Sweat dripped down my head, stinging my eyes. My clothes were soaked, and I could barely move my arms and legs.

"Is your dad in the cabin?" Mr. Kent yelled.

"I'm, I'm not sure," I mumbled. I couldn't remember much of anything. My brain wasn't working.

Mr. Kent grabbed me and somehow pulled me up off the couch and wrestled my useless body through the cabin door and out into the fresh, crisp air. I began sucking it in, coughing, my heart still pounding ferociously. Then he took off his coat, put it over his nose and mouth, and ran back into the cabin. Later, I found out he blew out the heater's flame. He probably saved our cabin, and he most certainly saved my life.

The neighbor stayed with me, and we sat at the picnic table in the cold, waiting for my dad, but he never returned. Mr. Kent invited me to sleep over at his place, just a block away, so he fetched his golfcart and picked me up. I could barely walk. He stayed up the rest of the night checking on me. He said if I didn't improve, he was taking me to the Medicine Clinic. My heartbeat returned to normal, and I eventually fell asleep. I remember Mr. Kent, his head resting on his hand while he sat in his lazy boy next to me, watching me closely as I drifted off.

My father never came back to the cabin.

Mr. Kent's son drove me home the next day.

So, yes, it is thoroughly ironic I'm using carbon monoxide to murder Cadie McLeod. Oh, the twists and turns of life! The mordancy! In fact, I'm even using my dad's old kerosene heater. It still works. I wish dad were alive, so I could tell him. That sick bastard would get a kick out of this entire thing.

I definitely turned out to be my father's son.

## CHAPTER 27

*Chuck*
*Rod K and his stepdad Ken*
*Mr. Dawson*
*The strange man at the dollar store*
*Karl, the sex offender who stays in the sub sometimes*
*Devon*
*The weird guy who DMs me*
*Blake*

Even though it was a dark, cold root cellar, there was a light and warmth emanating from Cadie McLeod. The young woman was upbeat and determined to extricate herself from this maddening situation. She had life to live. Goals to accomplish. People who cared for her, and a man who loved her. She was young and in the prime of her life. There was no way this monster – whoever he or it was – would get the best of her.

She knew in most every crime story, the woman was murdered, and the focus was on the man bringing the killer to justice. But in her story, Cadie planned to be the hero. The powerful protagonist. She would survive. She had to.
The moment she spotted that Great Owl looking down at her with soft yellow eyes, Cadie made a promise to Thomas and Aileen - mom and dad - that she would live.

So, just like Nancy Drew in *Curse of the Arctic Star,* a determined Cadie made a mental list of everyone who might want to harm her: boys and men who desired her or made unsettling comments and those who thought she wronged them. In one Nancy Drew book, the heroine sails on an Alaskan liner to find out who is sending threatening emails and is almost crushed by a falling moose antler – so Nancy Drewish! Yet, Nancy survives due to her deductive reasoning and strength of will.

Cadie knew it would take critical thinking, planning, willpower, and no doubt some luck to outwit her captor and free herself. A crucial first task of a good detective is to create a suspect list and motives; however, on modern crime shows, they toss red herring after red herring at viewers, wasting forty-five minutes of their precious time until producers reveal the true killer in the final minutes. Cadie and Aunt Marie had watched so many *Datelines* and *Forensic*

*Files* that they could figure out the guilty person in five minutes flat. If anything, the shows introduced Cadie to the wide-range of reasons why people commit murder – and how they do it.

She made another mental list:
*Passion*
*Lust*
*Mercy*
*Jealousy*
*Fear*
*Anger*
*Mental illness*
*Money*
*Thrills*
*Attention*
*Control*
*Rejection*
*Revenge*

As Cadie paced barefoot over the dirt and stone floor in the clammy cellar, she considered every name on her list carefully. She also thought about the reason each one might have to kill her and how they might do it. Of course, she was aware that it could be a random person, but in her case, the abduction seemed too planned with her as the focus. But why? What did she do that was so bad someone would kidnap her? Maybe rape or torture her? Even kill her? Those terrifying questions assaulted her brain. She commenced her analysis and began with the janitor at Scoops.

"Chuck presents himself as a tough guy, but I honestly think he's too cowardly to have choked me. At work, he's actually timid whenever I have to call him out. But if it was Chuck, why didn't he rape me? Why no sexual assault? He's had plenty of opportunity since my kidnapping, and he makes it painfully obvious he's into me, so why not act on his lust? Or is it just about control?"

Running her fingers through her long, red hair at an attempt to untangle it, she considered the Scoop's janitor further, then crossed Chuck off her mental list. Cadie did this, one by one, going through the names, so as to prepare herself for the perpetrator, their motive, and the possible method or weapon they might use to end her life.

"It could be a gun. A bullet to my head – front or a back."

Cadie shuddered at the thought. She walked purposefully the length of the narrow room, looking at everything, taking inventory.

"I can't turn my back on them at any time. I could try to rush them when they open the door and incapacitate them. Hit them with a mason jar, slice them with a piece of glass, or knee them in the groin. There's also the Adam's Apple or the area below the ribs."

While she mused counterattacks, Cadie looked upward at the slight light coming into the dark room through the rusted air vent. For some reason that was just out of her mind's reach, she was intrigued.

"They could try to kill me with a large knife, like a combat knife, and slice my carotid artery or stab me several times. Maybe I can find something more powerful in this room to attack them with first."

While she thought through the various counter responses that might save her life, Cadie began examining the wooden shelves that ran along the wall. She found several old, dusty mason jars; she knew a hardy shard of glass could come in handy. The young woman ran her hands along the dusty shelves, feeling in between jars, rotted vegetables, and, disgustingly, three dead field mice and one chipmunk carcass for a screwdriver or hammer long ago tucked away and forgotten.

"Maybe they'll choke me. They've already choked me once. I'd be unconscious in ten seconds and dead in five minutes, but at least I'd have a chance to struggle. I guess it's time to put my Women's Studies defense class to use," Cadie laughed. She recalled her instructor telling them to use their fingers like hooks to pry up their attacker's thumbs while kicking them and stomping their feet. Ms. Wrangler told the class, "This will buy you a few seconds to try something else."

*Ms. Wrangler, I am so thankful for you*, Cadie smiled, remembering her fifty-something, grumpy self-defense instructor who could take down a six-foot man, which she actually demonstrated in class.

Mr. Hunt, the dean of students, was on a power trip and treated the female students harshly. Cadie imagined Hunt thought he would get the best of Ms. Wrangler, so he agreed to her demonstration. Sadly for him, it didn't play out that way. Wrangler pinned him in thirty seconds. Cadie didn't have the proper appreciation for Ms. Wrangler in the tenth grade, but Cadie was extremely grateful for her lessons now. She continued her contemplation.

"Worst of all," Cadie stopped, "they could charge in here with a baseball bat or tire iron and beat me to death in the head."

That thought weakened her courage.

*I definitely need to find a weapon.*

As she finished checking the shelves and now the walls, running her hands along the rough field stones, trying to find a loose one, Cadie recalled the technique that made the entire class of teenage girls crack up.

Ms. Wrangler said, "You grab your attacker's two nasty fingers with both hands and pull those babies apart as hard as you can. Just rip them in two directions. Then you twist the asshole's wrist. That should stop them, so you can shove a knee in their balls."

Every girl in the room knew not to record Ms. Wrangler with their cell phones. Kitty was on their side – possibly saving their lives someday. No one minded the salty language in the least. It was their secret.

As she walked back toward the carpet, something was bothering Cadie. There was a thought in the back of her mind, running around, waiting for her to lasso it in. For some reason, she thought of the root cellar's air vent above her head once again and looked up at it, squinting - thinking.

"What? What is it" she wondered, frustrated. "What am I missing?"

Cadie closed her eyes and thought hard. She tried to imagine just how her abductor planned to kill her in this lonely room.

## CHAPTER 28

The last two days trying to locate Cadie McLeod were some of the most difficult and emotionally draining days of Sergeant Bakker's career. Six years ago, the days spent trying to find the hit and run killer of Cadie's parents Thomas and Aileen McLeod were equally horrible. This was personal for Bakker. She was emotionally invested in this family as was her body. Her flaring stress ulcer never let the McLeods get too far from her mind.

Few people in the office knew that six years ago, Bakker and her then husband lived on Alice Street, just a block away from the McLeod's bungalow. On her occasional evening walks, Bakker would wave hi to Aileen and stop to admire her flowers. Aileen's yard, surrounded by a crisp, white picket fence, was brimming with roses and pink hydrangea bushes as well as native Michigan perennials like Purple Coneflower, Bee Balm, Smooth Aster, and, of course, daisies.

Bakker was envious of the tidy, colorful yard and the happy family who sat on their porch swing with their daughter listening to music on warm summer evenings. Bakker didn't have a lot of time to tend to her own home, and she also didn't have many girlfriends – the byproducts of being a cop. She secretly hoped that she and Aileen might someday become friends. Bakker liked the happy-go-lucky young woman with carefree energy who was so different from herself. She and her husband had actually talked about inviting Thomas and Aileen over for a barbeque when the lovely young couple was murdered just days later crossing a road.

The fifty-year-old Bakker was exhausted and hungry, having slept only a handful of hours. Her body was poorly fueled by pots of strong coffee, a big bag of cheese cubes, and a package of Slim Jims from Delio's Deli a block away. Her ex always said they made her breath stink, but she loved them, so screw him. Anyway, Bakker knew she needed to eat better and planned on ordering in scrambled eggs, ham, hashbrowns, and toast from the nearby diner for her staff after the morning meeting. Later, she would buy them lunch. Everyone was working in overdrive and needed sustenance to be strong and sharp.

Now it was 6 am Monday. Bakker had arranged for her daughter to spend the weekend at her ex's house, so Donnie took Lila to school. The thought made Bakker jealous. Since her divorce, she had not had a man or any type of real romance in her life. Conversely, her husband had several profiles on dating sites and posted pictures of himself with various women regularly, enjoying concerts, dinners out, and traveling to Mexico and Florida.

Bakker didn't have the time or money for his lifestyle. Lila was all she had; the little girl was the center of her life. So, dwelling on Lila and Donnie laughing and having fun made Bakker sad. She missed being part of a family. The situation was made worse when Bakker imagined Lila being entertained by Donnie's flavor-of-the month bimbo from eHarmony or, more likely, Getababe.com.

*Soon, he'll be dating seniors off Silver Singles.*

The thought of Donnie in a mid-life crisis dating some elderly sugar momma with white hair and false teeth made Bakker smile.

*I know that's mean, but I'm hangry and damn tired.*

Time to change gears, she knew. This train of thought was wholly unproductive. She pulled her heavy wooden chair close to her desk and angled it toward her computer table to begin reviewing her many emails. The office was mostly dark except for the glowing computer screen and a petite gold lamp that cast a small light on the desk and lent a cozy feel to the room. As she read through her emails, taking notes, Bakker could hear the rest of the office come to life.

Debbie was at the sink filling up the coffee pot with water.

*Thank God. I am so in need of coffee.*

Bakker closed her eyes for a moment. She could hear Debbie singing along with a Christian pop rock song on 91.3 WCSG being broadcast from the speaker behind her desk.

"There's a better path with Jesus. There's no going back for me. I'm gonna live the way He says to live. Do what He says to do."

Bakker heard footsteps on the carpet outside her office, and Detective Brooke Field walked by.

"Morning, Sergeant," Field said as she passed Bakker's door. "Do you want a muffin? I have an extra."

"No, I'm good."

"When are we meeting? Field asked from across the hall, now in her office kitty corner from Bakker's.

"We'll meet at 7 am in the Conference Room," Bakker replied. "Kitchen and Brennan won't be there. I'll explain at the meeting. Also, I've got some info to share. I've just got to get through all these texts and emails first to see what other developments there might be."

"Sounds good. See you at 7."

Then Debbie appeared in Bakker's office doorway with a cup of coffee and set it down on a "Protect the Cove" coaster on the Sergeant's mahogany desk.

"Wow, that was fast," Bakker said.

"Oh, I already had a pot made. I was on the second. Detective Zielinski drank most of the first pot. So, I hope you have good news for us, boss. We could sure use some."

"Nothing right now, but I hope I hear something good soon," Bakker said. "Thanks for the coffee. And just to let you know, I'm ordering breakfast for everyone after the meeting. From Apple Tree."

"Oh, nice. I think everyone could use a good meal. Could we get some pancakes? I haven't had pancakes in forever."

"Sure, Debbie. Anything for you," Bakker smiled.

The Sergeant took a drink of the coffee and twisted her torso to face her computer screen on the side table. When she did so, her back tweaked.

*God, I need a proper office chair.*

Bakker opened her computer inbox and saw the familiar blue and yellow logo. She clicked on the email sent to her late last night from the MSP Computer Crimes Unit.

*Good evening, Sergeant Bakker:*

*This email is in regards to the cell phone video forwarded to us Saturday afternoon from the MSP and its K-9 Unit for enhancement and analysis. As you know, the FBI lab is also working to enhance the video.*

As I've mentioned before, improvement depends on the initial quality of the video: its spatial resolution, compression rate, and frames per second. Because your video had poor lighting and lack of detail and resolution, we could not identify a suspect's face. However, our analysts used newer software that was able to enhance the footage to some extent. We concentrated on the hat that the suspect was wearing.

The improvement to the video revealed that the top of the brim close to the cap is edged in a thin roping that is frayed. On the left side, the roping is more heavily frayed with three longer unraveled strands. These characteristics might allow the hat in question to be more identifiable.

Our analysis leads us to believe this is a rope hat that is a modern take on maritime headwear. Hat roping is a classic style worn by sailors that has been modernized. This type of hat might be worn by a casual boater, mariner, fisherman, or marina employee. However, clearly, as you are located in a coastal town, the suspect wearing the hat could be of any occupation or engaged in fishing/sailing/boating.

Last, there is a small logo or emblem or possibly letters on the hat. We are continuing our efforts at enhancing the video to see if any more detail can be ascertained. We will update you as to our findings ASAP.

Attached please find the enhanced video that shows the hat and the characteristics I mentioned. Don't hesitate to contact us with any questions.

Sincerely,
Meredith Cramer
Forensic Analysis
Michigan State Police Computer Crimes Unit

Bakker looked up from the screen. Those hat characteristics could prove useful, she thought. While there are lots of rope hats out there, our guy is wearing one that is fraying and has three long strands on the left side - a particular location. And maybe even an identifying logo.

The Sergeant reached down and took out a legal pad from her desk drawer. She was giving a press conference in front the police station at 4 pm, so she had to compile all of the information, leads, and evidence first for her staff meeting at

7. Then she had to create a short speech suitable for public consumption later in the day. She couldn't reveal their growing information.

Bakker began writing. Later, after the morning meeting, she would type her notes into a Word document for the digital case file that would become part of the record management system. Afterward, she would shred her notes. It's just that her thoughts and ideas flowed better when she went old school - writing by hand. Bakker knew cops who saw their careers come to an end over having shadow files in their possession and compromising court proceedings. Case files are heavily protected.

Bakker continued writing.

*Cadie McLeod Investigation: Notes by Sergeant Dana Bakker*

1. *No body or physical evidence of Cadie McLeod's (CM) body has been located by the MSP Search and Rescue and Marine Division or the US Coast Guard.*

2. *NamUs has not had any hits.*

3. *The FBI entered CM's name into the NCIC Missing Person File, including information from parents/loved ones of missing children.*

4. *CM's social media and bank accounts have not provided any clues.*

5. *A search of her home, property, neighborhood, and school (her school locker, etc.) did not provide any clues.*

6. *Phone records have not provided any clues.*

7. *We have interviewed over 75 people and continue to amass information.*

8. *The MSP K-9 Unit found the missing person's cell phone on Scenic Trail with a video of the possible suspect. It is being enhanced and analyzed. Some information has been gleaned by the MSP: characteristics about the suspect's hat (roping and fraying (on the hat's left side) and possible logo/emblem/letters.) It's also being enhanced at the FBI lab.*

9. MSP trooper found CM's flip flops on Scenic Trail, confirming she took that route the night she disappeared. The bike CM rode to Mariner's Beach was still locked to the bike rack after she went missing.

10. CM's Aunt Marie reported that CM had mentioned someone driving by their house a few times in the middle of the night and parking. CM couldn't sleep and would see a truck's lights shine in her bedroom window and then stop. She looked out her window and observed the truck sitting in the dark in front of her house on a few occasions. Dt. Rebecca LaCroix obtained footage from a nearby BP gas station and traffic light video from a nearby intersection. She also obtained footage from neighbor's home cameras. All footage was forwarded to the FBI office in TC.

*Suspects*

- Rod Keonig: There is a warrant out for his arrest for molestation of one child and possibly two. Koenig was present at the bonfire party, and there is an alleged incident between Koenig and CM. Koenig has a history of trouble with women as reported by school authorities and other people we interviewed. He has been missing since Friday night. His family property on Hill Valley Road was searched, and Det. Brennan shared concerning items including a zip tie were discovered. He may be hiding at a cousin's apartment in Corktown in Detroit. Dt. Craig Kitchen is investigating.

- Karl Kessler: He is a convicted felon for sexually assaulting three female children. He also has violated parole several times by loitering outside a middle school. It was reported by a waitress at Ted's that Karl made some suspicious comments. A search of his place of employment led to discovery of a Home Depot receipt/purchase of a shovel Thursday. Dt. Jake Brennan is investigating. He is driving to Karl Kessler's brother Richard's dairy farm in Leland, Michigan.

- Edward Dawson: CM complained about the high school teacher to the dean of students about inappropriate comments. The science teacher has a history of inappropriate interactions/relationships with high school females. He left his previous place of employment due to a supposed affair with a student. School authorities have reported more *examples of inappropriate behavior. They also report that Dawson was having questionable interactions with CM. Dt. Brooke Field is investigating.*

- *Blake Van der Velt: The high school senior once dated CM, but she broke up with him. It is reported that he took the breakup quite badly and spoke disparagingly about CM for a while. Someone described him as obsessed with her. We received an anonymous tip through our hotline that Blake threatened to hurt CM at a party once. He called her his "soulmate." From several accounts, Blake can be unstable in his personality and has mental health issues. Dt. Craig Kitchen is investigating.*

- *There are a few other suspects: Glen Boer, Larry Putnam, Chuck Winsome, and James Moore. Also, it was reported that Nick Brennan was observed yelling at CM Friday night. Dt. Dan Zielinski is investigating.*

Bakker hesitated a moment before she wrote down her final 'suspect.'

- *The Devil in the Dunes. Ten years ago, on the last weekend in July, six-year-old Emily Hadly disappeared from Mariner's Beach. Her parents Heidi and Louis Hadly were camping nearby and spent the afternoon swimming and sunbathing with their only daughter. Reports say Heidi and Louis fell asleep on the beach while Emily played with toys in the sand. When they awoke, Emily was gone. Kids playing volleyball on the beach said they saw her walk into the dunes. She was never seen again. An extensive search and investigation were unable to locate the young girl. The locals call her abductor the 'Devil in the Dunes.'*

Bakker stopped writing and looked over her notes. She studied the various men's names and her last entry. She sure hoped they didn't have a serial kidnapper on their hands.

*However, I do hope our guy is on this list. And I pray Nick has nothing to do with it.*

There's nothing worse for an investigation when absolutely none of its leads pan out. When the perp is some random person with their own agenda that's on nobody's radar, they're almost impossible to catch. They have no discernible link to the victim. If that ends up being the case, that it's just some rando who happened upon Cadie McLeod, a defenseless woman all alone in the sand dunes Friday night, then Bakker thought the young woman was as good as dead. She thought about the little girl who went missing. Some folks around Harbor Cove speak of an evil force that weaves its way through the dunes at night looking for female victims. Bakker didn't believe in such nonsense, but it troubled her that a second female disappeared from Mariner's Beach.

It was now 7 am, and Bakker walked to the conference room. Officers Brooke Field, Dan Zielinski, and Rebecca LaCroix, with Debbie poised to take notes, were sitting around the table listening to the young woman talk about her classes. Besides being their front desk receptionist, Debbie also was working on her Associates in Law Enforcement Degree from Northwestern Michigan College. Once she's earned it, Debbie planned on applying to the College's sixteen-week police academy. So, Debbie was definitely as asset to Bakker's investigative team.

Bakker sat down, and the conversation ceased.

"Good morning, everyone," Bakker began. "I hope you all got a good night's sleep because you're going to need it. We have a lot to review this morning and a young woman to find."

All heads nodded solemnly.

The group reviewed Bakker's notes and shared information – the fruits of their interviews as well as any new details or clues that had come to light since yesterday evening. Bakker filled them in on the day's activities of Detectives Jake Brennan and Craig Kitchen. Brennan was headed to the Kessler property in Leland, while Kitchen would try to locate Rod Keonig in Detroit. Everyone was somewhat apprehensive to hear this news. They knew that anything could happen out on the road tracking and interacting with suspects.

After a productive meeting, a delivery man from Apple Tree knocked on the conference door. He was carrying several plastic bags. The staff gathered around the table looked to the door, and smiles broke out all around when Bakker opened the door. They knew the driver well and smelled the hot, delicious food. Everyone's stomachs growled simultaneously, and the officers laughed in unison.

"Got you all some breakfast," Bakker said.

The officers immediately jumped up and grabbed the bags to help out. Within minutes, the conference table looked like a restaurant breakfast buffet with food spread out in a line. Debbie brought in a fresh pot of coffee. The staff ate well and made lively chit chat, allowing themselves a few minutes of breathing room from the intense Cadie McLeod case. The hot, hearty meal seemed to pump much needed energy into the tired staff, and they were revitalized. Bakker herself had a large helping of scrambled eggs with ketchup (she kept a bottle in her office refrigerator), one pancake, hash browns, and a piece of crisp rye toast with butter and mixed berry jam. Eating the comforting breakfast made her feel more upbeat and hopeful.

After finishing her breakfast, the Sergeant was headed back to her office, holding the ketchup bottle, when Debbie quickly walked up to her in the hallway.

"Sarge, Marie McLeod left us a voicemail. She said she found something in Cadie's room this morning that she thinks may be important."

Bakker's face registered her surprise.

"I wonder what that could be. We've already searched the house and Cadie's bedroom."

Bakker was quiet for a moment.

"Debbie, can you call Marie and tell her I'll be over there shortly. Then I have to run up to the FBI office in Traverse City. I need to check on the film footage Rebecca collected and the cell phone video MSP sent to Dority."

"*You're* going over to Marie's?"

"Yeah, I am," Bakker said, her voice catching. "And let's pray that whatever Aunt Marie found helps us locate Cadie. I can't imagine what that poor girl is going through."

Debbie was surprised at her boss's emotions. Bakker usually maintained a calm, reserved demeanor – even somewhat detached.

Bakker strode into her office and put on her utility belt, tightening it. She slowly ran her hand over the handcuffs, baton, and pepper spray before patting her Glock 22. The powerful gun gave her a sense of strength. In her career, she only had to fire her gun at a person once. She wondered if she'd use it again in the days ahead – maybe firing a bullet into Cadie McLeod's abductor. She hoped so. She wouldn't mind putting a bullet into the bastard that was causing so much pain. As she walked out of her office, Bakker stopped and leaned over her desk.

She grabbed a Slim Jim.

*Fuck you, Donnie.*

Bakker walked out the front door of the Harbor Cove Police Station with renewed energy - and extreme interest about what Aunt Marie had found. As she drove through the little town, the Sergeant observed that posters of Cadie McLeod were already nailed to almost every post and appearing in every store window. She continued driving and thinking about the aunt's voicemail.

*I wonder what Marie found?*

Bakker was extremely curious. Just what was waiting for her in the McLeod cottage on Waters Edge?

## CHAPTER 29

Nick continued to dream, intense images and emotions populating his unconscious mind. In the dream, Nick and Cadie finished their ice cream Pecan Ball, and Nick leaned over to brush away a speck from Cadie's face. Their eyes met briefly but powerfully. Then Cadie laughed a bit awkwardly while Nick was almost breathless when he looked at her glowing face. His heart ached at the sight of her.

They decided to leave the Grand Hotel's famous front porch that was surrounded by some 1,300 bright red geraniums. They stepped down the Hotel's front steps and walked over to the edge and took in the lush gardens below.

"It's so beautiful," Cadie said.

*You're beautiful.*

"Do you want to go down there? I read it's 79 steps," Nick suggested, his body suddenly flushing with desire.

Nick fervently hoped Cadie would say yes. He had something in mind for Cadie. The couple made the journey down the lengthy steps. The sun seemed to be shining even more brightly on the young couple, and a light breeze blew through the legendary 100-year-old vibrant gardens with over 150 types of flowers including lilacs, tulips, daffodils, roses, daisies, and begonias.

Nick and Cadie, talking and laughing, walked closely past a row of yellow lillies. The maple and white cedar trees provided welcome shade and playful shadows when they got too hot. As they searched for the Secret Garden, Nick couldn't take his eyes off Cadie. His body felt like it would burst from all the feelings it held tight. He longed to kiss her full, beautiful lips. He longed to do so much more.

Nick suggested they move into the secluded interior of the gardens. Nick found a spot out of view underneath a towering maple tree, and they plopped down in the grass, their faces pink and glowing from the sun.

Nick suddenly felt nervous, the weight of his feelings and desires overtaking him.

"Uh, I wonder if Mark Twain ever sat here," Nick said awkwardly, making small talk.

"He gave a lecture at the Grand Hotel in the 1800s, you know."

Cadie just tilted her head, studying him, and smiled.

"No, I didn't know that. So fascinating," she laughed. "You're just an onion with many layers, Mr. Brennan. So complex."

Nick knew she was just playfully teasing him, but his whole being felt on fire.

"Cadie."

"Yes?"

"Can we talk?"

"I thought we were talking," she grinned.

"No, I mean really talk. There are things I have been wanting to say to you." Cadie sat up a bit straighter and smoothed her hair. A slight, almost imperceptible frown crossed her face. They were having such a perfect time.

*What is he going to say?*

She began to feel nervous.

"Okay. Sure. What do you want to talk about?"

"I want to talk about us."

"Us?"

Cadie cleared her throat.

"Yes, you and me. I think you know. I mean, I think you know how I feel about you."

"I'm not sure I do," Cadie lied but wasn't sure why. She laid down in the grass and put her hands behind her head and looked up into the trembling trees, feeling uncomfortable.

*Why am I feeling this way? Ever since the death of mom and dad, I can't seem to feel anything. It's just so hard to be intimate. Why can't I let people get close to me?*

Nick laid down on the grass beside her. There was silence for a while. The two young people listened to the songbirds moving through the trees with their joyful, melodic whistling. The leaves rustled peacefully. The idyllic scene clashed with the tenseness Cadie was now feeling about the words Nick was sure to say.

"Cadie."

"Yes."

"This is not easy for me to say because I'm not exactly sure how you feel about me, but I think I do. I want to tell you what's on my mind. How I feel. What I'm thinking. What I've been going through. The plans and dreams I have for the two of us."

Cadie winced at the words plans and dreams.

*I have so many dreams of my own, though.*

"Okay," Cadie said.

"So, would you mind if I talked for a bit and you just listened? You can tell me what you think when I'm done. I feel like I need to get it all out or maybe I never will. And I'm nervous as hell. I just feel like right now is the moment I'm supposed to tell you everything."

Cadie closed her eyes and took in a deep breath, the warm breeze washing over her. "Okay, Nick, I'm listening."

## CHAPTER 30

Edward Dawson, the troubled biology teacher, sweated profusely as he drove his truck north on M-22. He drove up the sleepy Lake Michigan coastline past beaches, vineyards, rolling farms, orchards, and a thick forest of beech and maple trees. He finally spotted the Wilco Road sign and made a left. Dawson drove down the dirt road a half mile. He was headed for the isolated Empire Bluffs just south of the town of Empire - more specifically the secluded trailhead that would take him to a massive bluff towering six hundred feet over Lake Michigan.

He had been to Inspiration Point in Arcadia and the Bluffs at the National Lakeshore many times with Louise and Charles, his deceased parents whom he detested. Several summers, the trio left the Detroit suburbs behind and motored north up I-75 headed toward their cabin. The stops at the remote Bluffs always caused both fear and excitement in Edward.

The small, quiet, and strange family would hike the narrow, hilly trail, stepping over twisted, fallen trees and shifting rocks in sandy terrain until they reached the gigantic hillside and the panoramic views of the Lake Michigan and South Bar Lake. While the wind whipped his hair around, and he brushed the blowing sand from his eyes, the boy enjoyed the expansive view and turquoise waters. Sometimes, he looked down and had bad thoughts. He secretly wondered what it would be like to plummet to the rocks below, his body breaking into a hundred little bloody pieces. Sometimes he imagined what his father's body would look like broken and bloody on the rocks. The thought made him smile. Even at a young age, Edward Dawson had thoughts of death and revenge.

He parked his truck in the gravel lot at the entrance to the trailhead and grabbed the package on his front seat. The fifty-one-year-old Dawson was soon hiking the sandy trail that would take him to his destination. The sun shone on him, and he began to sweat. As he hiked, he looked down, always on guard for rocks and roots like he did as a child. His boots twisted in the sandy soil, while his mind was tormented with thoughts about his deviant life.

*What the fuck is wrong with me? Why can't I be normal and have a life like everyone else?*

The winds picked up as he hiked deeper into the woods, the cool lake breeze tossing leaves and stirring pollen. Up ahead, a mighty sugar maple had fallen over the trail, blocking it, branches sprawled in every direction. Dawson had to walk the length of the tree until it narrowed. Grabbing tree branches with bare hands, he fought to find secure footing and almost stumbled, but Dawson was fit and athletic. He hoisted himself over the tree and several large branches until he cleared it and continued on the 1.5-mile roundtrip trail, although today's troubled journey might only take him half that distance.

As he walked, his thoughts turned to Amber - as they often did - his prize student in Alpena. The girl was the end of everything good in his life. Sex with the 14-year-old cost him his teaching job, his coaching job, most of his family, and all of his friends. He was now a pariah. And even though things ended oh so terribly – he resigned in disgrace and left everything he had built to move across the state and begin anew – he couldn't help but find the memories of their sex utterly delicious.

*Oh, I am a monster.*

*But it was so good.*

He smiled as he recalled the shy brunette who caught his eye the first day of class. She sat in the back with her head down, wearing a black tee-shirt, jeans, and Converse sneakers, trying to hide herself from the world.
Dawson was sexually attracted to the girl immediately.

He liked the way she brushed her soft bangs from her hazel eyes. The way she nibbled on her pencil when she was thinking. The way her slender body flowed down the hallway when she walked. From that day forward, he was all in.
A few times a week, he would make excuses to hold Amber back after class.

"Hey, can you stay for a minute? I want to talk to you about your leaf project. You identified every leaf correctly. No one else even came close, Amber. I'm very impressed!"

Dawson would put his arm around her, and Amber blushed shyly but appreciatively. After many of these 'opportunities,' the teacher, who was now dyeing his graying hair a noticeable dark brown, began asking about Amber's personal life. He knew her father was ill with prostate cancer, so Dawson began giving the girl advice and support.

"You know, you probably shouldn't bother your dad with your stuff. You know he's so sick. When you need help with anything, just come to me. I'm always here to talk. In fact, why don't you give me your cell phone number? It'll make it easier for me to give you help with your homework. I'll send you a text, and then you'll also have my number. Amber thought his suggestion was odd, but she felt a slight excitement at his attention.

So, the texting began as well as the private FB messaging. The teacher also slid into her DMs as the young people call it. Dawson was cementing her trust in him one brick at a time. He became her confidante, her shoulder to cry on. They'd meet secretly at Coffee Hop and share a large cinnamon roll or sneak into Cinema One to watch one of Amber's favorite Marvel movies.

She got good at lying to her father, but it was to protect him, Dawson told her. Her lies were actually kindness, he said. That's right, Amber thought, I don't need to worry dad about my life.

Over the course of the semester, Dawson continually eroded normal boundaries and finally was able to supersede Amber's relationship with her dad. Dawson was now the main father figure. Whenever Amber had a question or needed help, she'd text Edward or stay after class. Dawson received a fair amount of grooming advice from an online site devoted to pedophilia that had since been taken down. The site, *Daddys' Girls*, said it catered to the "healthy, normal desires of both men and girls."

So, taking the site's advice, Dawson began making casual, offhand comments about sex; he even showed her some soft porn on his computer at school. One day after class, Dawson held her back and said he wanted to show her something. He led the girl by the hand into the back lab, closed the door, turned off the light, and kissed her up against the wall. Amber had never been kissed and didn't know how to respond.

In the dark, the teacher whispered, "You are so beautiful, Amber. I think about you all the time. In fact, I can't stop thinking about you. And you are so much more mature than other girls. You understand me. I really feel like I'm falling in love with you, sweet girl, and I want to marry you someday."

Amber was taken aback but couldn't deny her excitement. No one had ever talked to her this way. Shown her this attention. In the days and weeks to come, Dawson's repeated words and sexual overtures eventually worked, and Amber began to believe that she was in love with her biology teacher – a man almost three times her age.

"We're soulmates, Amber. You know what a soulmate is, don't you?"

"No. Not really."

"It's when two souls in all the world find each other. It's predestined. You and I were meant to be. Our souls belong together."

Sex soon followed. For Dawson, life was exceptional. He was sneaking Amber into his apartment or classroom lab for sex (also getting off on the secrecy), and he won Teacher of the Month for implementing a new computer tutoring program for athletes. The school district even featured him in its "Spotlight on Leadership" newsletter. To everyone, Mr. Dawson was a great guy - a role model. Hard working, caring, and respected. You couldn't ask for a better educator. Dawson's mask was securely in place.

Until that fateful day.

It was a Friday morning, 6:45 am, and students began pouring into the high school. Laughter, shouts, and banging lockers filled the tiled hallways. Dawson was at his blackboard writing the morning lesson, his back turned to the wooden door, when he heard a small noise that sounded like a kitten crying. He turned and saw Amber. She was sniffling into her science book.

He quickly walked across the room, looked both ways, put his arm around her, and ushered her back to the lab. "What's wrong, sweetheart?"

He gently brushed back her bangs. The young girl wouldn't look him in the eyes.

"C'mon, it's me. You know you can trust me. Here, sit down, and you can tell me what's wrong."

He pulled out a plastic and metal chair from under the lab table, and Amber gingerly took a seat. Dawson took a seat beside her.

"Now, what's got you so upset? Did you get a bad grade? Did you have a fight with Molly? Is your pet bird still sick? Or maybe it's something with your dad?"

"No. It's not any of that."

"Well, then, what is it? Tell me."

There was a long pause during which Amber looked down at the purple fingernail polish peeling off her nails and began pulling at a loose piece.

"I'm pregnant."

The two powerful words blasted into the air. They ricocheted off the floor and walls. They shot around the room until their energy was spent. Dawson grasped at his head. Sweat poured out of him. He felt weak. He might throw up.

"How do you know?! Maybe you're wrong! You could be wrong!"

Dawson's brain clawed for excuses. He felt frantic.

"I'm not wrong."

His heart thundered in his chest.

"And I told my dad."

KaBOOM.

And that. Was the end. Of everything. Life as he knew it was over.
Now, four years later, Dawson found himself in another predicament of his own making. All because of his dark desires. He had another young woman in his snare.

As the teacher walked the narrow trail heading toward the boardwalk, he wondered if today was truly the day he'd put a bullet in his brain.
Dawson had learned his lesson with Amber. No, he didn't learn to leave young women alone. No, he didn't learn not to act on selfish desires that stole the innocence of children and ruined their childhoods forever. What Edward Dawson learned was to not get caught.

So, everything of late had been going swimmingly. His current secret was firmly under wraps. Until yesterday afternoon. He got home from running an important errand, and the light on his answering machine was blinking red. It was a voicemail from Harbor Cove police.

"Hello, Mr. Dawson, this is Detective Brooke Field with the Harbor Cove Police Department. We need you to come down to the station. There's an urgent situation, and we have questions for you. Please return my call as soon as possible. This is extremely important. Thank you."

Dawson slowly backed away from the phone. The teacher was horrified. He'd been so careful to cover his tracks. No one was supposed to find out what he was up to. But had they? And how? He couldn't bear the thought. Dawson emerged from the canopy of trees and walked out onto the wooden boardwalk. Into the sunshine. The view was spectacular.

As far as he could see were massive, towering bluffs covered in trees, brush, and sand that sloped down to the water's edge. The mesmerizing blue waters of Lake Michigan glinted in the sun and rhythmically lapped against the sandy shore. He looked down the steep hill intently. He stared at the rocks below. Dawson was at a crossroads; he had a decision to make.

*Do I put a bullet in my head right now or follow through with my plan? I'm so very close.*

Dawson sat down on the wooden slats, his legs dangling, and placed the package containing the gun next to him. He caressed the package, feeling the sharp angles of the .38 caliber revolver. He contemplated the pros and cons of killing himself versus the deliciousness of fulfilling one last fantasy.

*She's waiting for me.*

As he looked out over the sweeping view, his mind spinning like an out-of-control film reel, the deviant had two thoughts flashing in his brain like screen images:

*I should have killed Amber when I had the chance.*
*What should I do now?*

## CHAPTER 31

Cadie lay quiet in the grass, almost holding her breath, and started to feel sick to her stomach. Nick stood up and turned away so he didn't have to look at her. Pacing back and forth, he began his 'speech.'

"First of all, Cadie, I have been thinking about telling you how I feel for so long - you have no idea. I think about you all the time."

He looked up into the trees, the sun speckling the leaves.

"I'm completely in love with you. I feel like you were meant for me, and I was meant for you. Like I have known you forever and loved you forever. When I see you, my heart comes alive. And whenever I'm with you, I'm a better version of myself. I feel like I could do anything, and together we could conquer the world – just you and me."

Cadie realized she was now holding her breath and inhaled deeply.

"I know I'm going on, but I've been thinking about this for a while. I shared my feelings with my dad, and he thinks a lot of it has to do with my mother and how she left us. Yeah, I'm heartsick over it. It's kind of hard to have your mother who you thought loved you and had your back just be okay with bailing on you, especially when you're still in high school, and just walk away from their kid. So yeah, it's a huge hurt. I'm not going to lie; it does make me emotional. It tears me up inside. But if anything, it's made me realize what's important in life - what I want - and what I want is you. My dad even said it: Cadie McLeod is an exceptional woman."

Cadie rolled over and placed her head on her arm. She closed her eyes.

"I know I'm getting far ahead of myself, *of us*, but sometimes I even think about a crazy idea. What if we got married before we went to college? I know you want to go to Michigan State, but what if we got married and went to community college instead? Why wait to start our lives? Or we could get married and go to college together? They have married housing at both State and Michigan."

Cadie felt like she was underwater. Her brain was becoming fuzzy.

"I just want to be with you, and I can't stand the thought of me being at UM and you being at Michigan State and us not being together and growing apart and meeting new people. I'm not going to ask you right now, I mean I don't even have a ring, but I want you to be my wife, to be my forever. It would make me the happiest man in the world."

Nick nervously ran his fingers through his thick hair.

"There it is. I said it. I said everything I've been wanting to say."

The young man sat down stiffly in the grass, his back turned, waiting for Cadie's response.

There was silence.

Nothing but wind blowing through the tall, leafy trees. Then the low-pitched boom of a foghorn off in the distance.

"So," Nick said, "what are you thinking about everything I said? Tell me."

"Uh, well, that was a lot. I, uh, wasn't expecting all of that," Cadie stammered, trying to process Nick's emotional monologue. "I really don't know what to say."

*Get married? Not go to Michigan State? Not follow my dreams? This is not the plan I had for myself! I have big goals. Most importantly becoming a forensic scientist and tracking down my parents' killer!*

"Yeah, I know it's a lot," Nick said, "and I'm sorry I dumped it all on you this way. I've just been carrying these feelings for so long, Cadie. I just needed to tell you how I feel. That I love you with my whole heart."

Nick turned to look at Cadie, his eyes open and imploring.

"Do you love me?"

Again, there was an uncomfortable pause and silence.

"I care about you very much."

"But do you love me?"

"You know, Nick, I think we should be heading back. I told Tori and Julie I would meet them at Murdick's."

"I asked you a question."

"I know, but I think I need to be getting back."

"That's all you have to say to me? After all I told you?" Nick said, his voice taking on anger. "I mean, I poured my guts out to you, Cadie. Tell me something. Tell me anything!"

Cadie stood up.

"Listen, we can talk later, okay? I really have to go."

*I care so much about you, Nick, but do I want – or need - a forever?*

Cadie jumped up and turned away from Nick. She began jogging, then running, through the massive trees until she reached the open garden drenched in sunlight, and she kept running faster and faster until she made it into town and far away from the pressure to live a life different than the life she had envisioned.

## CHAPTER 32

Cadie knew she could be killed at any time. Also, the water supply would run out soon. Her abductor could simply leave her in this tomb to die of thirst and rot away. He might just never come back.

*But why? What have I done? Why would someone want to kill me for no reason?*

Cadie remembered the truck and the strange note. Was it that guy? Did she cross him in some way? What were his plans for her? Was he just going to leave her here forever? It was a gruesome thought: her body shriveling up due to lack of water, leading to a painful, agonizing death. Cadie knew the body can typically only last three days without water as it requires a certain amount to keep cells alive and the body at the correct temperature. Whether it was death by organ failure, or death by some other means, Cadie knew she had to act quickly. Her water supply was almost gone, and she was becoming increasingly thirsty and tired. Her cell walls were beginning to shrink. Soon they would collapse.
It was time to save herself.

*I'll get myself out of here if it's the last thing I do.*

She was aware of the irony: If she didn't escape, trying to escape would indeed be that last thing she did. It was time to implement her game plan. First, she had to become thoroughly acquainted with every inch of the root cellar. So, she searched it from top to bottom. She ran her hands all over and around the walls looking for loose stones or any openings and weaknesses in the mortar. She meticulously searched the wooden shelves that lined the walls, looking for any items of value. When she was done, hours later, sweaty and exhausted, for her efforts she had amassed two large field stones that broke off the wall, one regular sized mason jar, three small jars partly filled with vinegar, and a loose board she pried from a barrel. She hid all her finds at the far end of the cellar. Cadie knew from her sophomore class trip to the 1921 root cellar in Leelanau County that every cellar has an air intake and an air outtake for proper ventilation – to keep air from getting humid and rotting the vegetables. The intake is always near the ground to draw in cooler air, while the outtake dispels the warmer air through a vent up above.

Her root cellar's outtake vent had provided her with slivers of sunshine, a meeting with a Great Horned Owl a fortnight ago, and moments of hope as she listened to songbirds fluttering up above. Regardless of these hopeful moments, Cadie knew she had to put her plan to work quickly before her mysterious abductor had a chance to kill her or leave her to die.

Earlier that morning, she heard noises nearby, perhaps someone on the property – her abductor? - running a machine that sounded like a generator or heater. Her mind finally provided another means of death. Was her abductor planning to kill her with carbon monoxide? Cadie and Aunt Marie had recently watched a Dateline episode in which a doctor in Ohio murdered his wife that way. At this point, Cadie understood her personal monster could return at any time and finish her off in any number of ways.

*I can't let that happen. I won't!*

Cadie searched the back of the cellar and located the lower vent. She found she was able to wiggle the vent a little. With her rock, she pounded on the vent for ten minutes, stopping to listen for any hint of her abductor. She sat down on the dirt floor and began pushing the vent with her bare feet until it finally broke free of the stone wall and landed out in the grass. Of course, it was a small opening, too small for her body. She would need to increase the size of the vent's hole, so she could hopefully squeeze herself through and escape to the other side.
She put her face into the hole, looking out; the exterior air smelled and felt wonderful against her skin.

A chipmunk running by suddenly stopped – most likely shocked to see her face peering out the cellar hole - and sat on its hind legs, studying her. Its curious head twitched back and forth. She admired the tan and blackish stripes on its back and face. They both observed each other for several seconds. Then the small creature became nervous and let out a little "wee" before it scampered down the hill, off to enjoy its freedom.

Freedom for Cadie also was on the other side. She could see the dense forest of birch and maple trees and hear the sounds of nature. But how could she enlarge the hole? None of the rocks around the opening seemed very loose. She pushed and pulled on them and banged them with her rock and kicked at them, and they moved slightly but still seemed largely anchored in place.

Cadie walked back to the other end of the cellar and sat down on the dingy carpet – which strangely had become like a bedroom – and ate the last bite of a granola bar and finished her supply of water.

*That's it. No more water. Two or three more days to live – if that.*

Cadie sat there for a bit, wanting to sleep, but knowing she could not. She thought about that saying, "You can sleep when you're dead."

*I need to get home to Nick and Aunt Marie. I have a whole life to live. Parents I made a promise to.*

What would Nancy Drew do, she wondered? Cadie knew it was silly to think such a thing – to wonder what an imaginary book character might do in her predicament - but somehow thinking about the fictional heroine gave her hope and strength. As she sat there thinking, a book she read in middle school popped into her head: *The Secret in the Old Attic*. In it, Nancy finds poisonous gas in some old blue bottles. There's also mention of a chemical with a particular odor – a clue Nancy uses to put two and two together.

*Why am I thinking about this book right now?*

Suddenly, she had the strangest sensation. She felt as if her father Thomas was there in the cellar with her, helping her. Thomas had been promoted to Lab Director the day he was killed, and he often joked and apologized to his only child for giving her his left-brain DNA.

*I'm proud to be like you, dad. And thankful for all your lessons. I just never imagined they might save my life one day.*

Her father was the smartest – and kindest – man she knew. Now Cadie felt that the spirit of her chemist father was with her, guiding her. Cadie continued to ponder, and the word 'chemicals' kept running around her brain. She knew it was only a matter of time before her neural pathways proliferated and presented the thought to her conscious mind. She recalled a visual about acid from her AP Chemistry textbook. (Mr. Dawson said she might have a photographic mind, but she knew the latest research indicated there's really no such thing. She probably just had the gene mutation that allows her to remember images for a long time.) Cadie also recalled a handout from the class trip to the historic root cellar in

Leelanau. The two images sparked her neurons into providing her brain with some curious words: lime, alkaline, caustic, acidic, and acetic acid.
She remembered their guide walking them through the old cellar and talking about lime putty mortar made from slaked lime and sand, the settling of root cellars, and the deterioration of mortar joints.

She got up and walked quickly to the end of the root cellar. Cadie reached the back wall, knelt down, and took hold of one of the small mason jars. They contained white vinegar. She knew that yeast feeds on the starch or sugar found in plant liquid from vegetables like potatoes or sugar beets, which she had found rotting in the cellar. The yeast and plant liquid ferment into alcohol. She remembered from AP Chemistry that when the alcohol is exposed to oxygen and acetic acid bacteria, vinegar is the result. All three little mason jars contained vinegar. Though exhausted, her face broke into a large grin. What she held in her hand was absolutely wonderful.

*White vinegar has 5-10% acetic acid with positively charged hydrogen ions. The ions should react with the alkaline in the mortar around the rocks and dissolve it!*

Cadie suddenly had a newfound excitement. She knew the vinegar's acidity had probably decreased as she had no idea how long the vinegar sat in the cellar. Thus, it was impossible to gauge just how acidic – how potent – the vinegar acid was. However, her rock, barrel board, muscular legs, and extreme will to live might combine to dislodge the large stones. If the acid could loosen the surrounding mortar enough for her to dislodge the rocks bordering the hole, she could escape!

Cadie sat down in front the hole studying the rocks, looking for mortar cracks the best she could in the dim light. She ran her fingers around the hole and rocks, feeling for fissures that had occurred over time from settling and water drainage.

*How am I going to get the vinegar into the cracks?*

Cadie sat on the dirt floor for a bit thinking. Neurons firing.

*I've got it.*

She tugged her filthy sundress off over her head and tangled hair. The sundress was a boho maxi dress made of four panels of yellow material sewn together. As she sat there in her bralette and underwear on the cold dirt floor, Cadie worked at pulling the panels apart. She decided a knife would do the job quicker, so she wrapped the larger mason jar in her dress and broke it against the wall. Carefully opening her dress, Cadie selected a large shard of glass that had a smooth edge so she wouldn't cut herself. She also knew she might need to use the large shard later to defend herself. She shook out the rest of the glass nearby and began tearing at and cutting her dress.

*I'll tear the panels into little strips and soak them in the vinegar. I'll shove the strips into the mortar cracks and then move them around with my glass shard. Finally, I'll pray they dissolve the mortar, even a little.*

Cadie worked on tearing the fabric into tiny strips for quite a while. She was extremely thirsty and even more tired, but she knew she couldn't stop. Not for a second. Sleep was her enemy. When all the fabric was torn, she soaked the pieces in vinegar, trying not to retch at the up-close, powerful smell and trying not to waste even a drop of the precious liquid. Next, she began shoving the strips into various mortar cracks that ran along the larger stones near the opening. She moved and twisted the fabric strips around with her piece of glass.

*If I can get the mortar to dissolve a little, I can hammer the larger rocks and push with my legs. All those hours doing calf raises and jumping rope at track practice just might save my life!*

The young woman now had a possible means to escape. With renewed energy and laser focus, for the remainder of the day Cadie McLeod struggled to dislodge three large rocks. She pushed and pulled for hours, every muscle – from deltoids and triceps to hamstrings, calves and quadriceps – burned and quivered. She could actually see them swell as the pain almost became unbearable. But she didn't dare stop. The 18-year-old who wanted to live more than anything never slowed. In fact, she worked harder than she had ever worked in her life.

## CHAPTER 33

It was noon, growing more humid, and the sun shone brightly – almost mockingly - overhead as Sergeant Bakker drove down the twisting Hill Valley Road – a street right out of a romantic *Lifetime* movie. Large oak and maple trees lined and canopied overhead while cheerful children rode by on colorful bicycles. Bakker was feeling increasingly nervous about Cadie McLeod's chances. The young woman had been missing since Friday night, now going on three days. She knew the odds of being found or even surviving decreased dramatically after day three.

Heavy hearted, Bakker pulled up to Marie McLeod's house and parked in the street, steeling herself for the upcoming meeting with the grieving aunt. It had been a while since she had seen the teal cottage with weathered wood and white dormer windows. The ground floor windows were adorned with window boxes bursting with orange zinnias. Bakker approached Marie's wide, welcoming front porch with its lazy overhead fan, porch swing with fluffy white pillows, and collection of driftwood. It reminded her of Aileen's porch, and the image of the deceased woman and her once happy family made Bakker choke up.

*Get it together, Bakker.*

She was walking up the first step when Marie, looking exhausted and unkempt in a long, wrinkled tee-shirt, opened the oversized front door with four small-paned windows.

"Good morning, Marie," Bakker said, climbing the remainder of the painted white steps.

"I think you mean afternoon, Sergeant," Marie smiled weakly.

She invited Bakker in and immediately walked her into Cadie's light blue room that was just off the living room at the front corner of the cottage. Bakker was surprised. She expected to see the typical teenage girl bedroom: clothes strewn about, pink stuffed animals piled on the bed, a dressing table with lipstick, blush, and movie stubs, and posters of boys and bands taped across the walls. Instead, what she found in the tidy room was quite different.

On the wall behind Cadie's bed was a large poster of the Periodic Table with perfectly arranged rows of chemical elements. Next to it was a whimsical yellow poster with E=mc2 across the top followed by red, childlike font: "Think like a proton: always be positive!" The third poster in the room was of hurdler Tobi Amusan of Nigeria in her green striped tank and arms outstretched. According to the poster, Amusan holds the women's 100m hurdles world record. Above that poster was a wood sign: "Girls just want to have fun-damental rights."

In one corner were Cadie's running shoes, track spikes, and leaning against the wall, her blue and green golf bag – the Harbor Cove High School Colors - with her numerous golf and track medals and trophies on a corner shelf above it. On one nightstand next to the single bed was a stack of books with *Hidden Figures* on top. Everything in the room spoke of an intelligent, curious, aware, and driven young woman.

Something silver caught Bakker's eye. She leaned in. On the nightstand next to the stack of books was a small black and white photograph in a silver frame. The picture was of a young Thomas and Aileen sitting on a quilt at Mariner's Beach. Thomas was holding a baby Cadie in his lap with his arms encircling her. Bakker had to bite her lip to keep from letting out a cry. Next to the frame was a small wood frame containing a vibrant watercolor painting. Bakker leaned in and studied the signature: A. McLeod.

Just then Marie tapped her on the shoulder, startling her.

"I'll show you what I found."

Marie pointed to the nightstand on the other side of the bed. On it was a brown leather journal with two gold buttons that kept the front flap closed.

"What is it?" Bakker asked. "And where did you find it? Our team said they thoroughly searched Cadie's bedroom."

"Well, every six months or so, I flip the mattresses. It's something my mom used to do – to keep the mattresses from getting worn down – so I do it, too. Anyway, when I flipped over Cadie's mattress this morning and stripped off the sheets, I found the book. It's Cadie's diary. I didn't even know she kept a diary."

Bakker pulled out sterile gloves from inside her vest, put them on, and then picked up the book. She flipped through the pages. Quickly reading a few, she thought the diary seemed fairly straightforward. Not a lot of gossip and drama. Just a recounting of her activities. More like a logbook or journal than a diary. Almost scientific.

"Have you read through it?" Bakker asked.

"I have. I wore my gardening gloves."

"Very smart, Marie."

Bakker continued to read.

"So far, in quickly glancing through it, I don't see much here."

"Let me help you," Marie said. "Keep going."

Bakker flipped through several more pages.

"Stop there," Marie said. She pointed down the page at a passage. Bakker began reading.

"I received a strange note today. I found it in the mailbox under some letters. It wasn't in an envelope. Just a little note folded in half with a cryptic message. I don't even know if it's meant for me. Maybe they got the wrong mailbox. It just unsettles me. It makes me think about the dark truck that sometimes parks in front of our house in the middle of the night. I might say something to Marie about the note, but I also don't want to alarm her. She became upset when I told her about the truck."

Bakker looked up.

"Do you have the note?"

"It's on the shelf. I'll show you."

Marie, with Bakker following, pointed to a small, folded note next to a Jade plant on a white, wooden shelf.

Bakker picked up the note, opened it carefully, and read out loud.

"It's almost time. I've waited for this moment for quite a while, and now it's almost here. So, I'll see you soon. And don't be scared. It will all be over quickly."

Bakker's lips pressed together, and her lower lip stiffened. Her eyebrows came together as a deep frown overtook her face.

"This is really odd," she said. "I don't like anything about this."

Neither do I," Marie said. "That's why I called you right away. But I don't know how it will help. It's so mysterious."

"I'm headed to the FBI office in Traverse City after I leave here. I'll hand over the note to them. They can compare the handwriting to our known suspects; it will just take some time."

*Time unfortunately we don't have.*

"Also, there may be fingerprints or bodily fluids on the note that could be helpful later."

Bakker instantly regretted saying 'helpful later'. She knew it meant bringing someone to justice and not necessarily locating Cadie.

"You just never know what the FBI techs will find. Let's hope there is something useful on the note. Thank you for contacting us right away, Marie."

"Of course," Marie said. "I just don't know what to think. I was pretty hopeful Saturday and Sunday that Cadie would be home any time. Today, I'm feeling a lot worse. It's really hitting me that she's gone . . ."

Marie suddenly choked up, and it became hard to finish her thought.

"or dead."

Bakker put her arm around the petite woman with bright blue eyes.

"I understand, Marie. But we have to stay positive. We have to believe that Cadie is out there fighting for her life. We are going to do everything in our power to bring her home."

"I know you will, Dana. Thank you so much for everything. Please just let me know when you hear something. Just anything, okay?"

"I will."

Bakker carefully put the journal and note into breathable evidence bags, gave Marie another hug, and left the cottage. As she walked down the front steps, she felt even more worried about the fate of Cadie McLeod than when she had arrived.

## CHAPTER 34

Nick texted his dad numerous times that morning from school and left two voicemails. He was growing more upset and slightly unhinged. It had been hours since his dad left their house and drove up to Leland to track down Karl Kessler. Nick kept sneaking his cell phone out of his jean's pocket and texting next to his leg, so his teachers wouldn't see. Using a cell phone during class was not allowed at Harbor Cove High School. He really didn't think they would confiscate his phone in light of the circumstances, but you never knew. Some teachers are on a full-time power trip. After third hour let out, on his way to the cafeteria, Nick ducked into the blue-tiled men's room and dialed his dad's cell phone again, recording a voicemail.

"Hey, dad. It's me again. Sorry if I'm being a pain. I'm just worried about you. I hope everything is okay. What have you heard about Cadie? I'm really freaking out. I mean, it's been almost three days. I keep thinking she must be dead. I know I shouldn't think that way, but it's hard not to. So, just please just call me and be careful. Nothing is going on here today. We're just watching movies, so I'm thinking about cutting out. What's the point of being here? Anyways, I love you. Hope you're okay. Hope you find Cadie today. Please, please call me."

After Nick sent the message to Jake, he saw that he had several texts from Blake, one from Blake's uncle, two from Dirk and one from Layne. He left the bathroom and began slowly walking down the high school hallway, oblivious to the noisy students all around him, and began reading the most recent text from Blake.

"Hey, it's me, your boy. Sooooo, are you coming out on the boat with us tomorrow? You'd better be! You know it's my B DAY!!! Uncle is getting us subs from Antonio's and a couple six packs. And, of course, the Glenlivet! It's going to be outstanding! Oh yeah! He's also got two surprises for me. Do you know what they are? I have no idea. I'm also pretty sure Dirk and his dad are coming. I've texted Dirk a couple of times, but that guy never texts back. Anyway, text me, dude. Call me. I mean it! Text me."

Nick finished reading the text and just leaned against the wall outside the library. He was already exhausted and the day had hardly begun. He thought about Blake's exuberant texts. Such odd behavior.

*Not one word about Cadie. The girl he supposedly loved is missing. Maybe even dead. And nothing. Not a word. Just all about his birthday. I mean, honestly, what is wrong with this guy? Did he do something to her? Is he involved?*

Next, Nick read the text from Blake's uncle Robert.

"Hello, Nick. It's Robert Van der Velt. Just checking in to see if you are coming out with us on the boat tomorrow. I'm ordering food and need to know how much to order. I really hope you can make it. I've got a big surprise for Blake: I just found out he's getting a tennis scholarship to Western. But don't say anything. It's a surprise. Thank you. And please let me know about tomorrow. Take care."

Nick read Layne's text; it just had to do with a sweatshirt Nick had borrowed and never returned. Apparently, it was Layne's favorite UM sweatshirt, and he wanted it back before he moved to Rochester in a couple weeks.

The last text was from Dirk.

"Hey, I don't know if we're going to make it tomorrow. My dad got asked to give a talk at Central and wants me to go with him. I really don't want to, but he said we can go check out the Towers where I'll be living in the fall. My dad lived in the Towers and is always talking about all the partying he did and how he ended up in the ER after the *End of the World* party lol. I'll have to tell you that story sometime. Anyway, I just thought I'd give you the heads up. I'm almost afraid to text Blake lol. He can be such a pussy about things. He just keeps texting me! I'll text you in the morning to let you know for sure. See ya. D."

Nick slumped further down the brick wall.

*Oh great: me, Blake, and Robert on the boat. Hopefully, my dad can go. This just gets better and better.*

Nick decided to send a text to Detective Kitchen to see if he knew anything. Then Nick called his dad again. No answer. He tried to leave another message, but the voicemail was full.

"Shit," Nick muttered to himself. "What is going on?"

## CHAPTER 35

The note Marie found in Cadie's journal had Bakker rattled. The lines, "Don't be scared. It will all be over quickly" actually made her tremble. She didn't want to show her fear to Marie, so she hid her response the best she could while in the cottage, but now, sitting in her SUV in front of Marie's house, adrenaline coursed through her veins. Bakker couldn't stop shaking.

*I've got to get this note up to Dority ASAP. We are running out of time.*

She checked her phone. One voicemail from Craig but nothing from Jake. She sent the detective a text.

"Jake, how is it going? I haven't heard anything from you. Please call me. I'm heading up to the FBI office in TC. If I don't hear from you within the hour, I'm sending Dan and Rebecca up to the Kessler property, so reach out soon."

Then she listened to Craig's voicemail.

"Hey Sarge, I just wanted to update you as to what's going on. I made it to Koenig's cousin's apartment in South Corktown and talked to his cousin, Ricky Blazis. He said he hasn't seen his cousin since Christmas, but I didn't believe him. Guy was super nervous. I walked around the block, talking to the neighbors, and several said they saw a dark truck parked in the cousin's driveway Saturday and Sunday, but it was gone this morning. Rod's mother drives a truck. One neighbor who said he parties with Ricky from time to time mentioned that Ricky has a relative – an uncle John Keonig – who owns a liquor store by Eastern Market. His apartment is above the store. I got the address from a neighbor, and I'm headed there now. I'll let you know what I find out. Just driving past Campus Martius right now. Any good news about Cadie? I sure hope so. Let me know. I'll call you soon. Thanks."

Bakker was glad to hear from Dan. It's always concerning when your detective is tracking a bad guy. Anything can happen. When Bakker was a rookie, she had a partner who was shot by a sawed-off shotgun walking up to a perp's front door in Kalamazoo. Just got blasted by a seventy-year-old man from the side of the house with no warning. Fortunately, she suffered only minor wounds to her leg, but she could've been killed. Bakker knew that on this job any day could be your last.

*What is going on with Brennan? I have a bad feeling about this.*

She sent Detectives LaCroix and Zielinski a text.

"Hey, Brennan headed up to the Kessler property in Leland a couple of hours ago. I haven't heard from him. I just messaged him and said if I didn't hear from him within the hour, I was sending you two up there. So be ready. I'll let you know."

Bakker put her SUV in drive, drove out of the idyllic subdivision, and headed toward Traverse City. Soon the Dark Ash Silverado was speeding east then north on M-31 past numerous farms and orchards, her SUV traveling well over the speed limit. She quickly reached the popular tourist town Traverse City and Grandview Parkway that runs along the southern shore of East and West Grand Traverse Bay. She could've taken M-22 north and over, but she never liked the fact that she had to go south on 610 to Almira Road before she could north again. Going out of the way that little bit bugged her. She like forward momentum – always. Plus, in normal times, she loved the gorgeous view of the Bay's turquoise waters along Grandview.

Now heading west, she quickly reached the FBI office – or RA (Resident Agency as they call it) - on East Traverse City Highway. No one would guess an FBI office was located in that building, Bakker thought. From movies like *Mississippi Burning*, *Silence of the Lambs*, and *The Siege* to the TV show *The X Files* and various books, people have developed a perception that FBI agents and their offices are glamorous, exciting, and even dangerous.

However, Bakker knew the job of an FBI agent is mostly the unglamorous task of gathering intelligence. Yet, she did recall when some sixty agents swarmed a home in Suttons Bay several years ago. There also have been attacks on federal offices and buildings, even bombings, like the attack on the Federal Building in Oklahoma City. So, yeah, an FBI office has the potential to be a dangerous place.

This Traverse City office, tucked away in a large, brown, nondescript professional center encased in rows of glass windows looked more like an insurance office Bakker thought as she exited her SUV. Moving quickly through the building, the Sergeant located the FBI office and strode through the standing metal detector. Of course, the machine detected her Glock, among other items, so, under the watchful eye of the woman behind the glass, she backed out, put her Glock and other objects in the tray as well as her attaché case, and came back in. Once cleared, she entered the reception area and nodded to the FBI agent behind the bulletproof glass.

"I'm Special Agent Lisa Benedict. Can I help you?"

"Yeah, I'm Sergeant Dana Bakker from Harbor Cove. I have a meeting with Dave Dority."

Just then, the tall, slender Dority appeared behind the glass.

"Hey, Dana, good to see you. Wish it was better circumstances, though. Come on in."

Bakker walked past Dority into the brightly-lit hallway. He ushered her past the agency's impressive weapons vault of semi-automatic pistols, rifles, shotguns, tear gas guns, and submachine guns and its evidence lockers of cash, jewelry, drugs, and guns to his largely sterile office. One personal touch was a photo of Dave with his wife and kids at Disneyland on the black metal credenza behind his desk. The only other personal memento was a wood and gold plaque on the wall: "NCAA Patriot League Division I Basketball Champions."

Bakker was thankful Dority was assisting. From past cases, she found him extremely intelligent and dedicated. She knew only three percent of applicants are accepted into the FBI Academy. She also knew Dority was a Naval Academy grad and a trained behavioral analysis expert. The 6' 6" basketball standout played for the Navy Midshipmen in Annapolis had helped the team win its league. He was driven in everything he did. Bakker had asked around and learned that the Special Agent worked two child abductions in his career, both with successful outcomes. She hoped his expertise and experience could help bring Cadie home.

"Dana, please take a seat." Dority said, "and we can get to it."

Bakker was more than happy to sink into the comfortable leather chair for a minute. The lack of sleep and recent adrenaline dump was getting to her, but she fought to remain sharp. Cadie McLeod needed everyone to be in top form.

"First, in your text you mentioned wanting a profile," Dority said, moving papers on his desk. "As you probably know, the majority of abductions are by parents. Of course, Cadie's parents are deceased. After that, the abductor is usually someone known to the child, or in this case, young adult. Also, research shows most kidnappers are Caucasian males between the ages of 30-59. And perps with numerous child crimes will typically be under 30. So, most likely, we either have a white kidnapper under 30 who was at the party and has a history of sex crimes – like Rod Koenig - or someone over 30 that targeted Cadie for sex purposes or some other reason. The good news is most people who kidnap for sex don't kill their victims. The bad news is that if Cadie was kidnapped for some other reason, the statistic is higher."

"Like what other reason?" Bakker asked.

"Hatred of women, resentment, power, dominance, control, revenge, dangerous incels. These are more likely to result in death – the ultimate control."

"Yeah, that's not what I wanted to hear," Bakker said, shifting uncomfortably in the comfortable chair.

"Most likely, Cadie was abducted by someone she knew and possibly someone who was at the party and left early. It could be a rando, but it seems unlikely that someone just happened to be on a deserted trail not known to the general public at midnight."

"I agree," Bakker said. "And to me it seemed planned. No one at the party heard Cadie yell out. So, it seems the suspect immobilized her almost immediately, which usually requires some planning, and Cadie was – I mean is - a strong girl – a top athlete. How did her abductor overpower her so quickly and easily? Also, Cadie was the only student at the party to ride a bike, which she often did, and that isolated trail leads directly to the bike rack, so it would seem someone knew Cadie's routine and waited on the trail for her."

Dority turned his chair to his computer and pulled up an email.

"So, let's talk about your videos. I sent them to the FBI Lab, and here is what they reported," Dority said, reviewing the Lab's pdf.

"Regarding the cell phone video, the Lab created a still photograph and conducted digital image modification. They were able to enhance the hat the possible suspect was wearing. It seems there's an image – maybe a small logo toward the top center of the hat with letters underneath the image."

"Yeah, we already knew that from the MSP techs," Bakker said, hoping that the FBI Lab was going to do more than provide information she already had.

"Okay, well, our Lab techs are still working on modifying the still. The report does indicate there appears to be three or four letters. The good news is they were able to determine two of the letters. They are a lowercase d and r. They'll let us know if they are able to enhance the other letters further."

Bakker cut in.

"Does the report say in what order in the three or four letters the letter d appears?"

"No, it doesn't. I'll email back to get an answer on that."

Bakker was dismayed that information wasn't included in the report.

"With regards to the footage collected by Detective LaCroix, just to review, Rebecca obtained footage from the BP gas station near Hill Valley Drive and the streetlight camera at Seneca Boulevard and Hill Valley Circle. Also, one neighbor two doors down from Marie McLeod had an Arlo front door camera that records 24/7, so it seems to have captured the truck in question on three different occasions. The other neighbor with a Ring camera installed a Ring Alarm sensor, so it also recorded 24/7; however, the lighting is insufficient in front of that home, so the infrared night vision was not able to capture a viable image of the truck."

Bakker sat up straighter.

"But one neighbor's camera did capture the truck?"

"Yes, it did. Unfortunately, the truck was blacked out."

"Blacked out?"

"Also known as a Chrome Delete. Some men – usually young men – like the look of a blacked-out truck. They replace the chrome or shiny exterior elements on their trucks with black. So, owners might black out emblems, grills, headlights and brake light rings, even window trim and badges. The goal is to make the truck completely black."

"Okay, so how it that a problem?" Bakker asked.

"Well, it just makes our job harder," Dority replied. "In looking at the Arlo footage and the footage from the gas station and street camera, it's hard to discern what type of truck it is. At this point, it could be a mid-sized Ford Ranger, Chevy Colorado, or GMC Canyon. These compact pickups are similar. It's just going to take our techs more time and effort to determine the exact model. On the other hand, you know you're looking for a blacked-out truck of some sort. Unfortunately, a lot of the young guys are into doing this to their trucks."

"We don't have a lot of time, Dave," Bakker said. "I know you know that."

"I'm really sorry, Dana, but our people are doing everything they can as quickly as they can. Unfortunately, the FBI Lab is working 35 cases right now. They're all serious, or they wouldn't rise to the level of needing the Lab's expertise. But trust me, my people are dedicated to providing as much intelligence as they can. I'll keep in constant contact with them and let you know as soon I get more information."

"Thanks, Dave. I hope I don't sound ungrateful. I know your people are working hard. I'm just really worried we are running out of time."

"It would be extremely helpful if you could get us the make and model of every vehicle driven by your suspects. And photos of their vehicles. As soon as you can."

"I will definitely do that. I'll text Debbie before I leave. With social media, we should be able to obtain photos. My ex has a two-seater MG, and he posted more photos of that sports car than he ever did of us."

"That rings true," Dority laughed.

"So, I have something else for you," Bakker said, reaching down into her attaché case.

Dority was surprised. He didn't realize Bakker had brought new material for analysis. He leaned forward, curious.

"What is it?"

Bakker removed the two evidence bags containing the journal and note and placed the bags on the desk in front of Dority.

"Cadie's Aunt Marie found a journal Cadie was keeping. It was hidden under her mattress. When Marie opened the journal, a note fell out."

"Okay. This might be helpful."

"It's scary is what it is. Cadie references the note in her journal. She wrote that she found the note in her aunt's mailbox. She thought it might have something to do with the truck, but she never told Marie. Cadie didn't want to upset her."

Out of his desk drawer, Dority removed sterile gloves and put them on. Then he carefully slid out the journal and the note. He opened the note on its evidence bag. Like Bakker did at Marie's house, Dority read the note out loud:

"It's almost time. I've waited for this moment for quite a while, and now it's almost here. So, I'll see you soon. And don't be scared. It will all be over quickly."

Suddenly, the seasoned professional who was always calm and cool seemed agitated. His eyes squinted, and his mouth set in a hard line. Special Agent Dority looked up from the note and stared at Bakker.

"This is not good. Not good at all."

## CHAPTER 36

Detective Jake Brennan slowly eased his Tahoe up the long dirt driveway, rocks crunching under his high-performance tires while his eyes scanned the dairy farm for any sight of Karl and Richard Kessler. Jake had to assume both men were dangerous. Karl was a convicted sex offender who did not want to go back to prison, possibly for life, and Richard was a sibling possibly protecting his brother. However, Richard owned a profitable business, so it was hard to gauge how much he was willing to risk for his wayward brother.

Jake pulled up in front of the oversized garage surrounded by high weeds. The large door was open, and Jake could see a front loader, tanker truck, manure spreader, and golf cart. A variety of old, rusty tools hung on the wall. Over the garage door was a long weathered, wooden sign that looked like it was hand painted with the same red paint as the mailbox: "Kessler's Crooked Creek Dairy."

Jake looked out both sides of his windows, continuing to scan the ageing farm for any sign of the brothers. Stepping out of his vehicle, Jake could hear the pronounced rustling of wind as it blew unfettered across miles of open farmland. In the distance, he could hear cows mooing and bellowing in their barn. Jake knew from studying Richard Kessler's website, which contained a map of the 1,000-acre farm, that the property contained several buildings: the farmhouse, a tractor garage/pole barn, a two-row steel dairy barn for some 300 cows, a milking parlor, small calving barn, and a silo for feed storage with Crooked Creek running along the north and east sides of the property.

Jake walked up the broken, uneven brick pavers and onto the sagging front porch with crooked railings and chipping gray paint. Still no movement anywhere. In the corner of the porch, he saw a fat Calico cat sleeping lazily on some dirty, wadded fabric. It opened one eye and regarded Jake warily. The detective walked up to the door. With his right hand resting on his Glock, he knocked decisively with his left hand on the wood surrounding the ripped screen.

"Hello, this is Detective Jake Brennan from the Harbor Cove Police Department. I'd like to speak to Karl Kessler."

He waited a minute. No answer.

Jake knocked again and repeated his announcement. Still, no reply, and no one answered the door. Jake walked over to the cloudy window with yellowish lace curtains and peered inside. He was looking into a filthy 1950s era kitchen with a red metal table and chairs and white metal cabinets. Empty beer bottles littered the room. Jake's eyes searched, taking it all in. Then they landed on the counter by a vintage toaster. There he noticed a tiny plume of smoke wafting up from a cigarette hanging just off the edge.

*Oh, they're home alright.*

He pulled back from the window slightly and continued to look around the kitchen. He could see through to the living room, but there was no activity, just an old brown couch. Jake walked off the porch and took a few steps back, scanning the upstairs of the gray, two-story house. For a moment, he thought he saw a curtain move in one of the windows, but he couldn't be sure.

He yelled out again.

"It's Jake Brennan from the Harbor Cove Police Department. I'm here to talk to Karl Kessler."

Just then, he heard a door shut on the backside of the house. The detective walked quickly to his right, onto the sparse grass underneath a large, overhanging willow tree, and began inching his way around the east side of the house with the cat hissing at him as he passed by. Jake walked quietly along the full row of tall yellow Lillies that bordered the old farmhouse until he came to the back corner. He stopped and slowly leaned forward, peering around the back of the house. He didn't see either man, but he thought he could hear low talking, perhaps on the other side of the calving barn some 70 feet away. He gradually came out from the side of the house. As he stepped into the sunlight, onto the small grass patio with rusty lawn chairs, a loud shotgun blast split the air.

CRACK!

"Oh crap," Jake shouted, throwing himself face first into the dirt. He quickly crab crawled over to a towering maple tree and positioned himself behind it, covered in dust, ears ringing. He could smell the gunfire's acrid, sour aroma like burnt caramel.

"Karl, Richard, it's Detective Jake Brennan," he yelled out. "It doesn't have to go this way. I'm just here to talk. I just want to ask Karl some questions. That's all. No one has to get hurt."

He could hear the men talking low.

CRACK!

Jake's ears were again assaulted by another explosion of powder as the pellet blasted out of the barrel and whizzed inches by the tree. He heard the high-pitched whoosh and immediately yanked back his head and tightened his body behind the maple, trying to make himself as skinny as humanly possible.

*The fight is on.*

"Richard," Jake yelled out, "do you really want to get involved in this? There's no reason you should go down with your brother. Just tell me where Cadie is."

Karl screamed back, "Shut up, mother fucker!"

"Karl," Jake answered back, "listen, I'm not here to take you in. I just want to talk. Maybe you just need your meds. I can help you. Just tell me where she is."

The detective tried to peer around the tree to get eyes on Karl.

"I'm not going back in. There's no way you're taking me in. You're gonna have to kill me first."

"No one is killing anyone, Karl."

"Well, I'm fucking killing you!"

Another loud shot rang out, and the pellet hit the trunk of tree right behind Jake's head, ricocheting off and hitting the picture window at the back of the farmhouse. A loud crack burst forth, and the large plate glass window instantly shattered, creating massive shards and shooting glass particles of every size and shape all over the patio.

"Fuck, Karl, you're gonna ruin my house," Richard yelled at his brother. "Do you know how much it's gonna cost to replace that? Jesus!"

"Shut up! Just shut up!" Karl yelled at his brother as he ran from this spot next to the calving barn toward the back of the property. Jake could hear the second man running after him.

Now it was quiet. Jake's ears were still ringing, and salty sweat dripped into his eyes, burning them. He wiped it away with his issued blue shirt sleeve. The shirt was soaked, and his heart beat profusely. Jake pulled out his cell phone to call for backup, but there was no signal. He tried to send a text, but the phone said it wasn't delivered.

"Fuck," Jake muttered.

He put his phone back in his pocket and reached down and removed his Glock from his holster, holding it at his side pointed down, his trigger finger outside the guard. Then, getting as low as possible, he ran over to the small calving barn where Karl had just tried to kill him minutes ago. He listened for the men's voices, for any sound. He noticed the wind picking up, and he hoped that would work in his favor, carrying their voices his way. He continued to stand still, listening for any tiny sound.

Then he heard it.

It sounded like someone crying out for help.

*Cadie!*

Jake moved quickly around the calving barn and surveyed the open land between himself and where the voice was coming from. A third of the way was a truck parked next to a tractor.

*I need to make it to that truck!*

The detective took off at a dead run, expecting to be shot any moment, but he reached the safety of the truck without incident. He crouched down behind the back of it, his eyes darting, scanning the area in every direction. All he saw was farmland and the long metal dairy barn some 30 feet away. The two men were nowhere to be seen.

*What if they're doing something to Cadie right now? Killing her before I can find her? Where are those two bastards?*

Then he heard the noise again.

*Is that a female voice? Is that Cadie? It sounds strange.*

He didn't know if the men were trying to trick him, pretending to be a woman to draw him out. Yet, if Cadie was in danger, he'd have to take that chance.

"Help me! Help me!"

Jake could hear the voice faintly coming from the other side of the steel dairy barn. It was hard to hear over the sounds being made by the cows. He ran to the barn and tried to move quickly but stealthily along the side of the long, white building, his Glock still out and pointed downward while he listened for the voice. Then he heard it again, off in the distance.

"Please, help me. Please!"

Across an open area of high, unmowed grass, Jake spotted a shovel leaning against a tree. Further away, he noticed a fence with a wooden door that was open.

*What the hell? What is that?*

Looking around constantly for the two men, Jake left the safety of the side of the barn, and, keeping low, his hand still clutching his Glock, ran across the grassy area toward the voice and up to the opening in the fence.

Immediately, he realized his mistake.

Actually, before his brain registered what it was, his nose did. Before him was a pit of animal waste for field fertilizer. Within seconds, he began to grow fuzzy from the toxic combination of methane, hydrogen sulfide, carbon dioxide, and ammonia. As he became disoriented, his hand opened, and he dropped his Glock in the grass. He tried in vain to focus.

Suddenly, Karl Kessler came out from behind a thick oak tree. Jake recognized his greasy ponytail and the red and black satanic tattoos covering both arms. The convicted pedophile ran full speed at Jake with a clear plan to push him through the opening in the fence and down the concrete retaining wall into the manure pit below.

Jake knew that was certain death. Everyone in Michigan can recall a story in which a farmer suffocated in his own liquid waste pit.

Karl ran hard at Jake to push him like a football tackling dummy through the opening and down into the putrid slime. But Karl didn't know something. What he didn't know was that Jake was a First Team running back in the Northwest Conference and had devoted hours of his youth to perfecting the spin move. As Karl ran up to Jake, Jake instinctively reacted to his direction, stepping into it with his hips, shoulders, and eyes turning at the same time as Karl's. As Jake's body began rotating, it brought Karl's body along with it. Not only was Karl not able to grab onto Jake, but his forward momentum, as Jake spun with him and then pushed him off, launched Karl through the fence's opening. Both men were operating on extreme adrenaline, and the more they sucked air, the more toxic fumes they inhaled.

Karl, now close to the pit's edge, became dizzy and disoriented. He took a few wobbly steps and began to fall backwards. He flailed his arms, his eyes wide with terror. They met Jake's for a fleeting moment. Then a second later, he was gone – screaming as he plunged 12 feet down the embankment and landing in the small pond of foul liquid animal waste.

Richard, who was watching from behind the trees, saw his brother tumble into the pit and came running full speed. Jake, who had fallen on his knees, was now laying on the ground just outside the opening, trying to stay conscious and roll himself away from the pit as much as he could. He was too disoriented and weak to get up. Richard ran madly up to the fence, through the opening, and without thinking, quickly scrambled down the side of the pit to save his brother. He, too, was immediately overcome with the poisonous fumes and passed out.

In three breaths, both men were dead.

Jake lay on the ground nearby, still trying to roll himself further away from the pit as the poisonous gases attempted to displace all the oxygen in his brain. He was able to formulate two final thoughts before he fell unconscious.

*I'm sorry, Cadie, that I couldn't save you. I'm sorry, son, that I didn't get to see you graduate; I'm sorry for everything.*

Then he was out.

# CHAPTER 37

Another hour passed, and still no one had heard from Detective Jake Brennan. No texts, no phone calls, no emails. Nothing. Detectives Rebecca LaCroix and Dan Zielinski raced north on M-22, passing cars and reaching speeds of 80 mph when no traffic was present. Unfortunately, as they approached Leland, a slow-moving combine caused the northbound lane to seize, so after waiting ten minutes for the oncoming traffic to clear, the detectives briefly turned on their blue light bar and drove around the line of cars. They then drove alongside the pristine Lake Leelanau until they reached North Eagle Highway and turned right. After a few miles, they turned east, and the Silverado picked up speed heading east on 626 or East Kolarik Road.

They soon passed the Gothic Revival St. Wenceslaus Catholic Church on their left. As they did, Zielinski, a devout Catholic and amateur historian, was reminded of the Czech Wenceslaus who was murdered by his young brother Boleslaus the Cruel. The story brought forth in Zielinski's mind the parallel to Richard Kessler being tormented endlessly by his younger brother Karl, a confirmed pedophile. Both older brothers, through no fault of their own, spent their lives grappling with challenging siblings. Finally, the Silverado reached the dead-end road Korbel Corners and continued east on the dirt road for a half mile.

"I don't have a good feeling about this," Detective Zielinski said, his hands gripping the wheel with his torso leaned forward. "It's not like Brennan to not stay in contact."

"I'm feeling the same way," LaCroix answered. "I think we're going to have our hands full today."

Minutes later, the detectives spotted the rotted mailbox, and the Silverado drove onto the quiet Kessler property. Adrenaline flowed through the detectives' veins as their fight or flight responses kicked in. A feeling of strength coursed through them as they stepped out of the vehicle. Instinctively, each touched their Glocks, readying for a fight.

They made their way to the front porch, stepping onto the sagging wood and knocking on the door. A cat was sleeping in the corner. After announcing themselves several times and getting no answer, the detectives left the porch and walked west. They could hear cows bellowing in the distance as they entered the cavernous garage, inspecting the vehicles and searching for Brennan and the Kesslers. Not finding anything, they left the structure and turned west and north, walking alongside the oversized garage until they came to the metal calving barn. They tread softy along the open-faced, 50-foot building that smelled like aged oak and rotten eggs, scanning the pens as they walked. There was nothing but old water and smelly bedding.

The dairy barn was nearby, and LaCroix and Zielinski could hear the cows snorting and mooing. They made their way over as a gust of wind swirled grass pollen up into the air, causing LaCroix to cough. Upon opening the barn door - despite the ventilation system and tip-in windows - the two gagged on the stench of decomposing manure and spoiled feed. Large fans spun lazily overhead to keep the cows cool, but they also spread the pungent smell throughout. Up ahead were two rows of 150 noisy, black and white Holsteins that were either sleeping, lounging in wood chips and sand, or munching on feed from their concrete troughs. The detectives walked the length of the barn covering their noses, sidestepping cow manure, and looking for anything amiss. At the end of the barn was a cluttered office, but again, no sign of Brennan or the Kesslers.

"I don't think I can take much more," Zielinski said, his hand covering his mouth and nose. "I don't know how these farmers do it."

"You get used to it," LaCroix answered. "Growing up in the Thumb, my neighbors were farmers. We smelled cow shit 24/7, but strangely we just learned to deal with it. If I'm honest, I even kinda like it."

"Now that's just gross," Zielinski said, the city boy from Detroit's Poletown shaking his head. Just as he was finishing his sentence, a 1500-pound Holstein let loose an enormous bellow that made Zielinski jump.

"Let's get out of here," he said, opening the door.

As they exited the north end of the long barn, they stood on the concrete pad and surveyed the rest of the property. All around, they observed rolling hills of farmland, a silo, and a grove of oak trees to the north west. South and slightly west of the trees was some sort of fenced-in area.

"What do you think that is?" Zielinski asked, pointing to the fence. Both detectives studied it, trying to determine what was fenced in. From a distance, it seemed to be a fence surrounding nothing. They began walking toward it.

"What's that blue thing laying on the ground? Zielinski asked, pointing up ahead.

Since Brennan was laying down with his head pointed toward them, from a distance all they could make out were two splotches of blue fabric on his shoulders. LaCroix was the first to figure it out.

"Oh my god! It's Brennan!"

The fit young detective took off at a dead run and sprinted across the grass with Zielinski in close pursuit until they reached the unconscious Brennan laying in the overgrown grass. LaCroix immediately knelt down and tilted back Brennan's head and looked and listened for breathing. Brennan was alive. She tried to roll Brennan's body on its side, but the tall man was too heavy, so Zielinski got down on both knees, and the two detectives rolled Brennan, so he wouldn't vomit and choke. Then Zielinski jumped up, grabbed his cell, and attempted to call 911. Immediately, both detectives began inhaling the toxic fumes.

"There's no service," he yelled. "I'm getting nothing," he sputtered, coughing.

"We've got to get out of here," LaCroix yelled back. "We're going to have to put him in our truck."

Zielinski jumped up and ran to the Silverado, while LaCroix moved away from the pit. Within minutes, the Silverado drove around the side of the garage and was tearing over the property until it screeched to a stop in front of Brennan. Zielinski jumped out and put his arms underneath the unconscious detective. LaCroix ran back over and grabbed his feet, and the two of them dragged the man to the truck and hoisted him in the back seat. The two detectives, gasping for air, jumped in the car, and Zielinski began to drive, when LaCroix yelled, "Stop!"

"Stop? Why?"

LaCroix grabbed a jacket, put it over her nose and mouth, and jumped out of the truck. Thankful the wind was now blowing northwest, she raced through the yard and into the gate to the edge of the pit and looked down. Immediately, she felt the effects of the poisonous gases; her eyes watered and burned. She then turned and was running back to the truck when she saw Brennan's Glock laying in the grass. She grabbed it and took off for the truck.

"What the hell was that about?" Zielinski yelled – exasperated – chomping at the bit to drive the hell out of there.

"The Kesslers," she said. "They're dead."

"What? How?"

"They asphyxiated in the manure pit. They're laying at the bottom, dead."

"What are you talking about," Zielinski spat out, sweating and maneuvering the speeding Silverado over the property and out onto Korbel Corners Road.

"The pit is full of toxic fumes. It kills within seconds," LaCroix responded, breathing heavily and wiping sweat off her face. "The pit killed them."

"Nothing wrong with that in my eyes," Zielinski answered testily, as the truck raced west. "Shit killed by shit."

"Except they may be the only people who know where Cadie is," Rebecca replied. Between heavy breaths, she said, "With them dead, Cadie might also be as good as dead."

## CHAPTER 38

After leaving school early, Nick lay on his bed, sun pouring through the tree outside his window and causing light to flicker throughout his room. He scoured his cell phone for any message from his dad or online news about his father or Cadie. Nick combed through his inbox, social media, and local news sites, but to no avail. He didn't know what else to do. No one had seen or heard from Jake Brennan since he left for Leland that morning. Nick called the police station and talked to Debbie several times, but she had no news to share.

While Nick searched his phone, he ignored the many texts from Blake Van der Velt. Finally, he read the text that told Nick to meet him at his boat at 10 am tomorrow. They were going to do some fishing and have lunch. Then, as Blake put it, "We're going to get SHITFACED!"

*Honestly, how are we supposed to celebrate a birthday and have fun when Cadie is missing? What is wrong with this guy?*

Nick was becoming increasingly worried about Blake and his odd demeanor. He placed his phone on the table beside his bed and lay back, closing his eyes for a moment. They were red and irritated and just needed a break. However, a minute after he laid his head down on the pillow to rest, his phone rang. Nick sat up immediately and grabbed it. He saw the call was from Detective Dan Zielinski.

"Hello?"

"Hi Nick, this is Detective Zielinski."

"Are you calling because something happened to my dad?"

"Your dad is okay, Nick, but he's at Munson Hospital in Traverse City."

"What? Why? Why is he in the hospital?" Nick cried out, jumping up and running out of his room. "What's wrong?"

"Do you know where Munson Hospital is? It's on Sixth Street in Traverse City. Can you head up here? Maybe get someone to drive you?"

"Yes," Nick answered, bewildered, "I'll head right up. But please tell me: Is he okay?"

"Yes, he is, Nick. Just get up here as fast as you can. I'll be waiting for you. Just come to Intensive Care."

"Intensive Care! Oh, god, that doesn't sound good!"

"Just be careful on the way up here, okay Nick? Try to get someone to drive you. I'll see you soon."

Nick grabbed the keys off the coffee table, tore through the kitchen, and ran out the side door toward his Jeep - the entire time praying Detective Zielinksi was being truthful and that his dad really was alive.

## CHAPTER 39

Jake Brennan was not dead but not out of the woods. After Detectives LaCroix and Zielinski met the ambulance at a restaurant parking lot on M-22 along west Traverse Bay, the EMTs immediately intubated Jake. Once he arrived at Munson Medical Center, a Trauma II Center and the largest hospital in the region out of nine Munson Healthcare system hospitals, the staff went straight to work. First, tests indicated his vital signs and arterial blood gas were within normal limits, but the trauma team moved him into intensive care to continue further resuscitation. Jake also showed no signs of being acidotic, his chest x-ray did not reveal pulmonary edema or hypoxemia, and there was no evidence of brain injury. He was no longer being intubated but was still sedated. Jake would not only survive but be okay. The winds shifting northwest saved his life.

In the blue, green, and gray waiting room down the hall from Jake's room, a group of law enforcement officials formed: Sergeant Bakker, Detectives Rebecca LaCroix, Dan Zielinski, and Brooke Field, Special Agent Dave Dority, and two local detectives who had worked cases with Brennan over the years. Detective Craig Kitchen was on his way up from Detroit. The northwest law enforcement community was tight knit and protective. As the men and women spoke in hushed tones, Nick Brennan was buzzed in, and he pushed through the wide, glass double doors looking distraught, his head twisting side to side as he searched for his father.

All eyes in the room turned in unison to look.

"Where's my dad?" Nick cried out, his red rimmed eyes scanning the people in the room. "Is he alive? Is Cadie alive?"

Dan rushed over and put his arm around Nick.

"Hey, hey, it's alright. Your dad is doing great. He's just down the hall sleeping. And no, we haven't found Cadie yet."

Nick buried his head in his hands and began crying.

Dan gently escorted the young man across the room to a chair by the window. He went to grab him a water bottle off a counter stocked with items, and on the counter was the Traverse City newspaper, *The Record Eagle*, with its headline, "Disappeared from the Dunes: Area Woman Missing." He turned the paper over so as not to agitate Nick further. As he did, Dan heard someone in the group nearby say quietly, "Has anyone called Laura? Jake's ex?"

"Where is she?" Rebecca asked. "Are they still married?"

"Down in Florida, I think. With Lou Carter. And yes, Jake and Laura are still married."

After a brief, quiet conversation, the consensus was that no one had Laura's cell number. Bakker said she would send Debbie a text when she got a minute.

Just then, the door buzzed again, and detective Craig Kitchen strode in. He walked over to the group sitting in a semi-circle in metal and plastic chairs. The group that was leaned in, talking quietly, sat up straight and looked over at him. Bakker stood up and walked a few steps to Craig.

"I sure am glad to see you," Bakker said, clearly relieved. "It's plenty hard having one man down. I didn't want it to be two."

"Oh, I'm fine, Sarge," Craig said, as the two walked over and stood by the group. "How's Jake?"

"Jake is going to be fine," Bakker said. "As you know, he was up at the Kessler farm and ran into trouble with those two assholes. Or should I say deceased assholes."

"Yeah, Dan filled me in," Craig said. "It's crazy. I didn't realize cow shit could kill you."

Despite the seriousness of the situation, the officers laughed. It really was surreal.

"So, now what? If Karl's our bad guy, how are we going to find Cadie?"

"I've got MSP on it. They've already got their K-9 unit on the property. Unfortunately, we found out the property is a lot larger than we thought. The farm map indicates about 1,000 acres. But Karl and Richard inherited their grandfather's property to the west and south behind the farm. So, it's a lot of land to cover. And a lot of hills, creeks, and trees. But the State Police is on it. The FBI is also sending agents over. How about you? How did it go down in Detroit with Koenig?"

"I wish I had better news."

"Fill us in," Bakker said, as she sat down, and Craig also took a seat.

"Well, as you know," Kitchen said, aware he was filling in the entire group, "I headed to Corktown this morning; Rod Koenig has a cousin down there. I spoke to the cousin, but he said he never saw Rod, that Rod was never there. I talked to several neighbors, though, and a few of them said they saw a truck parked in the cousin's driveway Saturday and Sunday. I think the truck belongs to Rod's mom. Anyway, one neighbor told me that Rod has an uncle who lives near Eastern Market and owns a party store. He knew the uncle's name and business because it appears on the sides of his business truck that is parked in his nephew's driveway sometimes. I looked up the address for the party store and headed over to east Detroit. I was able to meet with the uncle. Talked to him for a while. He's a decent guy."

"Did the uncle see Rod?" Bakker interrupted, already knowing most of this information from Craig's earlier message and wanting to get to the heart of the story more quickly.

"John, the uncle, said Rod did stop by his store. Rod was looking for a place to crash for a few days, but John told him he didn't want him staying with him. John has an apartment above his store."

"Why not?" Bakker asked.

"Well, the uncle has a friend in DPD, and he called him up. John said his nephew is always up to something. Anyway, the uncle's friend told him there was a warrant out for Rod for molesting little girls in Benzie County. So, in John's words, he told Rod to "fuck off and get the fuck out of here." Rod got pissed and knocked over some liquor bottles in John's store, but he left. Now here's the concerning part."

"What?" Bakker said, getting antsy from Craig's less than succinct delivery.

"Before Rod left, he was making a call in an aisle over, and his uncle listened in. John heard Rod say, "I'll be back soon. I've got some business to finish." Then he laughed and said, "Don't you just love revenge?" Anyway, I've got DPW looking for Rod, and they sent out a state-wide alert."

Nick got up and walked purposely over to the group.

"What does that mean? Revenge? Revenge on who? Revenge on Cadie?"

He looked at the detectives – waiting for an answer.

Dority stood up. "Nick, I'm Special Agent Dave Dority with the Traverse City FBI. I'm working with Sergeant Bakker on Cadie's case."

"Yeah, okay," Nick said, confused.

"Bakker and I met earlier today to discuss who might want to kidnap Cadie and their possible motivations. One obviously is for sex purposes."

Nick hung his head at that comment.

"Other motivations could be power, dominance, hatred of women, revenge – things like that. Do you know of anyone who was mad at Cadie? Anyone that would want to hurt her?"

Nick immediately thought of Blake. He wasn't sure he could bring himself to say something, though.

*Is my friend really capable of kidnapping Cadie? Of hurting her? Of even killing her?*

Nick didn't believe it.

"I already gave a full list of names to the Harbor Cove Police Department," Nick answered.

*I'm going out on that fucking boat tomorrow and getting answers. I'm getting to the bottom of this myself.*

Just then, an intensive care nurse walked into the waiting room.

"Hello, everyone, I'm RN Nichols. I want to give you the good news. Jake is awake and doing well. His vitals are good, and he has no brain injury. He's going to be fine."

Everyone stood up at once, smiles and pats on each other's backs all around.

"Can I see my dad?" Nick asked, quickly walking up to the nurse.

"Let's wait a little bit, okay? He's awake but still pretty out of it. I'll come back in a while and let you know."

Disappointed, Nick went and sat down by the window alone. Once the nurse had left, Bakker said, "Since we're all together, let's get updated on the case. I have some promising news to tell everyone. Nick, can you wait in the vending area for just a bit? The group of us need to talk privately."

Nick stood up.

"Cadie McLeod is my girlfriend. I love that girl with all my heart. I want – *I need* – to hear what's going on, especially something promising. I'm not leaving this room."

The detectives sat there quietly - stunned. No one realized that Nick and Cadie were together. This was definitely unknown information. The officials tried to quickly process the new information and how it impacted their perceptions of Nick. And Bakker remembered that someone at the party said Nick was yelling at Cadie Friday night. The Sergeant was torn. Yet, she went with her instincts. She really couldn't believe Nick was their bad guy.

"Uh, okay, Nick," Bakker said, finally speaking up. "But you cannot repeat anything you hear in this room. That is very important. Repeating any of this information could actually jeopardize the investigation and put Cadie's life at risk. Do you understand? You can't say anything."

"Of course I do. I'm the son of a cop."

Nick took a seat near the officials, and everyone drew near.

## CHAPTER 40

The imprisoned young woman struggled for hours at the end of the dark, dirty root cellar attempting to dislodge three large rocks and earn her freedom. As the day wore on, Cadie grew increasingly thirsty and tired but was able to break one rock free from the wall and kick it out the hole. The rock rolled down the grassy hill, and more sunlight entered the room. Cadie put her head to the hole and listened closely. She prayed her abductor was not on the property to hear her efforts and see a large rock rolling down a hill. But all she heard was the buzzing of cicadas.

After freeing the first of the three rocks, she rested for a while, careful not to sleep. She knew her body was in bad shape, her cells crying out for water as they shrank and began to malfunction. Her blood pressure was dropping, and she was becoming light-headed. She realized she was developing brain fog. The young woman was having more difficulty thinking clearly and focusing. Cadie stared at the remainder of the vinegar in a jar, possibly one fourth cup, and raised the small mason jar to her lips, drinking the sour liquid while the pungent smell made her gag. She had no choice.

Then she got back to work. Her idea of soaking strips of cloth in vinegar and working them into the mortar between the rocks had worked better than expected. But she also knew her strong legs played a part. Leaning back on both elbows earlier, for hours, she had used her bare feet to push on the rocks until her feet were blistered and bloody and her lower back growing raw. Her quads and calve muscles, starved for electrolytes, began to spasm and cramp. She knew she didn't have much time. Cadie picked up her stone and began banging on the second rock. She noticed it move slightly.

*That's more like it!*

The rock's movement gave Cadie a burst of hope and energy. The young woman continued banging on the rock that stood between her and freedom, pushing it back and forth with her hands and feet for the rest of the evening. Finally, as the sun set over Lake Michigan - with just a shred of red-gold light entering the cellar and cooler air traveling over Cadie's legs - the second rock broke free. However, Cadie was too exhausted to celebrate. She dragged herself back to the carpet, plopped down, and immediately slumped over and fell asleep.

In the distance, a car approached.

Cadie never heard a thing.

## CHAPTER 41
## The Weirdo

Tomorrow is the big day!

I peeked through the hole in the fieldstone wall, half expecting to see her dead. God, the smell coming out was awful. I have never liked sweat to begin with, especially on women, but the stink she created in that cellar was staggering. In only a few days. Did I say I despise sweat? I was honestly revulsed.

She just lay there, so very still. At first, I actually thought she might be dead. Just rotting away from lack of water. So, I wasn't sure at first. I had to watch her for a bit and really study her to see if she was breathing or not. But she was. I could see her chest rise up and down slightly. But where is her sundress? She was just laying there in only her dirty panties - like a whore. She does have long, shapely legs, though. I will give her that.

I'm feeling happier, if that's possible, and I find myself constantly humming, "Here's comes the sun." I'm enjoying the irony! And even though I am feeling good about everything – finally achieving my revenge – I sense that killing her will be the ultimate "living well" as in the saying, "Living well is the best revenge." I can only imagine how I'll feel once she's dead.

*Probably fucking ecstatic.*

I moved the kerosene heater and generator out of my truck and into the cellar's outer room. Everything is ready. Tomorrow night, I'll stop by and fire it up. Special thanks to my dad. He taught me everything I know about carbon monoxide and its ability to kill. May he rest in peace. Or not.

I'm so looking forward to tomorrow: It's the day I murder Cadie McLeod.

It's the day I gift myself.

## *TUESDAY*
### CHAPTER 42

Jake was released from Munson Hospital early Tuesday morning, so Nick drove his Jeep up to Traverse City and brought his dad home. Two TC detectives drove Jake's Tahoe from the Kessler property to his house in Harbor Cove, but Jake was told by his doctor not to drive for a day or two. The detective was still groggy – mostly from the sedatives the nurse said – but he was much better. Jake just needed to rest, but that was the last thing he wanted to do. Knowing that Cadie might be imprisoned, even hurt or dying on the Kessler property, tore him up. He believed he was so close to finding her. Nick told him what Bakker said, that the FBI and Michigan State Police with their dogs were searching the property. Right now, there was nothing Jake could do.

"Are you up for a coffee, dad?" Nick called out to his father from the kitchen. "I made a full pot, but I wasn't sure you'd be up to having some."

"Uh, do you even know me?" Jake laughed sleepily from the bedroom. "Of course I'll have a cup."

Nick poured the coffee, took a steaming cup into the bedroom, and placed it on the stand beside his dad's bed. Nick took a seat across from his dad in a floral wingback – a remnant of his mother's decorating style.

"I'm going out on the boat today with Blake and his uncle," Nick said carefully. "I wanted you to know that I'm doing this. I have to. I need answers."

"God, son, I'm still not sure this is a good idea," Jake said concerned, pushing himself to sit up. "How well do we really know Blake? I mean do *you* think he had any involvement with Cadie's disappearance? He hasn't been cleared as a suspect."

Nick didn't want to tell his father what Sergeant Bakker revealed at the hospital the night before or Jake might not let him go. He would find out soon enough.

"I don't think Blake is involved. Yeah, the dude can be weird. And he was really upset when Cadie dumped him, but it seems like he's moved on."

*I hope that's true.*

"Lots of dudes get dumped, but they don't kidnap their ex. I mean, you haven't kidnapped mom."

As soon as the words came out of his mouth, Nick regretted them.

"Yeah, okay. No, I haven't kidnapped your mom. But we're talking about Blake okay, and I'm serious."

"It'll be fine, dad. I'll have my phone with me, and I can text you if anything weird is going on. Plus, Blake's uncle will be there and maybe Dirk and his dad."

"Okay, but I'm also worried about that storm they're talking about. I got an alert on my phone a while ago that we might be in for a strong one. Where is Robert taking the boat? I don't want you guys going too far off shore in case this storm comes our way."

Jake knew a storm could whip up quickly, but it also could change course just as quickly and head to the UP instead of coming ashore. People along the west coast prepare for the worst but also make plans because, as often as not, it's blue skies and sunshine.

"I don't know. We might head over to the Manitou Islands."

"I wish you guys wouldn't even go that far," Jake said. "Just keep an eye out for a shelf cloud. News has it there's a powerful storm out west that might be coming our way. If it gets bad, head to Leland."

"I'll keep an eye out. And Blake's uncle won't keep us out if a storm comes. Plus, Blake said his new boat is fast."

"Yes, the Van der Velt money," Jake said somewhat cattily. "I also assume you guys will be drinking to celebrate Blake's birthday. Can you just promise not to drink too much? Stick to beer. Liquor and boating are not a good mix."

"I'll be fine, dad. Don't worry. And I don't care about drinking; I care about finding Cadie."

"Of course you do. I'm sorry I said that."

"Are *you* going to be okay?" Nick asked.

"Oh, sure. If I need anything, there's always Patty next door."

Nick went into the kitchen and finished packing his bookbag for the boat: a beach towel, a large water flask, a jacket, sunscreen, and a gift card he took from his mom's desk drawer for Blake.

"See you later, dad. I'll text you."

"Love you, son. Please be careful."

Nick walked out the house's side door and quickly ducked into the small wooden garage. He walked to the back of the garage and found Jake's red toolbox on his workbench. His dad's steel folding knife in a leather sheath was in the lower tray. Nick placed the knife in his bookbag. He had no idea what to expect when he confronted Blake today out on the boat, but he planned to be ready. The guy might truly be a sociopath. If so, anything could be possible.

After hearing his son's yellow Jeep leave the driveway, Jake felt incredibly tired. The events of the previous day were catching up with him. He could barely keep his eyes open. His brain ached. He decided he would grab a few minutes of sleep and then head to the police station. Nothing was going to keep him from finding Cadie McLeod.

## CHAPTER 43

As soon as Cadie awoke, she smelled the sharp, oily fumes. Alarmed, but at the same time tired and dehydrated, the young woman carefully stood up and shakily walked to the wall. She had noticed the peephole on day one and now peered through the opening to see what was going on in the exterior room with its tiny window. Her eye attempted to look around the outside room, but the hole would only allow a narrow width of vision. Suddenly, she spotted a hint of red. The smell permeating the room coupled with the partial image allowed her brain to recognize the item off to the side: a vintage metal gas can.

*Kerosene.*

"Oh god, no," she whispered.

Cadie stepped back. She could now more strongly smell the kerosene fumes working their way through the root cellar. And she knew.

*It's now or never.*

Cadie walked slowly to the back of the root cellar, holding on to the wall to steady herself so she wouldn't fall. She had sweated out most of her body's remaining fluids yesterday dislodging the two large rocks. Now she had one large rock to go. She hoped she had the strength to dislodge it. This was her last chance.

While she slept, she dreamed the two Great Horned Owls visited her again in the night. She saw their yellow eyes looking down at her from up above. Were the owls her parents, signifying they were there to help her break free from this dungeon? Or were they there to guide her somewhere else? Cadie wasn't sure she believed in an afterlife, but her scientific brain told her to stay open to what may be possible. However, her instinct to survive right now couldn't be diminished - not yet. She wasn't ready to die. She chose to fight.

Cadie sat down in front of the remaining rock – a large pudding stone from Lake Michigan - and studied her quartzite nemesis.

*It's you or me pal. What's it going to be?*

She laid down, her tangled red hair fanning out all around her, and stretched her long, athletic legs. She placed raw, blistered feet on the sizeable rock. It was smooth and cool to the touch. She began pushing on the rock. Her dehydrated calves were swollen, sore, and weak. She kept pushing, even when her legs began to spasm. What little sweat she had left beaded on her forehead.

She closed her eyes and pictured Thomas and Aileen. What did they want for her? Did they want her to survive this ordeal and live and thrive? To become a forensic scientist and solve their murder? To help other families obtain justice? To simply live a happy life? Or was it her time to let go? Did they want to bring her home to them, to keep her close and safe for all eternity? How could she know?

She continued to push, to move her feet around the rock. Finally, she mustered all her remaining strength and pushed as hard as she could.

Suddenly, the rock shifted!

"Oh my gosh!" Cadie screamed, her voice echoing through the stone cellar.

The movement gave her renewed energy. Cadie got on her knees, the cold dirt floor grinding into her kneecaps, and focused all of her body's might onto her two hands and left shoulder as she leaned into it, pushing the rock with everything she had left.

Suddenly, the rock broke free!

A loud CRACK blasted into the cellar and echoed off its dusty walls. Cadie felt the large stone surge forward as the dry mortar surrounding it crumbled. It dropped with a thud through the opening. Cadie almost hit her head on the rock above as the rock breaking free propelled her forward. She partially leaned into the opening and pushed the rock once more. It tumbled down the grassy hill.

The young woman sat there on the dark cellar floor for a second. Stunned. She had begun to believe she might die in this lonely tomb. Far away from Aunt Marie, far away from Nick Brennan, far away from everyone who loved and cared for her, and far away from her hopes and dreams.

"Goodbye, you stupid rock!" she yelled and cried simultaneously. "I win!"

Cadie shifted around and laid down on her back - moving her head into the hole. With her arms straight at her sides, she moved them backward and forwards, scooting her body by inches through the small opening. As she pushed through, she felt the sun discover her face. She couldn't stop smiling. Then she felt the cool grass on her neck, her shoulders, her back, and finally her upper legs.

She was through!

Placing one hand on the grass and weeds, she slowly pushed herself up to standing.

Freedom! It was the most beautiful feeling in the world.

Cadie stood there, wobbly on the uneven hill, and surveyed the spectacular view before her. She saw the High Rollways above the Manistee River, and the dense canopy of budding trees in most every direction. She smelled the fragrant Basswood trees. Their creamy yellow flowers dotted the landscape. Then she turned west and saw the storm clouds off in the distance, closing in rapidly, and felt the cooling wind. She wanted to cry, but she was too tired. She slowly and carefully made her way down the hill.

Now at the bottom, Cadie spied a narrow, winding dirt path reaching out in front of the cellar. She knew it was her path to freedom. She felt gloriously happy to be alive. She began walking, sometimes swaying from fatigue and lack of water, down the rolling path in front of the cellar. The path soon opened up into a larger, grassy area. She spotted a small, weathered wood barn up ahead to her left. A large padlock was clearly visible. Cadie reached the barn that was overgrown with tall weeds and began walking around it. The wind began to blow harder.

Then she spied it. A tarp covering a car.

*Surely, that car doesn't work. I could never be so lucky.*

However, Cadie felt that maybe her luck was turning.

With her biceps and triceps tight and depleted, Cadie tugged at the rotting fabric, moving around the dusty, blue car and pulling the tarp from several angles. Finally, she was able to remove all the filthy covering and pile it behind the car. She walked to the driver's side. Cadie noticed that the front left bumper was heavily damaged. In fact, as she looked closer, the entire front end was heavily damaged. Cadie even thought she could see dried blood, like the car had hit a deer. Maybe more than one.

*Oh, no. It's been in an accident. It will be a miracle if it works.*

Rain began to fall.

She opened the creaking door and got in the driver's seat. She noticed brown stains on the steering wheel. Of course, there was no key in the ignition. She looked over the dusty bench seats and saw another stain but no key. She looked all over the floor mats covered in dead flies and lifted them up and looked under them. Nothing. Then she placed her hand under her seat and began feeling around the scratchy rug. Her hand landed on a variety of unknown objects. Suddenly, it touched metal.

There it was!

Her hand grasped the set of car keys and yanked them up.

*If this car doesn't work, I might just die sitting here naked in my underwear.*

Cadie put the key in the ignition, and, praying beyond hope, turned the key.

It started.

"Oh, yes!" she yelled out. "Oh my god, yes!"

Cadie began to laugh hysterically and that turned into sobbing, her chest heaving and her eyes trying to form tears from her dehydrated body. Overcome with emotion, she put the car in drive and began to ease it around the side of the barn. Then she had a thought and stopped.

Cadie leaned over and opened the glovebox. There were some papers, and she pulled them out. On top was the registration. Cadie looked at the name on the document. She blinked. She leaned in and looked at the name again more closely. Cadie stared at the name for a solid minute, trying to process what she was seeing, then set the registration down on the stained seat.

*I can't believe he kidnapped me. And planned to kill me! Why? Why would he do this?*

Minutes later, as she fought to stay alert, she was driving across the large grassy property to an old dirt road. She turned right and headed west toward Harbor Cove. Her destination was its police station and Jake Brennan. She pushed down hard on the gas and began racing down that gravel road toward freedom and the rest of her life.

## CHAPTER 44

Nick pulled his Jeep into Van der Velt marina, which was coming to life with activity. The cheerful morning sun cast a happy glow over the sea of picturesque sailboats bobbing gently in Harbor Cove. The serene, aqua blue water glistened, and Nick observed several slender young men in blue marina tee-shirts and beige khakis completing various tasks on the docks sprawled out in front of him.

He drove to the back corner of the parking lot, behind large oak trees, in an attempt to isolate his Jeep and keep it from being banged into by people who didn't know how to park. As he rounded the tree, he was surprised to see Blake's truck parked there as well. Blake never parked there. He enjoyed his privilege too much and always parked in the spots reserved for his uncle. Nick grabbed the camo green bookbag off the front seat and exited his vehicle, uncomfortably conscious of the knife tucked in the interior side pocket.

He walked over to Blake's truck, remembering what Sergeant Bakker told him the day before.

"The FBI said the truck that's been driving past Cadie's house late at night is blacked out. All its chrome and identifying elements are completely covered black."

Nick looked at the blacked-out truck before him. He remembered when Blake told him he planned to do it. Nick said he thought it was a dumb idea, something that young men did to seem cool, but Blake went ahead and blacked out the truck anyway. Now Nick was approaching a truck similar to the one in a video at an FBI lab. He could recall only a few other blacked out trucks in Harbor Cove. He walked up to the Chevy Colorado's driver's side door and peered in the window. There was nothing too interesting, but then his eye caught on something around the rearview mirror.

*What is that?*

Nick studied it for a moment. Then it came to him.

*Is that a zip tie?*

Nick felt a wave of cold pass through him.

*Why is there a zip tie around the mirror?*

He began to sweat, and his anxiety multiplied.

As he walked away from the truck, he also remembered all that he had heard yesterday. Special Agent Dority told the group that the FBI further enhanced an image of a hat taken from Cadie's cell phone the night she disappeared, and the hat appeared to have three lowercase letters, two of which seemed to be "r" and "d." Nick didn't say anything to the group, but his mind immediately went to "der." Nick knew people in Harbor Cove with "der" as part of their last name; many people of Dutch descent live on the west coast of Michigan. However, there was only one person with "der" in his last name – Blake Van der Velt - who had professed to love Cadie McLeod and claimed to be heartbroken when she dumped him and who now seemed completely carefree. Oh, and who drove a blacked-out truck.

Nick adjusted the bookbag, pulling it closer to him, and made his way to the front of the marina. He walked onto the wooden planks and under the large green and teal welcome sign with its smiley-faced sun and seagull that stretched over the entrance.

"Dude, you made it!"

Blake Van der Velt walked briskly toward him wearing his signature aviator Ray Bans, tan Sperry boat shoes, and light blue J. Crew swim trunks. He had a blue and yellow Oberon already open in his hand. In that moment, Blake reminded Nick of Tom Cruise in *Risky Business*.

"Happy birthday, buddy," Nick said, leaning in to give Blake a half hug. "Looks like it's going to be a great day."

Nick looked up at the innocent, white puffy clouds, but saw something darker farther out. He knew his dad had mentioned a possible storm, but Robert's million-dollar Pursuit could go 50 mph. He felt confident they could outrun any storm and make it to shore safely.

"Oh yeah, it's going be an awesome day," Blake said, grinning broadly. "I'm really glad you could make it. I guess Dirk and his dad aren't coming. Luuk had to go to Central and dragged Dirk along with him. But no worries. We're going to have a blast. Now let's get you a beer."

The two young men walked down several docks until they reached the mini-yacht, Robert Van der Velt's new offshore cabin cruiser named *Best Revenge*. They entered the massive, gleaming boat from the stern, stepping alongside the bulwark onto the narrow passageway next to three Yamaha V8 motors and four long trolling rods with silver reels and brightly colored mono line. Blake walked over to the white built-in cooler and dug his always tanned arm into the ice until he pulled out a cold Oberon and handed it to Nick.

"Man, this is a fantastic boat," Nick said, admiring the impressive, 46-foot fiberglass, white and light blue cruiser. He knew that Robert Van der Velt, who had inherited the marina from his grandfather years ago, was wealthy, but this boat was something else.

"Oh yeah, it's got everything," Blake said. "It's got a galley for cooking, berth for sleeping, and a sic sound system. The bridge deck is so sweet. I'll show it to you."

Nick opened his beer and took a drink, still holding his bookbag firmly over his shoulder. The two young men walked past the livewell, a 75-gallon fishbox, and a white vinyl couch to their left and stepped up and through the aft's large glass door onto the bridge deck. The nine-foot-high windshield and tall side windows allowed the bridge to be awash in bright sunlight. Robert Van der Velt was sitting in the white and gray helm seat, his back to the young men. He was checking to see that the steering, throttle, and electrical system were operating properly. He heard the young men enter the bridge and rotated his seat.

"Hey, Nick, good morning," Robert said, putting out a tan, weathered hand for a handshake.

"Good morning, Mr. Van der Velt," Nick said politely, shaking his hand.

"It's Robert. Haven't I told you that before?" Robert laughed. "Mr. Van der Velt makes me feel like my grandfather. So, how do you like my new boat?"

"Oh, man, it's awesome," Nick said. "Thanks so much for having me out on it. Blake says it can go 50 mph and planes almost immediately."

"Yeah, that's right. It can hit 20 mph in 14 seconds."

"Wow, that's amazing. So, I have a question for you. Why is it named *Best Revenge*?"

Robert smiled. "When I was trying to come up with a name, Blake mentioned an old saying of his dad's – my brother – that 'Living well is the best revenge.'"

"Oh, I get it," Nick laughed. "Well, it's too bad Dirk and Luuk couldn't make it. This is an awesome boat."

"They choose not to come," Blake said, an angry look passing over his face like a fast-moving storm cloud. Then it was gone – quickly replaced by his perfect white smile.

"Well, okay, then. Looks like it's just us. Why doesn't someone get me a water, and we'll get going. We've got a birthday to celebrate," Robert smiled.

"Oh sure." Nick walked down the step to the cooler and dug a bottle of water out of the ice. Robert and Blake followed him onto the stern as they began to ready the cruiser for departure. Robert had turned on the blowers, and now he and Blake began removing the synthetic lines that moored the boat to the dock. Once the boat was ready to leave, Robert returned to the bridge with its panoramic views of the marina and began easing the large cruiser out of its slip. Minutes later, the boat was cutting through the placid waters of Harbor Cove on its way out to the mighty Lake Michigan.

"Let's go hang out on the cabana," Blake said, leading Nick alongside the bulwark to the foredeck where there were two built-in lounge chairs with headrests.

"Hey, Robert, can you put on some tunes? I hooked up my phone."

Minutes later, the two seemingly lucky men lounged on the foredeck, sipping cold beer, warm sun on their faces and bodies, while the lengthy cruiser smoothly passed through the narrow channel and out into the 321-mile-long and 118-mile-wide Great Lake.

As the cruiser cleared the channel and transitioned into the large, dark Lake Michigan waters, the boat began to pitch slightly. Nick's mind turned to his plans. What exactly was he going to say to his friend? When would he say it? And how would Blake react? Nick had witnessed Blake's temper before. So had Cadie. Nick looked over at his bookbag that was lying to his left next to the bulwark. Suddenly, a strong gust of wind blew into his face. As Robert turned the boat northwest toward the Manitou Islands, Nick looked toward the horizon and thought he could see, off in the distance, the dark clouds coming closer.

"Hey, let me get you another beer," Blake said.

"I haven't finished this one."

"Jesus, pound it already."

Blake got up and walked to the boat's stern. Nick took his cell phone out of bookbag and saw he didn't have service.

*I hope I can reach Jake if I need to.*

Blake brought back two fresh beers and took a seat, laying back.

"So where exactly are we going?" Nick asked.

"Robert's taking us to north Manitou Island. Fishing there is good for Lake Trout and Salmon. We'll probably anchor offshore on the north side. There's a drop off, and we can anchor on the edge."

"Oh, that's cool," Nick said, watching his friend quickly put away another beer.

"We need to break out the Glenlivet," Blake laughed. "It's my birthday for crissakes. Robert, can we open the Glenlivet?" he yelled over his shoulder.

"Let's wait until we get to the island," Blake's uncle yelled back from the bridge.

North Manitou – three by three miles long and 22,000 square miles altogether - is an island rich in forests, tall dunes, and breathtaking shorelines that would rival any beach in the US. The Island is some 35 miles northwest of Harbor Cove, so it makes for a good day of fishing. Their trip would take them north to South Manitou Island, east around the island, and then west through Manitou Passage and the Manitou Passage Underwater Preserve, which surrounds both the North and South Manitou Island next to Michigan's Sleeping Bear Dunes National Lakeshore.

Once known for shipping, boats of the past sought safety from storms in the lee of the Islands. Thus, the preserve was rich in shipwrecks, underwater docks, and other artifacts. Robert planned to take the young men past a cool shipwreck south of South Manitou that rose above the waterline.

"My uncle said there's a river that dumps into Lake Michigan on the north side of North Manitou. It's supposed to be good fishing there," Blake said, "as long as it isn't too windy."

Nick watched the young man drain his second beer and began to more seriously contemplate the wisdom of them being that far out when a storm might come ashore. The winds were picking up and becoming louder.

*At least, we'll only be 15 miles or so from Leland.*

Nick laid back, trying to calm his anxious mind. He thought about Cadie and said a prayer for the beautiful woman he adored.

*God, please bring her back to me. Please let us find her.*

Nick began to think about what he was going to say to Blake - who had never once asked about Cadie since Nick stepped foot on the boat.

*What exactly do I say? 'Hey, why don't you seem to care that Cadie's missing? Did you kidnap her? Maybe you killed her? The FBI has your truck on video. Are you some kind of psycho?'*

Nick was thankful Robert would be on the boat in case Blake got angry and things went bad. He was also thankful for his dad's knife, although he prayed to god he wouldn't have to use it.

Nick closed his eyes, feeling the growing pitch of the boat as it moved through the deep blue waters that seemed to be growing more restless. He then felt cold raindrops. He readied himself for the storms that were headed his way – storms he would have to endure if he was ever going to see Cadie McLeod alive again.

## CHAPTER 45

After his short nap, Jake got dressed and drove to the police station. It was now raining and the sky getting dark. As he pulled into the parking lot, he noticed the tall row of arborvitaes along the parking lot swaying back and forth in the strengthening winds. The best he could, Jake jogged across the parking lot. He pulled open the heavy police station door. The detective hoped to sneak back to his office and get on his computer. However, just as he stepped through the door, a chipper Debbie walked into the reception area with her steaming cup of black tea.

"Jake! What are you doing here?" Debbie yelled, quickly setting her cup down on the reception desk and running over.

"Are you okay? I heard what happened. I thought you'd be taking a few days off."

Debbie leaned in and gave Jake a big hug.

Before Jake could even respond, Sergeant Bakker yelled from her office.

"Brennan! Is that you? You're not supposed to be here!"

A second later, Bakker was in the reception area, hands on her hips, not looking at all happy, her ponytail seeming tighter than ever.

"Why are you here? You need to be at home resting."

"You know I can't rest. You of all people should understand that. I need to be here. I need to know what's going on with Cadie."

Bakker just closed her eyes and shook her head deeply.

"Honestly, does anyone around here listen to me? You almost died, Brennan. From a big pile of crap," Bakker said and couldn't help the smile that slightly curled at the corner of her mouth.

"Oh, you're never going to let me live that down, are you?" Jake said.

"Well, you're here now, so come on. Let's get you up to speed. We'll go to the conference room. You want a coffee?"

"Of course."

A minute later, Bakker and Brennan took a seat at the large mahogany table in the conference room, rain pelting the window. Brennan looked out and saw dark storm clouds churning and thought of Nick out there on the boat, but knew Robert would keep them safe. He turned to Bakker.

"First, I want to say I'm sorry about how things went down at the Kesslers. I never wanted that to happen. It was a chaotic scene. And I had no idea there was a pit of shit that was going to kill them."

"Hey, let it go. That was a crazy situation. No one could plan for something like that. Plus, you didn't create that pile of shit, they did."

Jake smiled at her turn of phrase.

"So, no word on Cadie?"

"No. MSP and their dogs are still up there. It's a big property. FBI has some agents, too. But, no, they haven't found anything."

Just then, Debbie brought in two hot coffees and set the steaming cups down.

"You're the best, Debbie," Jake said, moving his coffee closer to him. "Thank you."

He turned to Bakker, "So what is new? Tell me everything."

"Well, there are some important pieces of information, but I'm almost hesitant to tell you," Bakker said.

"What? Why?"

"Because they seem to point to Blake Van der Velt."

The color in Jake's face drained.

"Blake? Why Blake?"

He leaned in, increasingly worried as he thought about his son currently on Blake's boat miles offshore, a storm clearly on its way. Just then Detective Craig Kitchen entered the conference room and put a wet bag of beignets on the table. His intense green eyes and shaved head always got everyone's attention.

"Hey, buddy, how are you doing? You gave us quite a scare."

"I'm fine. Honestly, Craig? Beignets?"

Somehow, Jake felt that enjoying treats right now was inappropriate.

"Yeah, I stopped by Scoops. I wanted to check in. See if anybody had heard anything. I talked to Alcee for a bit. She feels horrible about Cadie. Gave me this bag of beignets to share with everyone. Told me to give you all her best." Jake immediately felt bad for giving Craig attitude. He was a good man.

"That was nice of her. Thanks, Craig."

Turning back to Bakker, Jake said, "Okay, so, why are we settling on Blake? What about Rod Keonig? Edward Dawson? Even Karl Kessler? Or the creepy janitor?'

"There's a few other names floating around out there, too," Kitchen added.

Craig took a seat at the table. Just then a strong gust of wind rattled the window. Everyone looked and wondered just how bad the storm was going to get.

"As you probably know, we have a warrant out for Keonig, but we really don't have anything to tie him to Cadie," Kitchen said. "Yeah, he was at the party, and yeah, he's a loser, but he isn't known to wear a hat. He does drive his mom's truck from time to time, but it's not blacked out."

"Okay, so now I need to know exactly what's going on. This is all new information," Jake said, shifting in his chair. Kitchen leaned forward and grabbed a powdery beignet from the white bakery bag.

"As I was telling you," Bakker said, also grabbing a beignet, "there's information that points to Blake. One, the FBI enhanced the image taken from Cadie's cell phone the night she disappeared. The suspect was wearing a boating hat with roping that was frayed on the hat's left side. The hat is similar to what the employees wear at Van der Velt Marina. They also were able to determine letters. In the middle of the hat we now know were three letters, two of which were identified as the lowercase letters d and r. As in der. As in Van der Velt."

"Well, that seems to be a stretch. Everyone has one of those hats. And Jesus, there's a ton of people around here with der in their names," Jake said "The whole westside's Dutch."

"Yeah, maybe," Bakker said. "But the videos that Rebecca pulled from Marie's neighbors, the nearby streetlight, and the BP gas station show a blacked-out truck going by the McLeods late at night on several occasions and parking in front of their house."

"Okay," Jake retorted, "but this town is full of black trucks."

Jake so badly did not want it to be Blake.

"No, not a black truck. A blacked-out truck."

Bakker carefully enunciated the word blacked so it almost sounded like two syllables.

Jake sat for several seconds, not saying a word.

"A blacked-out truck? A truck that someone covered all the chrome and emblems black?" Jake said out loud, processing the information as he spoke the words, but already knowing the answer.

"Yes," Bakker said. "A blacked-out truck like the one Blake Van der Velt drives. That is the truck in the FBI video. The truck even had a bull bar, just like Blake's truck. But there's more. Let me call Rebecca in here. She's better at this forensic stuff than I am."

Bakker sent Detective LaCroix, who was in the back of the station sorting files, a text, and she joined them in the conference room, taking a seat next to Craig.

The winds outside were growing louder, stronger.

"Rebecca, explain to us again about the note Marie gave us. The one Cadie found in her mailbox."

"Well, you know how when you have a pad of paper, and sometimes what you wrote on one sheet also leaves an impression on the sheets that follow?"

"Yeah, okay," Jake said.

"The FBI has a machine, an EDD – Electrostatic Detection Device – that can make out an indented impression that's not visible to the naked eye," Rebecca said. "When they used the EDD on Cadie's note, four letters were detected. Dority said it appeared they were a person's initials, like someone signing off."

"What were they?" Jake asked.

"Capital B and V, then lowercase d, and then capital V."

Craig whistled. "Blake Van der Velt."

Jake was stunned. He looked down at his hands, now trembling, and tried to ingest all the information – to process it. Struggling to believe that Blake Van der Velt kidnapped Cadie McLeod. Maybe even murdered her.

"I really don't want to believe this. I can't believe this."

Jake shook his head. With this new information, fear for his son was escalating to horror.

"Guess where my son Nick is right now?!" Jake said weakly.

"Where?" Bakker responded, cocking her head, staring - almost glaring - at Jake and his now obvious emotions.

"He's on Blake Van der Velt's fishing boat out on Lake Michigan!"

Bakker stood up.

"What?! Why?! Why is Nick with Blake?! On his boat?! You've got to be kidding me!"

"Jesus, Dana, they're friends. There's no way I really thought Blake was involved in this! If I did, I would never have let him go! I mean, Blake's just a kid."

Jake was now shaking, his adrenaline coursing as fear overtook him. He stood up and began pacing the room.

"This is just great!" Bakker yelled. "And now there's a storm!"

"Let me pull up the radar on my phone," Craig jumped in. "I've got a good weather app."

The room became silent.

"Uh, yeah, it doesn't look good. Some pretty strong straight-line winds might be coming our way. Possibly 50-70 miles per hour."

"Fuck!" Jake yelled. "I've been trying to text Nick, but I can't get through. No service out there. I can't believe I let him go!"

Jake abruptly stopped talking. His head dropped.

"And there's more."

Bakker walked over to Jake. Her eyes narrowed to slits. She crossed her arms in front of her.

"What do you mean, 'more'?"

Jake swallowed hard and looked up at her.

"Nick is planning to confront Blake on the boat."

"WHAT?!" Bakker yelled. "No, no, no! He can't do that!"

"I know, I know!" Jake yelled. "I feel like shit! Jesus, Dana, he's my son! He's all I've got!"

Jake jumped up and strode forcefully toward the door.

"Where are you going, Jake?" Bakker asked, forcibly quieting her voice and trying to remain calm. She knew how much Jake loved Nick. She knew her attitude wasn't helping.

"I'm going to the marina. I might be able to get service there and get a hold of Nick. If I don't, I'm grabbing a goddamn Coast Guard boat myself and heading to Manitou."

Jake dashed out the door, and Bakker immediately pulled out her cell and started making calls.

## CHAPTER 46

Nick nervously watched the horizon; he saw the line of dark storm clouds coming closer. The other two men on the boat seemed oblivious to the approaching bad weather. Blake was over drinking and chatting nonstop, while Robert was up on deck looking over the controls. Nick gripped the side of the boat, scanning the distant sky and feeling the sharp westerly winds whip his hair and tee-shirt. He looked down into the deep, black waves that were increasingly rough and choppy and prepared himself for the conversation ahead. He hoped Blake would give him answers. He prayed those answers would lead to Cadie.

Robert decided to bypass the Manitou Passage, known for its aggressive waters and shipwrecks, and steer the cruiser around the western side of South Manitou Island to the northern Island. The skies above were cloudy, and the waves getter higher – about six feet. Robert ran the boat at six knots, heading northwest. After about 17 nautical miles, the cruiser reached the waters off North Manitou, near the island's river mouth. Blake's uncle turned off the boat. The large cruiser swayed slightly but held its own in the choppy Lake Michigan.

"Is it time to break out the Glenlivet?" Blake yelled up to his uncle on the deck.

"Okay, okay. Let me get it."

"I'm going to put my jacket on," Nick said as the cooler winds made him shiver. He walked toward the boat's bow, holding on where he could, and dug his jacket out of his bookbag. He saw the knife poking out of the pocket. Then he thought about Cadie and what might be happening to her.

*Is she injured somewhere? Wondering why I haven't come to save her? Is she dead? Why hasn't Blake said anything?*

Nick tried to push all the dark thoughts and questions from his mind. He had to if he was going to get through this afternoon – to get the answers he came for. Nick thought about what he was going to say to Blake in the next hour. Then he remembered the gift card at the bottom of the bookbag and dug it out. Heading back to the stern, Nick handed the card to Blake.

"Here you go, buddy. Happy birthday."

"Oh, wow, thanks. Fifty bucks. Nice! You're such a good friend," Blake said, grabbing Nick in a slightly drunken hug. The men stumbled a bit as the boat lurched in a larger wave.

"Oh shit," Blake laughed.

Robert appeared on the top step with a distinctive aqua blue box with gold seal in his hand.

"Here we go, gentlemen. Are we ready for some Scotch Whiskey?"

He removed the similarly colored bottle from the box and walked down the steps.

"Hell, yes!" yelled Blake. "Finally! Let's do this!"

Robert opened the bottle and handed it to Blake who took a long drink of the deep gold liquid. He handed the bottle to Nick who took a shot. Blake then grabbed the bottle back and took a second shot.

"Slow down, Blake. We have all afternoon," Robert laughed, taking a seat.

"Hey, fellas, why don't you guys sit down? I have some good news I want to share."

Blake and Nick took a seat on the bench seat across from Robert. Blake smiled broadly and a bit sloppily. He was enjoying his birthday so far.

"I got good news this week," Robert grinned. "It looks like someone got a full-ride scholarship to play tennis at Western."

"What?" Blake jumped up. "No way!"

"Yes way," Robert laughed. "You got a full ride. Alec Patterson called me this week and gave me the news. It was down between you and that player from Grand Rapids, but Alec said the committee thought you were the stronger overall player."

"Oh my god, that's awesome!" Blake hollered. He threw back another shot of the whiskey.

"Congratulations, Blake. You deserve it."

"That's just crazy," Blake said beaming, sitting back down with the bottle and taking a fourth shot. He finally handed it to Robert who took his own shot of the expensive, floral-smelling whiskey.

"I also have another surprise."

"More surprises? This is the best birthday ever," Blake whooped.

"So, you know how we've been having problems with your truck? Well, guess what? I bought you a new one! I ordered you the Raptor. It's got a great engine. Perfect for off roading. We're going to pick it up this weekend. You're going to love it."

"Oh my god! No way! Really? I can't believe it! Thank you, uncle!"

Blake jumped up and hugged his uncle. He then turned to Nick.

"Can you believe it? Robert bought me a Raptor!"

Nick smiled through gritted teeth. He wasn't feeling at all enthusiastic for Blake's happy news.

"I can't believe it. Robert, you're the best! A Raptor! We are going to be doing some serious wheeling, Nick! This calls for a drink!"

Blake grabbed the bottle from a surprised Robert and took another shot.

"Hey, slow down, Blake. You're going be drunk and puking before we even catch a fish. Why don't we get going?"

Robert stood up.

"You guys check the trolling lines, while I start up the boat. Nick, why don't you fish with the rod in the starboard outrigger while Blake uses the port-side rod? Once we get underway, I'll use sonar to find some schooling baitfish. I see some birds swooping over there, so we'll head that way."

"Look at those clouds, Robert," Nick said. "It looks like it's getting bad out there."

"Oh, no worries. If a storm blows in, this boat can outrun it. If it gets too bad, we'll head to the Leland Marina and wait it out. I've got a slip there."

Nick felt slightly better, but his anxiety was growing. Blake was on his way to drunk, and Nick knew what that meant.

*How in the hell is this afternoon going to play out?*

Nick pulled his cell phone out of his pocket. Still no service.

Robert climbed up onto the bridge deck while Blake headed portside and shoved the Glenlivet in a crevice. The boat began to move, almost immediately reaching the trolling speed of two miles per hour. Blake picked up a rod and nestled it under his left arm and elbow. Nick took up the starboard rod and shoved it into his hip. The waves were rolling pretty good now, and the boat tossed.

"Hey, Blake. So, you were having problems with your truck?" Nick yelled over the wind. He was perplexed about this new information.

"Yeah. Robert noticed something off with the engine. He's been driving it for a few weeks. He's been trying to figure out what's wrong. If it's something serious."

"I didn't know that. What have you been driving?"

"Robert had another truck he kept at some family property. I've been driving that truck for a couple weeks."

Nick pondered this.

*Robert's been driving the blacked-out truck?*

It didn't make sense.

"So, you haven't been driving your truck at all?"

"What is this? No. I told you. Robert's been driving my truck," Blake yelled over the wind from the other side of the boat.

The cruiser moved toward a squabble of seagulls circling and swooping down into the waters. The winds were growing stronger. The cruiser swayed. Nick saw the dark clouds advancing. Small raindrops began to fall.

"Is that a shelf cloud, Blake? Sure looks like one."

Blake, fairly inebriated, turned unsteadily to look.

"Nah, that's nothing. We see that all the time out here. It'll blow north," Blake said.

He picked up the bottle and drained most of the remaining whiskey.

"Dark clouds are always blowing through out here. If a storm does whip up, this boat can handle it, and we can always go down below."

As the cruiser trolled through the black waters, Nick looked out over the increasingly large waves. His mind feverishly attempted to process the information he had just learned and what was told to him yesterday by Bakker.

*Robert's been driving Blake's truck? So, it's been Robert who's been driving past Cadie's house late at night? Why? And Cadie got a threatening note with the initials BVdV impressed on the paper. It has to be Blake: Blake Van der Velt. What about the hat in the video? It had the letters d and r for der. It's the same hat Robert's employees wear. Just what the hell is going on?*

Nick's mind twisted and turned. Just then a tremendous wave washed over the bow, spraying water everywhere.

"Blake," Nick yelled over the increasingly loud wind. "Don't you think we should head in? It looks like it's getting worse. Why don't you talk to your uncle?"

The raining was picking up.

"Dude, chill! It's fine!"

"Maybe I should say something to Robert?"

"Don't! It's my birthday, goddammit! Don't ruin it!" Blake barked, fully drunk and agitated now. "You always gotta fuuuuck everything up," he slurred at Nick.

Nick knew this behavior was coming. Yet, he felt powerless to not respond in kind. His suppressed fear and anger began to break free.

"Fuck everything up? What does that mean?" Looking at Blake's contorted face, Nick could see his friend's darker side taking hold.

"You know what I mean! Don't pretend you don't!"

Suddenly, the boat pitched hard.

"Oh crap," Nick yelled out, grabbing on to the side so he didn't fall.

Blake was undisturbed. He just swayed drunkenly and began yelling into the wind.

"I'm talking about Cadie, you asshole! We had a good thing going until you ruined it! Ruined my life!"

"What?! I didn't ruin your life! You guys were already broken up by the time I liked her. You know that."

The increasing winds rattled Nick's thin jacket. He shivered uncontrollably as they sliced through him and rain fell from the sky. Looking to the west, he saw the shelf cloud stretching north and south coming closer.

"Hey, we really need to get going! Let's go to Leland and dock. We can always come back out after the storm passes."

"Fuck, you're an asshole sometimes!" Blake screamed. "It's my birthday, and you always want to make it about you! Typical Nick!"

Nick just looked at him, fists clenched. He fought to stay calm. He was afraid what he might do if he let loose all his pent-up feelings.

"Listen, I'm going to talk to Robert. We need to head for shore!"

Nick took a step up toward the bridge deck when Blake suddenly grabbed his rain-slickened jacket and yanked him powerfully. Nick was thrown backward and landed hard on the fiberglass stern.

"What the hell?" Nick screamed at Blake, who was now drunkenly standing over him, swaying as the boat pitched in the strong waves. "I can't believe you just did that!"

"It's my birthday! We're staying out here! You're not going to ruin another goddamn thing in my life!"

Nick pulled himself up to sitting. Sharp pain pulsated at the back of his soaked head from hitting the stern. His jacket and shorts were drenched from the lake water swishing around the back of the boat. Nick looked up at his drunk friend.

"Dude, you're delusional! Cadie's breaking up with you had nothing to do with me!"

Nick stood up. His icy hand grabbed onto the cooler handle to steady himself. The wind whipped his hair into eyes. Rainwater slid down his face.

"I can't see what she sees in you, man," Blake slurred, his eyes narrowing. "I mean, you didn't even get into college. What kind of loser can't get into college? I just got a scholarship, and you can't even get in. And you live in the tiniest, shithole house in town. I mean it's fucking small. So, you're stupid and you're poor!" he spat out. "Even Laura took off. Your fucking mom doesn't even like you!"

Nick just glared at Blake. His head throbbed. He had reached his breaking point; fury coursed through every vein and capillary in his body. Nick took a deliberate step. The two men were now face to face. Only inches separated them as both glared.

"Oh, really, Blake? Let's talk about you for a moment. How about I tell you that the police think you kidnapped Cadie! Maybe you even murdered her, you sick fuck!"

At that, Blake's face visibly changed. The angry smirk slid off his face, and his hateful eyes opened wide with shock.

"You haven't said one word about her since I got on this boat, but somehow she was the love of your life?! Instead, you're acting like you don't have a care in the world. Just getting drunk. Not one word about Cadie! Not. One. Fucking. Word! What's that about?! Where is she, Blake?! What did you do to her?! Did you kill her?!"

The boat pitched hard. The two men struggled to remain upright.

"What are you talking about?!" Blake screamed back, water spraying across his face.

He stood there drunk, shaking his head. Trying to process what Nick had just said. He sat down roughly on the bench seat and dropped his head in his hands. Overcome. Then, after a few seconds, with glassy eyes, he looked up slowly at Nick.

"I didn't have anything to do with Cadie going missing. I would never hurt her. I loved her. Why would you even think that?"

"Because Sergeant Bakker told me a few things yesterday. She said you're their number one suspect. The night Cadie went missing, her phone took a video. The guy is wearing one of your marina hats with a d and a r on it. As in der. As in Van der Velt."

Blake, shaking his head profusely as the boat swayed, yelled, "That's your evidence? Dude, hundreds of people have that hat, like all our employees. I think I even gave you one!"

"Except there's more. Cadie found a weird note in her mailbox, something threatening. The FBI took it and was able to find an impression on the note. They were initials, like someone signing their name. Guess whose initials were on the note: BVdV? How many people in Harbor Cove do you think have the initials BVdV in that order, huh? Just you, Blake! Those are your initials! What did you to do to Cadie?! Tell me!"

Nick was shaking, seething with anger. He was holding onto the side of the rolling boat. Water rolled down his face and into his boiling eyes.

Blake looked down, shaking his head, trying to work through Nick's words. The winds grew louder, more intense. He sat there, his brain processing wildly. Suddenly, he looked up at Nick. His eyes were huge and bulging. Sheer terror stretched across his face. His entire demeanor radiated fear.

"There's someone else with the initials BVdV!"

"Yeah, right! Who?!"

"Robert! Blake yelled into the wind. "My uncle!"

"Robert?" Nick answered, confused. "What do you mean?"

"Robert sometimes signs his name Bob! Bob Van der Velt – BVdV!"

Both young men froze. They stared at each other, neither saying a word as the cruiser pitched more violently. Water continued to splash over the sides of the stern, but neither noticed.

"And you just heard that Robert's been driving my truck."

Their eyes locked and darkened. Both men suddenly understood. It was Robert who drove past Cadie's house late at night, parking in front of her bedroom. It was Robert who wrote Cadie a threatening note. But why? Why in the world would Robert do this?

Just then, the tall, imposing man appeared on the top step. Nick and Blake immediately looked up.

"What are you boys talking about?" Robert called down calmly. He gripped the railing and stood there stiffly, legs wide, as the strong winds rattled his coat.

Nick saw that Robert was now wearing a hat. The Marina's nautical hat. The one Bakker said was spotted in the cell phone video. Nick stared at it. The left-side roping was frayed just like Bakker had mentioned.

He stared up at the unsmiling man, and his mind filled with horror. Nick felt he couldn't move. Like a statue, he stood still and mute, gaping at Blake's uncle while the older man glared down at him. Suddenly, in the silence of the overhanging moment, the hairs on his neck stood up, and Nick had an uncontrollable realization: he was standing in the presence of pure evil.

## CHAPTER 47

Cadie was now hypertonic. Extremely dehydrated and mentally foggy, on sheer willpower alone she drove north and then west down miles of twisting, rolling, rain-soaked roads, trying to stay conscious while rain blew into her line of vision. Finally, she reached concrete and turned left, and headed west for Harbor Cove. She wondered exactly where she was; it was hard for her to concentrate. She couldn't think clearly. She thought she might be north and west of Buckley because of the Rollways she viewed from the hill above the cellar.

The road was deserted. She pushed down harder on the gas. In what was now a downpour, Cadie fought to see through the windshield and thought she saw the red sign for the Cherry Bowl Drive-in.

*I'm almost there! I have to stay awake. I have to get home to Nick and Aunt Marie. I won't die like this. I won't!*

Cadie imagined the scene if Nick and Marie found her dead in the car. It was too terrible a thought to entertain. She drove as fast as she dared. The rain and winds were picking up. She also didn't want to kill someone if she fell unconscious behind the wheel. That is not how she wanted her life to end. Five miles later, she crossed into Harbor Cove.

*Oh, thank god! I'm going to make it! I am!*

In her momentary celebration, she passed a wooden pole, and something caught her eye. She quickly glanced over and saw a wet poster, its ink dripping, nailed to the pole.

*Was that me? Was that honestly a picture of me? Are people looking for me?*

Feelings of happiness and joy flooded through her.

*Oh, thank you, everyone! Thank you! I'm going to make it home! I promise you I will!*

Cadie moved her head back and forth, trying to stay awake. She knew she was on the verge of unconsciousness. She checked her seat belt. She drove three more miles and turned left on Sandy Shore. After a mile, Sandy Shore ran closely along Lake Michigan, and now, through the foggy side window, she could see the massive waves pounding the shore of Lake Michigan. Storm clouds swirled overhead. Winds buffeted her car. It seemed to be raining even harder. With everything she had, Cadie struggled to stay awake.

She drove down the deserted street, the extreme winds pushing her car into the northbound lane. She fought to keep the car on the road. Up ahead was Van der Velt Marina. The parking lot was largely empty. Most of the boaters had left before the storm got bad. She passed the marina and went around a bend. She accelerated, praying she would reach the Harbor Cove Police Department before she passed out or died.

Suddenly, she became nauseous; she was sweating profusely. Her ears began to ring. She realized she was going to pass out. She could last not even one more minute. She was at the end.

*Goodbye, Nick. I really did love you.*

In her final seconds of consciousness, the young woman pressed down hard on the brake, then she was out. She slumped against the wheel. Now, with no driver, the full-size car swerved across the left lane and entered the ditch. The front end hit the ditch hard and then popped up, and the car continued driving quickly across a grassy, sodden field. It continued on toward a large marsh full of cattails and bulrushes. Just then, the car's anti-lock brakes kicked in. The brakes pumped in quick bursts, emitting a loud grinding noise. In front of the tires, rainwater, grass, and weeds combined to create a dam effect, slowing the car, and within four seconds, the car came to a stop.

Under the dark sky, the headlights turned on. They glared at the tall, reedy plants in front of them. Just inches away was the edge of a deep, flooded marsh - bloated from rain and snowmelt. At ten feet deep, the marsh could easily swallow the blue LeSabre whole. The car began to inch forward, sliding on the slippery grass. As rain pummeled the field and cold winds whipped across the land, the front wheels of the car slowly entered the swollen wetland.

## CHAPTER 48

"Oh, boys, I really wish it hadn't come to this," Robert yelled over the howling wind.

He stood on the bridge deck looking down at Blake and Nick. Neither said a word. They were shocked into silence.

The *Best Revenge* was now rolling side to side. The low, ominous shelf cloud had closed in, leading the powerful thunderstorm that was close behind. The temperature was a frigid fifty degrees. Upper clouds swirled wildly, while gusts of winds 60-70 mph besieged the cruiser.

Nick and Blake attempted to stay upright in the heaving boat while swirling waters washed back and forth across the stern. Robert, on the top step, stood steady, gripping the side rail tightly. He continued to stare down at the two young men. His eyes darted around like he was contemplating the universe. After what seemed like forever, Robert yelled again.

"And we were having such a lovely time!"

Suddenly, without warning, Robert jumped. The older, but agile man bypassed the steps and landed on the stern below. He took three large steps toward Blake. His nephew, drunk and taken off guard, quickly retreated backward toward the side of the boat and immediately lost his balance on the slippery stern and slid downward. Robert advanced and grabbed Blake.

Blake screamed, "Robert! What are you doing?!"

Robert grabbed his nephew's head and slammed it hard on the side of the fiberglass boat. The force of his head hitting emitted a loud crack.

"Robert! No! Please! No!" the injured, disoriented Blake begged as blood poured from the gash on his head.

Robert then lifted and shoved his nephew – who was now whimpering and crying - backward, his head and neck whiplashing. Blake fought to defend himself and tried to form a sentence, but Robert quickly propelled him up and backwards while never saying a word. Within seconds, the newly-turned 18-year-old was flipped over the side of the cruiser. He was immediately engulfed by the raging waters below.

Nick, frozen in place, couldn't believe what he had just witnessed. He heard his friend screaming and pleading for help above the wind. For seconds that seemed like hours, Nick stood still; he was shocked into silence. He stood there wordless, gripping the other side of the boat with all his strength, rain pelting his face, watching Robert push Blake overboard. It happened so quickly; his mind couldn't process what his brain had just seen.

Robert then turned to face Nick.

His clammy face was slick with rain water; his shirt drenched with Blake's blood. Nick looked into Robert's eyes and saw nothing there. No feelings. No humanity. Just empty and black. He knew he was looking into the eyes of a sociopath – a monster. He wanted to help his friend, but Blake's uncle stood between him and the portside. Nick couldn't hear Blake's screams anymore.

"Robert, we need to help Blake! We've got to help him!

Robert took a step forward – a slight smirk taking over his face.

*He's enjoying this.*

"I'm so sorry, Nick. I've always liked you, and that's saying a lot since I don't like most people."

Robert took another step forward.

"But Blake's dead, and now it's your turn. Unfortunately, I have to kill you, too."

## CHAPTER 49
## The Weirdo

Twenty-eight years ago, on a warm autumn evening, I went from Weirdo to Monster. After I yanked Thomas McLeod – TJ to his friends - from his car that fall evening, I beat the shit out of him. I beat him until he bled. I beat him until he was unconscious. He was supposed to be my friend, but instead he betrayed me. He stole my girl. My soulmate. The woman I planned to grow old with. I can still hear his screams as I landed blow after blow on his perfect, handsome face.

"Why, Robert? Why are you doing this?!"

*Why! Why am I doing this?! Because you stole Aileen from me! You ruined my life! You destroyed my hope for any chance of happiness! You have everything, and I have nothing! You are EVERYTHING!*

I can still picture Aileen hanging out the Camaro window, eyes wide in horror, screaming, begging me to stop. So, what did I do? I beat TJ harder. The moment I punched him in the eye, I heard his bone crack and remember hoping I disfigured his face so he would be ugly like me forever.

Thomas and Aileen were hugely popular students at Manistee Harbor High – voted *Most Beautiful Couple* - and I was nothing to nobody. At school, behind my back and sometimes to my face, classmates called me The Weirdo. I was awkward and insecure. I really didn't know how to communicate with people, let alone women. They never gave me the time of day. I was ugly and strange and spoke with a slight stutter. People actually moved away from me in the hallways as I walked by.

From a young age, I knew something was seriously wrong with me. It didn't help that my father loathed me. To him, I was a total disappointment. Sometimes, he hit me in anger. Other times, he called me vicious names and taunted me with The Weirdo nickname. Mostly, though, he just ignored me. So, practically overnight, I went from The Weirdo to being regarded as a full-blown monster. Everyone hated me - despised me.

TJ was in Manistee General for a week with a broken orbital bone and contusions on his liver and spleen. Doctors were even concerned he might have a brain bleed. Of course, at the hospital, I assumed TJ had a steady stream of well-wishers. I imagined the smiling throngs grasping their ridiculous balloon bouquets: "We love you, TJ!" "Get well soon, TJ!" "You're the best, TJ!" An endless line of hugs and kisses.

It made me want to puke.

Obviously, I was arrested at the scene. The tree-lined street was crammed with nosy neighbors and my shocked classmates, while the ambulance workers tended to the bloody Thomas lying unconscious in the grass. I was handcuffed and placed in the back of a Manistee patrol car and whisked to the local station. When dear old dad walked up to the holding cell to take me home, I was sitting on the metal bench, covered in TJ's dried blood, grinning profusely.

I'd never been happier.

Dad just cocked his balding head and studied me with black eyes. He knew I was evil. Minutes later, after we'd left the station, I slid into the front seat of his LeSabre. Looking straight ahead, he muttered, "I wish you had died that night." I knew immediately what he meant: the night he tried to murder me with carbon monoxide. I was only ten, and already he hated me and wanted me dead.

After beating McLeod, I was ordered by the Manistee County Court to be placed in a ten-unit facility for high-risk youth. So, until I turned 18, I lived in a center for juvenile delinquents surrounded by some quite nasty and violent young men. I recall attending Hopeful House Academy and its course "Social Skills 4 Life." That amused me to no end since I had zero capacity to learn social skills. When my placement ended, my records were sealed, and I looked forward to a fresh start. My plans were to leave Michigan where nobody knew me and begin again. Then the bastard got sick. (Mom had abandoned us years ago, although I do sometimes wonder if dad actually succeeded at murdering someone and getting away with it.)

*Where's her body, dad?*

So, it was just me and my dying dad as he wasted away from lung cancer. Daily endless coughing, wheezing, and hacking blood all over our living room sofa and carpet. I felt nothing but disgust. Months later, my foul-smelling and emaciated father died.

That made me so happy.

Now I was utterly alone.

Dad did leave me money, though. Enough to attend college out of state, so that's what I did. I moved to New York where no one knew me, and I started a new life. I enrolled in NYU's business program and lived in a small apartment in Chelsea. I liked the many art galleries and well-known market. I often took long walks alone by the Hudson River at night. But mostly, my years in the Big Apple were all about work. I didn't have time for a social life. Or friends. Or women. People don't like me, and I don't like them. Especially females. They're nothing but cruel creatures who torment men. Aileen taught me that.

New York also taught me a lot. I learned to wear a mask. I observed others closely: how they talked, how they interacted, how they showed they cared about each other. I watched them smile and say nice things. Hold the doors open for women. Say please and thank you. This might sound weird, but I would mimic them at home. Just practicing, really. I'd stand in front of my bedroom mirror for hours and pretend to be someone else, someone people liked. "Oh, how are you today? My, don't you look lovely. Can I get you a coffee? What a beautiful dress."

Over time, my mask improved, and people actually began to think I was the nice, polite person they saw before them. In reality, there were two of me. One night, I was having a cocktail at the Lobby Bar in the Chelsea Hotel when someone called my name.

"Robert! Robert Van der Velt!"

Naturally, I was startled. No one outside of work had called my name in a long time. I looked up from my magazine and saw Marissa standing in front of me. I hadn't seen her since that night I beat TJ. She had put on a few pounds but wasn't wholly unattractive. For a while, we made the smallest of small talk, and Marissa told me that TJ and Aileen got married and were living a "sickeningly sweet life" in Alma, Michigan, where they went to college. It was obvious Marissa didn't like Aileen. I think she was always jealous of her.

Anyway, since that night and as the years went by, I tried hard not to think about TJ and Aileen. Unfortunately, I thought about them 24/7. I woke up thinking about them, and I went to bed thinking about them. My dad once called me a vindictive prick. But why should I forget? Why should I forgive them? They have all the happiness while I have nothing but an empty apartment and an empty, lonely, miserable life. I deserved more.

Then, one day, everything changed.

I was sitting in my apartment, finishing a puzzle, and sipping my expensive Glenlivet when I got a call from a lawyer in Harbor Cove, Michigan. She called to inform me that my Grandfather Diedirik Van der Velt had died and left me Van der Velt Marina in his will. I never even knew the old man, but he was a goddamn Van der Velt, and so was I. That's all I needed to know. I also knew someday my luck would change. It had to.

In short order, I moved to Harbor Cove. I met with lawyers and took possession of my family's marina. I purchased a modern condo with outdoor fireplace and massive glass windows facing Lake Michigan. I assembled a wardrobe of custom Brioni suits, a cashmere Tom Ford overcoat, seven pairs of Gucci loafers, and two pairs of Dior boat shoes (Clearly, I have penchant for well-made leather shoes.) Soon, I became an admired business owner running a major marina along Michigan's west coast. I was wealthy. I wore fine clothes. People respect that. Then I made it my goal to become a pillar of the community.

*Just have to keep that mask firmly in place.*

The *Benzie County Record Patriot* and *Lake Life* wrote glowing articles about me. I then created a foundation for at-risk youth. (Comical, really. Oh, if they only knew!) The picture of me and Mayor Clark at the opening reception made the cover of *Lake Life*. There I was in my gleaming, hand-crafted tuxedo, Clark's arm around me like we were best friends. I had arrived! My life was finally prosperous and successful, and I found myself thinking about Thomas and Aileen McLeod less and less.

Until that day.

It was a Saturday morning, sunny and 75 degrees. I drove my newly washed, obsidian black Mercedes down Main Street, a warm breeze blowing through my expensive car, and I tapped along to Bob Seger's "Hollywood Nights" playing on my 31-speaker surround sound.

*I was beginning to feel, well, normal.*

Then something seized my attention.

There she was.

I would recognize her anywhere.

Aileen McLeod.

The dream girl of my youth drifted across Main Street right in front of me – like an apparition. I froze. I couldn't twitch a muscle. I watched, utterly transfixed. Aileen entered Bell's Diner, her luxurious, crimson hair flowing behind her. I hadn't seen her since that night I almost killed TJ.

I quickly pulled to the curb, my brain shooting fireworks. I was glued and stared at her every movement through the restaurant's large glass window. Smiling and laughing, Aileen floated over to a table. Then I spotted TJ. The handsome, tanned Thomas grinned back at his lovely wife as he jumped up and pulled out a chair for Aileen.

*He was always so polite.*

Seated next to him was their angelic daughter – the spitting image of Aileen – silky red hair tumbling down around her small shoulders. After Aileen sat down, TJ leaned over and kissed his child on the top of her precious head.

*God, he was always so perfect. Then I noticed the scar around his eye. Did I cause that when I punched him in the head? I sure hope so.*

I slipped on my Ray Bans and slouched down in the leather seat for the next hour, my guts twisting, observing the happy McLeod family enjoy their breakfast. All my buried feelings resurfaced! Dark, suppressed feelings burst forth in every direction: jealousy, sadness, hatred, anger. All my years of being alone. Of being different. Of being overlooked and ridiculed. As I sat there sweating in my two-hundred-dollar golf shirt and $100,000 car, the smell of my own sour stink permeating the vehicle, I grew smaller and smaller and smaller.

*Oh, how I despised the McLeods and their happiness.*

I sat there for quite a while – in utter misery. Then, like a gift, it came to me. A solution. I contemplated my idea for a long while. I had no other choice.

That morning, I made the necessary decision. It was time. I could no longer afford to be tortured by these people. How was I to continue on with their perfect life plaguing me at every turn?! They had toyed with me long enough! So, I began to formulate my plan. I recalled my family's favorite quote, "Living well is the best revenge," and the thought came to me like Christmas morning as I sat in the hot car.

*Dying is the better revenge.*

My plan was simple, really. Nothing fancy or complicated. It only called for the complete and utter destruction of the McLeod family – TJ, Aileen, and their little girl who looked just like her beautiful mother. Every last one of them needed to die. No one would be spared. Finally, I began to feel hopeful. Finally, I knew happiness was within reach.

From that morning on, whenever I could, I stalked the little family. I found out that they had just moved to Harbor Cove. I also was careful to always drive my dad's LeSabre so as not to be detected. I quickly learned the McLeod's daily routines, and I contemplated how I would kill them.

Then one day, I just got lucky.

It was a June evening. I was parked down the street from their cottage, watching the house from under an oak tree, and I saw Thomas and Aileen celebrating something. Both of my front car windows were rolled down, and I strained to hear. All I could ascertain was their joy as they talked loudly and animatedly on the front porch. I saw Aileen high five Thomas while he grinned happily like he always did. Then Aileen threw her arms around him in sheer joy. I watched them under their front porch light as Thomas pulled back from the hug and kissed Aileen deeply. Their love sickened me.

I decided I would kill them that night.

They walked hand in hand down the cobblestone front path to their Camaro parked on the tree-lined street. Minutes later, I was following them. Thomas made several turns, and soon we were driving up the coastal highway M-22, dark trees on each side rushing by in a blur - the moon hidden by clouds. Then it came to me.

*They're going to Frosty Bar.*

I sped up and passed them, keeping my eyes straight ahead, hoping they wouldn't see me. I drove quickly for two miles, and when I saw the ice cream shop's colorful OPEN sign cheerfully blinking on and off up ahead, I pulled to the opposite side of the road and waited. It was a Monday night, and the street was quiet. Deserted. Soon, I saw their headlights in my rearview mirror. I watched their white Chevy Cruze slowly pass me and pull farther down the road into the parking lot. A minute later, Thomas and Aileen exited their car, again smiling broadly and walking hand in hand like young lovers. They crossed the parking lot.

I throbbed with adrenaline.

All the many years of hurt, pain, and anguish, the loneliness, the nicknames, my father's hatred, my mother's abandonment, TJ's betrayal, and Aileen's indifference all came crashing together and fomented into a massive, pulsating pit of pure rage. I would not let them win! I jammed my car in gear. I maneuvered the vehicle out onto M-22 and got in position. Then I pushed down hard on the gas, pushing as hard as I could without flooring it and squealing the tires. The car quickly ripped down the street. I timed it perfectly.

When they entered the road, the happy couple was looking north, toward the small ice cream shop. They were engrossed in conversation. Their backs were to me. They were still holding hands. Aileen was tossing her red hair about as she always did.

I continued to accelerate. Then they were right in front of me. I think when I hit them, I was going 50 miles per hour. Thomas must have heard me at the last second because he snapped his head around and looked back in sheer terror.

*Did he recognize me? Did he understand it was me who was killing him? I like to think so.*

That night, as I slowly drove away from their decimated bodies, their fluids dripping off my car, my headlights caught on something shiny. I slowed, opened my door, leaned over, and picked it up. It was a necklace. It was Aileen's half a heart necklace covered in her blood and body tissue. I tossed it on my front seat and drove away - my now blood-stained hands gripping the steering wheel. As I did, a smile spread across my sweat-soaked face. In fact, my whole body vibrated with exhilaration.

It was then I felt an emotion surge through me that I hadn't felt in decades. It was happiness. Pure, sweet, long-chased happiness.

Killing them had set me free.

*Well, almost.*

## CHAPTER 50

In the downpour, under black skies, Jake raced along Main Street headed toward Van der Velt Marina. Suddenly, his Tahoe began hydroplaning in a deep trench of water that ran along the curb, and he wrestled with the steering wheel. Finally, the SUV finally righted itself. The Tahoe continued to barrel down Main Street until it reached Redding. Squealing his tires, Jake careened around the corner, slightly skidding, and ripped down Redding Boulevard. He drove the next four miles as fast as he dared in the pouring rain and then turned right. He tore down Sandy Shore that would run along Lake Michigan in a half mile. In the distance, he saw the turbulent Lake Michigan waves terrorizing the empty beach.

He was rounding a bend when, to the right, something caught his eye. His brain registered that something was amiss. He quickly glanced over and saw headlights out in the grass. There was a car sitting far out in the field next to the marsh. He grabbed his two-way radio and called for assistance.
In that moment, he was profoundly torn. He needed to get to the marina and reach Nick, but he couldn't not stop. The person in the car could be in jeopardy. He felt he had no choice but to pull over and help. He wouldn't let another person die. He couldn't live with that if he did.

Jake slowed and parked on the side of the road. The detective jumped out of the Tahoe and looked east through the driving rain. He could see the white smoke exhaust curling from the car's tailpipe. The car was still running. The cold rain quickly soaked his jacket and pants. The wind howled and whipped his hair. He tried to run through the rain-soaked grass, but his feet immediately sank in mud. He fought to pull up his feet and tried to run again, but both of his shoes got stuck, and he fell over into the mire. He knew he was weak from the chemicals he had ingested the day before, but he was determined to reach the car.

The detective struggled to his knees and wiped mud off his face. Digging both hands into cold, wet mush, he pushed himself up. Then, he moved as fast as he could in the mud that was turning to quicksand. He inched toward the car, fighting to pull his shoes from the sticky mud one plodding step at a time. His calves burned, and his brain throbbed. He was drenched in rain and sweat. He looked up and saw the car's right headlight casting an eerie glow on the row of cattails. The car's left headlight, in fact the front left corner of the car, was submerged in the marsh. He worked his way through the downpour to the back of the LeSabre and placed his hands on the cold metal to steady himself. Through the foggy rear window, Jake saw a figure sitting in the front seat, leaning against the steering wheel. The person was completely still. No sound or movement. Fear rose up in him. He felt that unwelcome nausea in his stomach.

Jake braced for what he might find.

*God, please don't let this person be dead.*

Suddenly, the car's left front corner began to slide deeper into the water. Jake knew he had minutes – maybe seconds – to open the door before the pressure of the water would hold the door closed tight. He moved his way along the left side of the tilted car, his shoes and ankles sinking into the cold, spongy wetland. He was almost to the door handle, when the car shifted. It quickly jerked forward. Jake grabbed the icy handle, praying he wouldn't accompany the car as it dropped into the marsh. He recognized he was in a life-or-death moment. Jake pulled the handle just as the vehicle began to slide. He pulled as hard as he could, and the heavy, wide door swung open, flinging Jake backward with it. He clung to the door handle with all his dwindling strength. The rain continued to beat down. His arms and shoulders burned.

Now Jake was in the frigid water up to his chest, holding onto the door handle with one hand. Rain poured down his head. The shock of the cold made it suddenly hard to breathe. He felt his legs growing numb. He pulled himself to the car door and carefully and slowly maneuvered around it. Finally, Jake, still in the water, was between the car door and the front seat.

The detective knew he had to somehow remove the driver from the car before it slid fully into the marsh. Jake saw there was a black seat belt over the driver's waist. He knew he had to unbuckle it if he was going to pull the driver out. As he was reaching toward the seat belt, the door swung away from the car and Jake, now too far from the car, missed the belt. Jake was suddenly plunged into the bone-chilling water - completely submerged.

He reacted with shock. He began to flail his wooden arms. Everything was gray and cloudy. In the muffled water, he could hear the rain beating against the surface above. Jake's legs tried to push off the bottom, but there was nothing below him. He began to fight for his life.

Somehow, he found the ability to calm himself and began swimming upward. His head broke free of the murky water, and he grabbed onto the bottom of the car's door opening, coughing and choking. He held himself there for a minute, soaked to the bone, freezing, trying to breathe and get his bearings. He shook his head like a dog to throw off the rain. In that moment, Jake was keenly aware the car could slide down into the marsh any second, taking him with it.

After a few moments, once he could breathe somewhat normally again, Jake looked up and saw that the occupant still was not moving. Their face, covered in long hair, was pressed against the steering wheel. Jake stared at the driver. He took notice of her long, red hair. He knew he had seen it before.

Then Jake's body began to tremble violently. He suddenly felt the urge to vomit. The neurons in his brain fired wildly, and his shocked cells passed their messages with fervor as they interpreted the image before them. Finally, the unbelievable thought burst forth into Jake's conscious mind like a red-hot explosion.

*Cadie McLeod.*

## CHAPTER 51

Nick stared back at Robert in complete confusion.

"Why do you have to kill *me*? What did I do? I don't understand!" The young man screamed into the wind at what he now knew was a sociopath.

"Stop this, Robert! We have to save Blake!"

Then, a terrifying realization took hold. A thoroughly horrendous thought.

*Robert kidnapped Cadie.*

The monster standing right in front of him stole his beloved Cadie.

Nick fixed his eyes on the evil, soulless man before him and glared with rage. Then a deep, primal scream erupted from his shattered heart.

"Did you take Cadie, Robert?! Tell me! Did you take her? Did you kill her?!"

Nick was now shaking and crying, cold straight-line winds and sheets of rain pummeling his face and body. The large cruiser rolled and heaved in the monstrous waves. Robert, brown hair plastered to his head, rain water pouring down his long, angular face, simply smiled. An empty, evil smile without human feeling.

He reached deep into his pants' pocket and pulled out something gold and shiny. He held it up for Nick to see, and it twirled violently in the sheeting winds. Nick thought it looked like a necklace. He saw a gold half a heart. Nick then realized it was two necklaces, each with half a heart, tangled together and blowing in the wind. He was confused. His mind raced. Were these Cadie and Aileen's necklaces? How could Robert have both women's necklaces? His mind tried to comprehend.

"Where did you get those necklaces?!"

Again, Robert smiled - slyly.

"Like my boat says, Nick, it's all about revenge."

The two necklaces continued to twirl crazily in the shifting winds. Rain continued to pour down on the two men. Robert went to shove the necklaces, dripping wet with old, crusted blood, back into his pocket, but they slipped from his wet hands onto the stern.

"Revenge?" Nick yelled out, shaking his head madly, utterly confused. "What did Cadie ever do to you? I don't understand!"

There was a moment of quiet between the two men that seemed to last forever. The winds howled. The yacht shook. Each took stock of the moment. One man wondered what would happen next. One man planned his next move. Then the moment broke.

Robert suddenly ran across the stern. Nick instinctively knew Robert planned to shove him to his death just like Blake minutes before. However, Robert didn't know one thing. Robert didn't know that Nick, whose father wanted him to play football just like his dad, spent hours in the front yard learning numerous defensive skills. One skill in particular made his dad most proud. It was the spin move that earned Jake Brennan All-Conference honors.

Just as Robert reached Nick, his rain-drenched arms outstretched to shove the young man overboard, Nick's muscle memory kicked in, and he stepped to the side and turned with him. The men's eyes met and locked as Nick rotated his body with Robert's. The older man looked at Nick in surprise as he twisted alongside him.

Time slowed. At about three quarters of the turn, Nick grabbed Robert's arms and, in that instant, the young man's heart cracked open, and all his pain and anger tore loose. His father's sadness, his mother's abandonment, the murders of Thomas and Aileen, and the abduction of Cadie poured forth, and Nick, gripped with an extraordinary strength, shoved Robert with ferocity. He propelled the tall man up and backward, flinging him starboard, and Robert crashed into the side of the boat.

Then, just like Blake, Robert toppled backward over the gunwale – screaming profanities - his expensive deck shoes kicking the air, and his tan hands clawing for his expensive mini yacht. He hit the black water and was immediately sucked in by the raging waves like his nephew.

Nick quickly looked down. He saw Robert fighting to stay afloat, flailing his arms at the waves that crashed at him from every direction. The older man was screaming and battling to stay alive. Finally, Nick saw what he had never seen before in the older man's eyes: fear.

Nick turned away as Robert's screams were swallowed by the gale. He ran to the other side of the boat and furiously scanned the cavernous lake and mountainous waves.

"Blake! Blake! Where are you? Blake! Blake!"

His eyes darted endlessly, and he yelled over and over until his throat was raw, but he did not see his friend. Only the roiling and indifferent Great Lake that stretched for miles. His face and hair drenched, Nick raced around the perimeter of the cruiser, stern to bow, several times screaming and searching for Blake, but to no avail. His efforts were futile. The cruiser began to pitch violently. The bow began to take on water. The *Best Revenge* didn't have long.

Suddenly, Nick spied a red and white lifebuoy and frantically removed it from the buoyant line. With all his might, he threw it overboard against the pressing winds. It caught a breeze and blew out of sight. It was Blake's last hope. Nick knew he would not be able to locate his friend in the massive storm waves that crashed in all directions. He saw the cruiser taking on even more water. He knew he had no choice but to find safety.

Nick ran to the stern and was just beginning to head up the steps to the bridge when he saw the necklaces floating in the swirling water. He grabbed them and headed up to the bridge. With cold, trembling hands, he pulled his cell phone from his pocket and called 911.

Nothing.

*OF COURSE THERE'S NO SERVICE!*

He was exhausted and shaking. He sat down at Robert's seat at the helm. He spotted the cruiser's radio and turned it on. There's was no noise. He turned the knob until he heard a faint crackling sound. Then he picked up the microphone, pushed in the button, and yelled frantically.

"Hello! Hello! Is there anyone there? I need help! I'm north and west of North Manitou Island. People are overboard! Please send help!"

Nick wrapped his icy hand around the boat's stainless-steel throttle and pushed it forward. Under the dark skies and pelting rain, it was hard to get his bearings. He scoured the control panel until he spotted the black, mounted compass. He maneuvered the throttle until the magnetic needle pointed to 90 degrees, and Nick hoped he was headed toward Leland.

Suddenly, the complete and utter irony flashed bright in Nick's mind. In the end, the *Best Revenge*, Robert's symbol of hoped-for success and validation, had afforded him nothing but a lonely, watery grave.

The battered young man held the throttle firm, and the cruiser moved east of the island in the choppy Great Lake. Enormous gusts of wind buffeted the boat. In the distance to his south, Nick thought he saw Sleeping Bear Point, and his hope increased. Nick knew Sleeping Bear was special to Cadie; it always provided her comfort. Seeing the 450-foot bluff rise up through the mist like a stalwart sentry suddenly gave Nick a burst of fortitude.

With renewed strength, Nick pushed the throttle, and the cruiser, at one hundred percent load, battled the fifth largest lake in the world. While the cruiser pitched back and forth and fought its way through the towering eight to ten-foot waves, Nick prayed. He prayed harder than he had ever prayed before. He wasn't praying for his own life, though. He was praying that somehow, someway, he would see Cadie McLeod alive again.

## CHAPTER 52
## Michigan State University

Nick maneuvered his yellow Jeep through the twisting street under a canopy of colorful trees until he saw her blue Camaro in the parking lot. The car always made him smile. He pictured the many times she drove that Camaro into his driveway, red hair blowing in the breeze, with a big grin on her face.

"What are you waiting for? Get in," she would always call out and tap the horn.

He pulled in next to it and parked his Jeep. Through her ground floor window, Cadie saw him arrive. She grabbed the quilt off her bunkbed and raced down the dorm's hallway and through a side door – her face beaming. The two young people met on the maple-covered steps outside historic Landon Hall – the Tudor-style dormitory with high-pitched, gabled roofs.

"Hello, beautiful," Nick said, enveloping her in a huge hug. "College life looks good on you. I've missed you!"

Cadie McLeod beamed and pulled her head back from the hug and kissed Nick deeply. Both could feel the love and passion between them. The moment seemed to last forever. Then Cadie took Nick's hand.

"C'mon," she said, "let's walk."

It was a bright Saturday morning in early September on the Michigan State campus as the two walked along Red Cedar River. Redwoods, Elm, White Oak, and Norway Spruce created a lush canopy of vibrant fall colors. Red and orange autumn leaves swirled in the tender breeze. At 11 am, happy students on blankets already dotted the large expanses of grass. Nick could hear the MSU marching band practicing nearby with its proud, brass instruments echoing throughout campus.

"Let's sit here," Cadie said, and began laying and straightening the small quilt. "A homemade gift from Aunt Marie when she came to visit Tuesday," Cadie smiled up at Nick as she perfected the last corner and sat down. "We had such a wonderful day together. I don't know what I'd do without her."

Nick smiled. Everyone loved Aunt Marie.

He then noticed a new ring on Cadie's right hand. It had a little brown and white owl on it.

"What's with the ring?"

"Oh, this? I'll tell you about it sometime."

Nick sat down on the quilt across from her.

"My dad wanted me to tell you he sends his love. He said he hopes you are doing alright."

Cadie looked down. She tried to compose herself, but she began to cry quietly.

"What would I have done without your dad, Nick?" she said, her voice shaking. "I really don't know how he did it. Rescuing me from that car. Carrying me all that way across the field in the middle of a storm. If it wasn't for your dad, I'd be dead. Your dad saved my life."

"That's my dad," Nick smiled through tears of his own. "You know, I heard the whole story from Detective Kitchen. He said my dad pulled you from that car right before it sank. You were seconds from death. He grabbed your hair to pull you out of the water."

At that, Nick smiled mischievously.

"That mess of hair on your head actually saved your life."

Cadie playfully slapped his arm, her tears ceasing for the moment at his attempt at humor. But turning serious, Nick added, "You have to know he really loves you. We both do. We'd do anything for you."

Cadie nodded.

"I'm just so grateful."

Then the magnitude of it all struck her, and she began to sob, deep, wrenching sobs from the depth of her soul that poured out all the pain and anguish she had suffered for so many years and the trauma she had just endured. Nick grabbed her and embraced her fiercely, fighting his own tears. All of his own pain flooded to the surface as well. The two of them hugged and cried for a long time, Nick stroking her hair, rocking her until their tears subsided.

Finally, the two young people laid down on the quilt, hands behind their heads, neither speaking for quite a while, just looking up into the towering trees and letting their feelings quiet.

"I wanted to tell you that I signed up with a therapist through the university," Cadie said. "Maybe it's something that would be good for you, too, Nick. We have both been through so much. I think we need help going forward."

"Yeah, my dad and I have been talking about it – for both of us actually," Nick responded. "I never thought I'd see the day that tough Jake Brennan would see a shrink, but I agree: I think we all need as much help as we can get."

Nick looked over at Cadie and once again marveled at her luminous green eyes, lush red hair, and sun-kissed cheeks. She was utterly exquisite.

Nick was finally accepted into the University of Michigan in early July, but he decided to change his major to Law and Public Policy. It was a selective program, but he got in. Nick wondered if the admissions agent had been swayed by pictures of Nick and the heroic Jake Brennan splashed across the front pages of the Detroit papers. There was even talk of a second Medal of Honor for the hero cop.

After attending Blake's memorial, Jake, his truck crammed full of Nick's stuff, including Nick's old PlayStation, drove his son to Ann Arbor and moved him into East Quad. After they finished, the men sat on Nick's bunk and shared a shot of Glenlivet in honor of Blake – a person who did nothing to deserve his circumstances. As they remembered Blake, the coast guard was still searching Lake Michigan – still trying to locate the young man who would be in their minds forever eighteen.

After Jake left, Nick settled in. He spent the summer interning for a professor in the School of Public Policy. After all he and Cadie had been through, Nick realized he wanted a career that would allow him to make a significant difference.

Meanwhile, Cadie took it easy. She spent the summer reading chemistry textbooks at Aunt Marie's cottage and getting her strength back. She enjoyed convalescing in Marie's backyard and, like her father Thomas, growing her love of Goldfinches and Chickadees. Cadie and Marie even adopted a Red-bellied Woodpecker that was nesting in an old hardwood at the back of the property. A highlight of the day was catching a glimpse of its red crown and hearing its rolling kwirr. Cadie also enjoyed the numerous well-wishers who stopped by the cottage. Marie always had a pitcher of ice-cold strawberry lemonade at the ready.

There were definitely tough days, though. Some days Cadie lay in bed for hours replaying her life history, crying, and struggling to make sense of it all. Nothing Marie could do or say would coax Cadie out of her room when her dark moods dominated.

Thankfully, other days were spent with Nick. He would travel home whenever he could, and the young couple tried to let go of their worries at their favorite spot: Mariner's Beach on the shores of Lake Michigan. They took turns driving Nick's Jeep or Cadie's Camaro up the twisting roads. It was a blessing that Cadie never regained memory of what happened to her in the dunes that night. Toward the end of summer, Nick helped Cadie move into MSU. After everything that had happened, both young people just wanted time to process the events, try to heal, and hope to be normal. So, for the most part, they avoided talking in depth about all that had occurred and was ongoing. It was probably time for a bit of closure.

The bells of Beaumont Tower began to ring in the distance. Cadie waited for the peal of bells to end before she began. She sat up, and Nick joined her.

"The prosecutor said it was Robert Van der Velt who beat up my dad in high school," Cadie said. "He was utterly obsessed with my mother, but my mom loved my dad. So, one night, after a party, Robert found them together in my dad's car. He pulled my dad out and beat him in front of my mom. It was a terrible scene. Robert put my dad in the hospital. Then he was arrested and placed in a juvenile center until he was 18."

"God, that's crazy," Nick said, incredulous. "I always wondered where your dad got that scar around his eye. I wonder if Robert gave it to him? It's insane that Robert had been holding this terrible grudge against your parents since high school."

Cadie looked down for a moment, quiet. Then she looked up, her eyes meeting his.

"I didn't know if you heard this, but it was Robert who murdered my parents. It wasn't some random drunk driver who killed them. It was Robert. He ran them down in cold blood. The tests on his car were positive for my family's DNA."

Nick sat there. Stunned. The news was too much. He thought about poor Thomas and Aileen, and, of course his friend Blake who had done nothing wrong but want to celebrate his eighteenth birthday.

"Oh my god, Cadie. I don't know what to say. Robert truly was a monster."

"It's impossible to comprehend hating people so much that you would run them over. Then try to kill their daughter. And kill their own nephew. What kind of person does this? I truly feel like I'm living a *Dateline* episode," Cadie said wryly.

"No one who is happy with himself and at peace could do what Robert did," Nick said. "He was deeply, profoundly disturbed – mentally ill."

Then Nick reached into his jacket pocket.

"I have something for you. I would've given them to you earlier, but they were at the jewelers, and I wanted them to be perfect. I also wasn't sure how you would feel about getting these back, but they belong to you. You need to have them."

He pulled out a shimmering gold box and placed it on the quilt in front of Cadie.

"What did I do to deserve this," she smiled. "You're too good to me."

She picked up the box and slowly removed the lid. Then she saw what was inside: two sparkling gold necklaces, each with half a gold heart.

"Robert had them on the boat that day. He showed them to me right before he tried to kill me but fell overboard. I couldn't figure out how he came to have your mother's necklace. I remember you telling me her necklace went missing the night she was killed. Now, unfortunately, I know."

Cadie sat there stunned. Saying nothing. Just looking down.

"I can't believe this. Thank you so much, Nick. I was heartbroken when I awoke that morning after being kidnapped and found my necklace was gone. You have no idea. It was a link to my mom and dad. I thought I'd never see it again. And now to have it back? And my mother's necklace? This means everything to me."

"I know it does," Nick replied.

There was silence as Cadie stared at the necklaces – almost in a state of shock at their return. Nick uncrossed his legs.

"So, now what?" he said, changing the subject to lighten the mood. "What's next for Cadie McLeod? What are your classes?"

Cadie's face brightened a bit, and she resituated herself on the quilt.

"I'm just ready to get going!" she said enthusiastically. "I've got Forensic Chemistry, Social Science and the Law, Intro to Forensic Science, and Principles of Chemistry."

"Wow. You're really going for it! You're going to be the Amazing Cadie McLeod: Crime Fighter!" Nick grinned. "I'm so proud of you! I can just picture you hosting *20/20* someday. Nothing is impossible for you."

Cadie laughed, shaking her head and tossing her beautiful hair in the autumn sunlight.

"I think I'll have my own show! And solve crimes! And nothing is impossible because the word actually says, I'm possible."

"Did you just make that up?" Nick laughed. "That's pretty good."

"Maybe I did, maybe I didn't," she winked.
Then her demeanor changed, and she looked Nick in the eye.

"In all seriousness. I just want to make my parents proud, Nick. I could never give them the justice they deserved, but at least through my work I can get justice for other people."

"I know you will, Cadie."

"I believe my mom and dad would want that. It's the kind of work that would honor them."

Nick watched the lovely, talented, and strong young woman talk and hung on her every word. It was great to see her laugh and her eyes light up. To see her passion. To see her strength and resolve.

As he watched her face glow in the bright autumn light, he knew one thing for sure: Cadie McLeod was going to be alright.

## *EPILOGUE*
# Cadie McLeod

Robert Van der Velt murdered my parents. He murdered his nephew. He tried to murder me.

I got away.

My second semester at MSU, I took the course "Psychopathy: The Dark Core of Personality." From it, I learned the dangerous traits of the psychopathic narcissist: sense of entitlement, lack of empathy and remorse, grandiose sense of self, and a constant need to obtain a goal, which, in my case, was murdering my family. He saw us not as human beings but objects in his game of a twisted life.

In Ovid's *Metamorphoses*, Narcissus, the handsome young man, forsakes everyone to focus on himself. One day, he sees his reflection in a pool of water and falls in love – with his own image. Day after day, the young man sits on the edge of the pool, consumed by love of self, until, without food, water, or sleep, he succumbs to death.

Robert Van der Velt was consumed with self, and it led to his destruction. My parents, Thomas and Aileen McLeod, were the opposite: they were consumed by love and life. They lived with happiness and focused on other people. Everyone has a choice to make: light or dark. Good or evil. Robert chose evil. He chose to make dark, terrible choices over and over that hurt the ones I loved.

I can't let evil like that continue unchecked.

I can't let monsters like Robert Van der Velt keep destroying innocent lives and getting away with it. My professor said I was the most determined student she'd ever taught. I guess you could say I gained my motivation the hard way.

Aileen and Thomas McLeod never received the justice they deserved. But I can get justice for others.

*And I will.*

## ACKNOWLEDGEMENTS

The author wishes to thank the following people for their help and contributions to this novel: Dot Byard, Gerald Byard, Haley Korbel, Keith Byard, Kellee Byard, Shannon Byard, Sharon Clark, Jim Froehlich, Lyn Froehlich, Mitch Gill, Leigh Mass, Kacie Watt, and Dave Webster. She also is grateful for the many friends and family members who have supported her on this journey.

## ABOUT THE AUTHOR

Wendy Byard is the author of *Teach and Reach for Classroom Miracles*. She taught college English and composition and high school English and history for over 25 years. She wrote for *On the Town* Magazine and was a Special Writer for *The Flint Journal*. Byard also was a marketing and advertising executive for Grey Advertising in Chicago and Group 243 in Ann Arbor. Byard currently writes the column "Beyond Our Backyards" for a Michigan newspaper. She resides in Metamora, Michigan.

Made in the USA
Monee, IL
02 June 2025